'Was it rea[...]
whispered.[...]

'What?'

'The rabbit. Up your sleeve.'

Suddenly Luke was laughing, filling the warm, steamy tavern with richly infectious laughter, his hands reaching over the table to grasp hers, still sticky from the cake. 'Oh, Estrellita! What an innocent you are! No, of course it wasn't there—look, see for yourself...'

She smiled as he bared his forearm. She was too entranced to see the thoughtful expression that abruptly appeared on his face. 'You're almost too good to be true, Estrellita. A child out of the gutter who'll believe anything—a skivvy with stars in her eyes and a natural talent for the boards... I wonder...'

Although born in Essex, Christine Franklin now lives in Devon. An avid reader since childhood, it seemed only natural to her to write stories as she grew up, and in the late 1960s this urge to write became all-important.

Happily married, with a grown-up son, Christine is the author of several contemporary romances, children's books, and books of folklore and walks. She has an absorbing curiosity about the past, and enjoys researching and writing for Masquerade.

A CERTAIN MAGIC

Christine Franklin

All the characters in this book have no existence outside the imagination of the Author, and have no relation whatsoever to anyone bearing the same name or names. They are not even distantly inspired by any individual known or unknown to the Author, and all the incidents are pure invention.

All Rights Reserved. The text of this publication or any part thereof may not be reproduced or transmitted in any form or by any means, electronic or mechanical, including photocopying, recording, storage in an information retrieval system, or otherwise, without the written permission of the publisher.

This book is sold subject to the condition that it shall not, by way of trade or otherwise, be lent, resold, hired out or otherwise circulated without the prior consent of the publisher in any form of binding or cover other than that in which it is published and without a similar condition including this condition being imposed on the subsequent purchaser.

First published in Great Britain 1992 by Mills & Boon Limited

© Christine Franklin 1992

*Australian copyright 1992
Philippine copyright 1992
This edition 1992*

ISBN 0 263 77597 6

Masquerade is a trademark published by Mills & Boon Limited, Eton House, 18–24 Paradise Road, Richmond, Surrey, TW9 1SR.

*Set in 10 on 10½ pt Linotron Times
04-9203-80481
Typeset in Great Britain by Centracet, Cambridge
Made and printed in Great Britain*

PROLOGUE

THE bear-boy, holding his huge charge at arm's length, stared down at seven-year-old Essie, grinning at her fear with huge sea-green eyes.

'Give us a penny!'

'Haven't got one.' Essie's face crumpled with disappointment. The boy, dark-haired, with a look about him that had made her quick imagination spark immediately into fantastic dreams and images, was proving to be all too human and greedy. A penny, indeed! He was bumping her back into the uncomfortable reality of what she ought to be doing, which was pegging out the family washing on the wasteland beside the river, not staring, entranced, at the little troupe of clowns, tumblers, ladies in feathers and tinsel, men and boys on stilts, all of them in strange, outlandish clothes. And, most captivating of all, this shabby, hot-eyed, shambling bear.

How dared the boy break up her dreams? Life with Aunt Beattie and Uncle Tom was hard enough. If she didn't have dreams she'd die of hopelessness. At seven years old she knew it already. The bear-boy was a terrible disappointment to her.

'I wouldn't give you a penny, not even if I had one!' Her country voice shrilled upwards like a nagging fishwife's, but he only smiled more broadly.

'Keep your hair on, or I'll let old Rastibus loose on you—likes a bit of screaming girl, he does. . .'

The bear's chain rattled, and the animal, hearing its name, shuffled a step nearer. Essie smelled the rancid breath, saw the matted brown fur ripple in movement, and felt panic overtake her.

'He won't, will he? Oh, lawks. . .!'

5

'Don't be silly. He won't do nothing 'less I tell him. Take a joke, can't you?'

Essie calmed down. Such power. She forgot her fright and began dreaming again, dreams of becoming as powerful as the bear-boy. Power to stop Aunt Beattie ordering her about, to stop Uncle Tom hitting her. Power to make people look at her and be kind. Perhaps even love her...

The hurdy-gurdy music was being blown away by the wind. A trumpet cracked on a high note, and a grubby-looking child stared back towards Essie. The little procession of entertainers straggled on, laughter and chatter fading as they reached the bridge and disappeared down the street.

Only the boy and the bear were left. Already Rastibus was shaking his head, rattling his chain, anxious to follow the motivating music.

'Where're you going?' asked Essie yearningly. And then, very anxiously, 'Coming back, are you?'

The dark boy looped the chain around his arm to restrain the restless animal. He grinned at her carelessly. 'Goin' to the fairground in St Thomas. Then off to Crediton. No, we shan't come back here.'

Essie stared, wanting him to stay for ever. He wore tattered breeches, one leg red, the other yellow, a tunic split into similar colours, and, on his shining, raven hair, a tall pointed hat decorated with peeling silver moons and stars and crescents. Her face lit up. 'Who *are* you?'

Leaning forward, he tweaked her tangled carrot-red hair, and let his grin curl upwards into joyful mischief. 'A magician, of course.' Uninhibited sauciness broadened his thin face. 'An' who are *you*, madam?'

He was only teasing her, of course, but no one had ever shown such personal interest before. Proudly, she told him, 'Estrellita.' The name Aunt Beattie never used, never mentioned because, for some reason, it was the wrong name. Essie—short, ugly, meaningless, was the right one.

'Estrellita? That means Little Star, doesn't it?' The boy yanked the bear's chain and started running over the waste ground after his friends. The animal fell on all fours as it shambled behind him.

Essie stared, never to forget the sight, or the boy's voice, as it faded slowly, echoing back to her, finally blown away for ever by the wind that tunnelled down the river.

'Estrellita! Es-trell-it-a. . .'

CHAPTER ONE

ESSIE DART plunged her hands into the cooling washing-up water and fished out the last remnant of the mistress's supper.

'There! That's done. Now I can get off.'

Beside her, Grace, the middle-aged parlour-maid, sniffed disapprovingly as she piled shining plates and dishes into the wooden racks overhead, stretching the length of the gloomy, gas-lit scullery. 'Where you going, then?'

'Out.' Essie was in no mood to share her plans. She knew Grace too well—always ready to make uncalled-for criticism, even sneaking to Mrs Grindle, the cook, if she had something worth the telling.

'Hmm. Mind you're not late back—door's locked at ten.'

'I know that.' Essie scrubbed at the greasy tide-line on the stone sink with lumps of soda, thoughts wandering as the longed-for freedom drew nearer. 'I'm only going down to the river——' From the corner of her eye she saw Grace's peaked face sharpen with curiosity, and bit off the words quickly. 'I mean, where I'm going finishes before ten. I'll get back in time.'

She heard Grace sniff again, sensed the woman's hesitation before leaving the scullery, knew the sudden wicked joy of hating her, hating the cold, damp scullery, and the whole basement kitchen, most of all hating Mrs Grindle with her red face and bulging stomach beneath the huge white apron.

To get out. To slip away from this drudgery and spend an hour in that other world of lights and music and excitement—oh! *Oh*! Suddenly, Essie could not keep it inside her a second longer. She must tell someone, and so it had to be Grace, come what may. Turning around with a whirl, she smiled fiercely into the alarmed eyes that watched so closely. 'I'm going to the gaff! The fishboy said as how there's one tonight—down by the quay. Only a penny to get in. That's where *I'm* going!'

'What's a gaff, then?' Clearly, Grace considered it the work of the devil, whatever it might be.

Essie rinsed the dishcloth and hung it triumphantly on the one water tap. 'Theatre, stupid! Haven't you ever heard o' penny gaffs? Like music hall they are, only cheaper. Oh, it'll be lovely—there'll be singing and dancing and——'

'And sin everywhere. You mind you don't get picked up, Essie Dart.' Grace looked down her pinched nose and her face took on what Essie privately called her 'do-gooding' look. Essie leaned back against the sink, torn between desire to leave and at the same time feeling the awful need to torment her tormentor.

'Maybe I'll run away and never come back. I'll go for a dancer, that's what——' Teasingly, she began to sway her thin body from side to side, skinny arms floating upwards in an ecstasy of uninhibited movement until suddenly they touched the flaking plaster of the scullery walls and fell again. 'Or a singer,' she elaborated, spurred on by the expression of horror on Grace's face. 'Tra-la-la—la-la-la!' Her small, true voice rose effortlessly, soaring around the grimy ceiling.

'Essie?' came a grim voice from the kitchen, just down the passage. 'Stop that row this instant. An' take care as you don't smash any of Madam's plates—Doulton, them are. Cost you a year's wages if you breaks one.'

'Yes, Mrs Grindle, no, Mrs Grindle.' Essie's brown eyes gleamed with rage and mirth and she stuck out her tongue at the invisible cook, more to shock Grace than to be the rude little guttersnipe she appeared.

Grace swallowed the bait instantly. 'Essie Dart, there's no hope for you. You'll end up in trouble, just like your aunt Beattie said, when she brought you here last year. "Only sixteen," she said, "and wicked already. . ."'

Essie's face fell. 'Oh, her! Mean old skinflint.'

'That's no way to talk of the good woman who's brought you up.' Grace hung the wet tea-towel on a string secured to the wall.

'On'y took me in 'cos my ma wasn't there,' said Essie grudgingly, already untying her damp apron and preparing to fly upstairs.

'And why wasn't she there?' demanded Grace, righteously indignant. 'Because she ran off with a man, that's why—an ice-cream seller, your aunt Beattie said. . .'

Again, Essie's natural caution was overrun by her quick irritability with old sobersides Grace. 'My ma was in the theatre before she had me,' she bragged. 'She left me with Aunt B. because she wanted to go back there, to sing and dance, just as I want to do——'

'And she came to a bad end. As you will.'

'Oh, you——' Essie mouthed a rude word, brushed past Grace, stuck her head around the kitchen doorway to say more politely, and in one long, rushed breath, 'Washing-up's all done, Mrs Grindle; I'm off now, and I'll be back before ten.' Then she clattered up the wooden stairs, through the baize door, and on up to the attic bedroom she shared with Grace.

She didn't feel the chill of the March evening as she threw her cap on the bed, releasing a ripple of soft carroty hair around her shoulders, before stripping off the ugly skivvy's dress that she hated so much.

And then, before reaching for her one good outfit, hanging behind the door, she picked up the small hand-tinted photograph of her mother that Aunt B. had ungraciously given her when she left the tenement at Tan Court last year, and stared at it appraisingly. She saw a small, slightly foreign-looking face with a snub nose, like her own, dark, liquid eyes that smiled and dreamed, and rich hair—red, she knew, like her own—curling untidily out of its restraining coiled knot.

For no good reason, Essie's heart began to beat faster. She didn't remember Ma, but there was something in this faded photo that she would never tire of looking at—some rare quality that excited her.

Not beautiful. No, she wasn't beautiful; but there's something in her eyes—a sort of longing. Something she can see? A dream, maybe. . . Essie thought hard as she stared at the photo.

Yes, that was it. A dream. Satisfied, Essie slipped the little photo in her pocket after she'd put on her old dark blue woollen dress. She thought she knew what Ma's dream had been, because she, too, had her own dream. And getting away from the scullery and Grace and Mrs Grindle, going off to the gaff to hear music, to watch conjurors and acrobats, was all part of it.

Eagerly, Essie knotted her hair and got ready for her evening out.

Slipping out of the back door into darkness, threadbare coat pulled tight, boots in hand so that Grace and Mrs Grindle, drinking tea in the kitchen, shouldn't hear her, Essie paused on the path leading to the front of the house. She laced her boots, skewered her hat, with the drooping cotton violets hanging over the brim, more firmly to her wiry hair, and set off at a trot.

In this residential part of the city she had to stop once or twice to peer at unfamiliar road names, half hidden beneath the street lights. Once a new-fangled motor-car scared the life out of her as she crossed in front of it, and she wondered how much longer the horse-drawn traffic that still crowded the country streets would last, now that the new century was producing such sights and surprises.

Once down Fore Street hill she came into her own, for here, beside the flowing, murmuring river, she had grown up. The sleazy old tenements with their shadowed alleys and courts, the factories and warehouses, the cranes and moored boats with soaring masts and jibs, were home to her.

Soon she left the road, cutting down on to the quayside. For a moment she hesitated. The tavern at the side of Exe Bridge served strong tea and a plate of thick yellow cake for only a few pence, and she hadn't waited to eat her supper—but no. Money mustn't be wasted. Food wasn't important. Theatre was.

It was easy to find the gaff. A half-torn poster flapped on a hoarding, pointing the way. Essie stopped to read it, slowly saying the difficult words aloud, for schooling had been infrequent, living with that slavedriver, Aunt B.

> MONSEY'S PENNY GAFF THEATRE. EVERY NIGHT EXCEPT SUNDAY. PAY YOUR PENNY AND TAKE YOUR PICK. SHAKESPEAR. COMEDY. SONGS AND DANCING. GIRLS. MR HAROLD KENNET'S WORLD-FAMOUS MAGIC ACT.

She turned down the quayside, seeming to sense the way she must go. Now she could hear noise blown down the river, voices rising above a background of tinny music. Unerringly she tracked it down to a cellar-like entrance built into the surrounding red sandstone cliffs that rose a stone's throw from the riverside.

At the dark doorway she produced her penny, which was snatched by an invisible hand, while a thick voice grunted, 'Performance began ten minutes ago. You're late.'

Inside the crowded cellar, despite the fishy stench of its daytime use, a magic world revealed itself to Essie's rapturous senses. In front of a makeshift stage of trestles balanced on a couple of barrels, the packed bodies of the audience clung together in hot huddles—boys and girls mostly, with only an occasional adult.

Here and there a babe in arms yelled, its thin wail instantly hushed. Briar pipes glowed and hearty voices shouted comments on the acts being performed beneath critical eyes.

As Essie blinked in the semi-darkness, the woman on the small, dust-enshrouded stage wheezed out the last verse of a song in a tired voice, curtsied and then disappeared, to catcalls and boots thumping on the beaten earth floor.

Gradually, as Essie became used to the half-light of the guttering candles and oil lamps, she ignored the heat, the smoke and the smell, and wedged herself more comfortably into a convenient corner in the back row, watching with undiluted pleasure as act followed act.

Acrobats clad in threadbare lionskins. A dancer, all tinsel and smiles, whose fixed grin had a look of desperation about it. The singer, with another song which the audience joined in, singing lustily, if not in tune. Applause, catcalls, boots thumping, voices shouting, 'Get off', or 'Encore'—briars re-lit with spurts of sulphurous yellow in the shadowy darkness.

Essie hugged herself, all thoughts of her former life beneath Mrs Grindle's heavy thumb fading. What else would she see in this enchanted place? She held her breath, waiting for the next revelation.

Another man, but this time old and silver-haired, shoulders drooping, his black suit green with age and use. Essie thought he looked ill, and her expectant smile faded. Was this the world-famous Mr Harold Kennnet of the poster? She saw how he fumbled with the Chinese rings, fudging the trick of joining them. Her heart sank as hoop after hoop fell on to the stage, the jangling descent echoing with great boos from the unfeeling audience.

'Oh, poor man! He shouldn't be up there; he's not well——' In her dismay, Essie spoke aloud, and her words were overheard.

The girl next to her, whose bony elbow had already

stuck into Essie's side in the crush, leaned closer. 'Not well? Come off it, stoopid—drunk, that's what he is.' She grinned knowingly.

Essie said sharply, 'He's still a poor man. And I'm sorry for him.'

'Then you'm a fool. Us've paid our money and us don't wanna see broken-down acts, do us?'

Essie was about to retort with her usual zest, but suddenly the catcalls ended as a younger man came on to the stage. He was tall and thin, dressed entirely in black. His raven-dark hair and light eyes seemed to emphasise the pallor of his face, and in the flickering light a silver earring shone in the lobe of his left ear. He looked strange—unusual... But it wasn't only his appearance that quietened the audience. Essie was immediately aware of his presence. It was as if he held invisible power within him. Her mouth dropped open and her eyes widened. As she watched, her amazement grew, for clearly the man had the unruly, noisy audience in the palm of his elegant hand.

He smiled gently at the tottering Harold Kennet and then led him off-stage, returning quickly before the audience could resume its loud clamour of disapproval. Essie was unable to take her eyes off him. She sensed, too, that the rest of the audience felt the same.

Casually, he picked up the fallen Chinese rings, shot an amused glance at the faces watching in the shadows, and then proceeded to demonstrate perfectly the trick that Harold Kennet had been unable to perform. Hoop after hoop linked up until he had a chain of them, jingling through his hands. And then, just as the watchers let out their breath and began to murmur with approval, down they all fell—a heap of brass rings, untouched, but magically separated.

Essie thought the roof of the cavern must fall in, so great was the applause. Her own hands were hot and sore with clapping, and all she could think of was what would he do next, this clever and astounding magician?

He rapidly ran through several other tricks. A flow of silken scarves from a pocket. A wand hovering in the air at his command. Even a rabbit from his black sleeve.

The girl beside Essie said dreamily, 'Oh, isn't he lovely. . .?' and Essie knew just how she felt. All those tricks, and the man himself, so still, so quiet, so—what was it?—well, no other word but magical.

And then he was gone, casually walking off into the darkness, the silver earring a small, glittering star before that, too, faded away. The stage was suddenly, disappointingly, empty, and the audience once more a crowd of noisy hooligans, shouting and clapping. But Essie was still transported with delight, and so excited that when, a few minutes later, a shifty little chap with a battered hat clamped down over mean eyes climbed on to the stage and shouted, over the echoing boos, if there was anyone in the house who'd like to take the opportunity of coming up and showing his or her talent, she stood up immediately, shouting back at him, 'Yes! I will!'

Bravely she pushed her way through the mocking crowd until she stood in front of them all below the stage. The man looked down at her, gappy teeth showing as he forced a smile in his puffy face. 'Excellent! A pretty young lady here—just what we was all hoping to see. Come round the side, my dear, and I'll fix you up for your act. . .'

Shifty-face disappeared, and Essie was handed down the front row until she met him in the darkness at the side of the stage. His hand, moist and hot, came out of the shadows to grasp hers. 'Monsey's the name—Ned Monsey. I'm the proprietor here. Now, what you gonna do, eh? Sing? Dance? Why not? Nice little body you got, gel. . .'

Alarmed, she fought off his invading hands. 'Stop it! Yes, I can sing—*and* dance. . .but—but——' Suddenly, the enormity of what she was about to do overcame her natural exuberance and self-confidence. 'But I'm not sure. . .'

Too late. He had pulled her into the shadows, was leading her behind the stage, among dim figures busily changing, or leaning against the wall, drinking and chatting.

'Come this way, my dear.' He pulled her into a tiny alcove behind an upright piano, and she looked about her uneasily. Tattered clothes hung on the walls. An oil lamp illuminated a bespattered mirror on a bare shelf. She smelt powder, sweat and the lingering fumes of spilt gin. Something inside her asked fearfully what she was doing here—and for a second she faltered. But then she remembered her mother and the photograph she had snatched up before she left the attic bedroom. Like a soothing hand on a fevered brow, it came to her that Ma had known places like this. She might well have changed in such a squalid little alcove before going on to a similar, rough stage, and performing for a noisy, rough audience.

And if she did it, then I can too. The thought gave Essie fresh confidence. She turned, staring composedly into Ned Monsey's speculative, near-set eyes.

'Well? Got some music, have you?' she asked cheerfully. 'Tell the man at the piano I'm gonna sing that one about the old cock linnet—you know, the one Marie Lloyd does. I'll do a verse and a chorus, see, and then I'll dance through the next verse before the last chorus. All right with you, Mr Monsey?'

She saw, with hidden glee, that he was taken aback by such youthful arrogance. While he was still staring and chewing at a dirty fingernail, she went a step further. 'And I'll wear that dress—that red one; get it down, will you? I can't reach up that high.'

He did so, muttering something she wasn't interested enough to hear. But when his hands touched hers, passing over the soiled red satin costume, her smile faded. Sharply, she said, 'And don't you watch while I change, see? I'll come out when I'm ready. Go on, then—off you go. . .'

She supposed that no one had ever spoken to Ned Monsey like that before, but reluctantly he did as she ordered, disappearing from sight before she unbuttoned her blue woollen dress and changed into the thin, slippery red satin concoction. Bootlace shoulder-straps barely held up the befrilled bodice, and the frothing skirt of net and lace stuck out like a piecrust, but to Essie it was perfection. She smiled at her reflection in the stained mirror, pinched her cheeks to make the colour come, and pushed her fingers through her unloosed hair until the dark red curls fell in soft tendrils around her exposed shoulders and upper arms.

Then she heard voices just outside the alcove, heard the pianist trying out the familiar tune she had suggested. Excitement grew. Another few minutes and she'd be on that stage! Singing! Dancing! Just like Ma had done. . .

She gave a last quick glance at the mirror. Her face glowed. Her eyes sparkled. Her body was shapely—a bit thin, maybe, but her legs were good and the two little bumps at her breast showed off her tiny waist. Yes, she'd do, all right. Ma would have been proud of her, looking like this.

Out of the alcove, she stopped suddenly, aware that the men lounging backstage were staring, and their expressions offended her. Most of all, Ned Monsey's eyes alarmed her. He was looking at her as if she was something he wanted to own, to have for himself, to possess. . . He came sidling up, grinning, showing his gappy, stained teeth, and put an arm around her waist, pinching her too tightly.

'Lovely! What a pretty gel! Tell old Monsey what yer name is, dearie—must have a name to announce you, eh?' His hands pawed hungrily at her body, and she side-stepped quickly, slapping at them.

'Leave me alone, can't you?'

'All right, all right.' His tone changed and he looked around sheepishly, scowling at the bawdy laughter from the watching figures. 'Keep your hair on—proper little tiger-cat, you are. Well, got a name or not, eh? Come on, don't keep me waiting, or I'll change me mind and you won't go on——'

'My name is Estrellita. Estrellita Dart.' She said it loudly and confidently, drawing herself up, proud of the name, proud to be here, sure of herself as never before. It all felt wonderfully right, in spite of Ned Monsey and his filthy old theatre and the men staring at her in the shadows. She couldn't explain how she felt, but she knew, somehow, that Ma had felt the same—this strong urge to leave home, this easy acceptance of smelly bodies and stained costumes and leering eyes, this excitement at hearing the music, the voices cheering and catcalling—the wonder of the drumbeat of applauding boots on the floor when it was over. Oh, yes, she was in the right place at last. And her audience was waiting. . .

She ran towards the stage in a flurry of thrilling excitement, hearing Ned Monsey's thick voice shouting her name.

'Ladies an' gennulmen, I gives you Miss Estrellita Dart. . .'

And she paused briefly, realising that her lifelong dream was about to come true. And then, through the ill-lit shadows and wreathing smoke that filled the little theatre, she became aware of a pair of brilliant, moody eyes watching her. Deep, blue-green eyes that stared, making her catch her breath in wonder, making her senses tingle, her legs wobble. The magician stood there, his presence reaching out to her through the crowds as if he and she were alone.

He smiled briefly, and the moment was past. Eager hands helped her climb up on to the dusty trestle, and she walked out into the hot, smelly patch of light that came searing up from below.

There was no time to be nervous, for the piano was already tinkling out the tune she knew so well and there she was singing. Thoughts raced through her mind, even as she sang. She was amazed that her voice could fill the space all around her. Surprised that she had the courage to smile down at the shadowy faces in the audience, and, above all, blissfully happy that she had found the nerve to take this first step towards her future.

Oh, if only miserable old Grace could see her now! At the end of the chorus, she began to move, gracefully flitting around the stage, dancing as she had danced all her life, doing what was second nature and enjoying every moment of it. Her bare legs twinkled and pirouetted beneath the blaring lights, and she heard the audience begin to applaud, hand-claps beating in time with the saucy rhythm of the music. Her smile widened. The satin dress stuck uncomfortably to her body, she felt on fire with heat and emotion, and her legs would surely never quieten down again after this ecstatic moment of cavorting around the stage. As the last chorus began she heard every voice in the theatre join with hers, and knew she was a success.

Watch out, Marie Lloyd! Estrellita, 'Little Star', was already on the first rung of the ladder to fame and riches. No longer was she Essie Dart, the skivvy, for ever washing up, with soda-red hands and damp apron!

And then, as the music stopped and the audience began its boot-thumping applause, she knew something was wrong. A dark figure rushed on stage and pulled her off. In the middle of a triumphant curtsy she stumbled and would have fallen over the edge of the trestle, had she not been held in a strong grasp.

'Hey! What you doing? Let me go, damn you!'

Her immediate fear was that it was old Shifty-face, Monsey, coming to get her—so great was her panic that she kicked out wildly, and felt the small red shoe land on her assailant's shin.

A low, rich voice swore in her ear and the arm

grabbing hers grew rougher. 'Stop it, you silly child. I'm not going to hurt you.'

'But you are! Let me go—oh, help, help. . .' Her shrill voice rose above the shouts and cries that now filled the theatre, and rose into a fierce scream, until a hand came out of the darkness to cover her mouth.

'Stop that noise, or we'll all be in trouble.' The voice was still low, but it had an authority that made Essie change her plan of biting the fingers so harshly gagging her. Instead, she struggled even more and once again kicked out at where she thought her captor's legs must be.

But, before she knew it, she was being half carried, half pulled out of the heat of the theatre and hustled away through the chill darkness of the quayside. Feet tripping and stumbling, unable to cry out further because of the hand over her mouth, Essie could do no more than wonder fearfully what was happening to her.

She heard wild shouts in the distance, and could only imagine the uproar in the theatre, and then, abruptly, she was freed, being none too gently impelled through a door into welcome warmth and the smell of food.

'Put this around you and sit down. Be a good girl and I'll get you some tea. And don't move—if you run off dressed like that you'll end up in the nick, and I shan't be around to rescue you a second time. So stay there—understand?'

Breathless, and, for once in her life, not knowing what to say, she slumped in the chair she'd been pushed into, staring up into the amused sea-green eyes of the man who now towered above her, darkly bearded face set in a tight smile that was half amused, half annoyed. Very slowly her pulses settled, her thoughts quietened. They were in the tavern beside the bridge. Beneath the heavy coat thrown across her shoulders she still wore the skimpy red dress, and her legs were bare, goose-pimpled from the night air.

And the man looking down at her—the man with the low, rich voice, the tall, handsome man dressed all in black, whose pale face was illuminated by those extraordinarily brilliant, all-seeing eyes was——

Essie sucked in a deep breath and said in a tiny, disbelieving whisper, 'You're—why, you're the magician! Aren't you?'

He stared into her wide eyes before turning away to the counter, saying casually over his shoulder, 'Yes. And you're Estrellita. I always knew we would meet again, one day.'

Her mouth dropped open and she gasped, unable to think straight, for long-forgotten images and sounds had now taken possession of her. The river, long ago. That cruel wind, biting through a small child's threadbare clothes, snapping the sheets that hung overhead. Dancers and musicians trailing across the wasteland, a moment of magic, and a boy with a bear on a chain. Ras—Rasti. . .?

A mug of steaming tea appeared on the table in front of her, and the tall man in the elegant black frock-coat sat down opposite. He pushed a plate bearing a thick wedge of yellow cake across the table. 'You look half starved. Get your teeth into that.'

'Rasti——?' She was still wandering in the never-never land of childish memories. Quickly he broke off a chunk of cake and ate it, himself suddenly grinning, and showing perfect, shining teeth.

'Rastibus, my old bear. Not forgotten it all, have you?' A pause, while he leaned over the table searching her astonished face with his brilliant, keen eyes. 'I never did—not for a moment. All the time I was working up and down the country, in London——'

'London?' Another gasp of amazement. Surely London was a golden city.

'And in Paris——'

'*Paris*!' She was even more flabbergasted, and showed it.

He smiled, mysterious and mocking. 'We are in the twentieth century, you know. The world is getting smaller every day.'

She was lost in his smile. It seemed to her bewildered eyes that a curtain had abruptly been lifted, revealing the beauty and gentleness that hid behind the casual, rather cold mask of his lean face. Here was the friendly boy from the past, teasing her again—surely not the awesome, worldly performer she had just seen at the gaff.

'You silly goose! Don't look at me like that!' Clearly, he misunderstood her radiance for something more commonplace. 'Paris isn't the end of the world—there's nothing much to going there. In this business we have to move around, you know.' And then, when she still seemed unable to speak, or take her eyes away from his, he broke off another small piece of cake, and fed her, as if she were a baby.

Obediently Essie opened her mouth, shut it, chewed the stale, dry cake. She didn't even taste it, it went down so unthinkingly.

'That's better. Now drink your tea.'

The hot, sweet liquid was more successful in returning her to reality. She caught her breath, choked, then gasped as he leaned across to pat her gently on the back and then, finally, let loose the glory of her smile. And, with that release, she found her tongue again.

'I saw you! On the stage—back there. . .'

'At the gaff? Yes, I'd heard old Kennet was in trouble, so I came down to see if I could help. Poor old devil—he was good once. Taught me the rings when I was just a nipper, starting out. It was the least I could do, helping him just now.'

'But——' Essie's thoughts flew in all directions '—but why are you here? In Exeter? I mean, after London? And *Paris*?'

Again, the teasing grin enclosed her. 'You obviously

don't go to the theatre, Estrellita—I'm on the bill at the Royal for a fortnight. Come and see me, wiil you?'

The mockery made her spirits rise in delight. 'I'm only a skivvy! *I* can't go to the theatre!'

'But you've been in one tonight. Singing. Dancing. . .' Suddenly he was serious, the unsmiling, brooding man again, watching her with those deep, strange eyes.

She tried to explain and it all came tumbling out. Aunt B. And Uncle Tom. The scullery, Grace and Mrs Grindle. The wish, that had grown to a need, then an all-powerful urge, to get up and perform for an audience. Her fervour quailed a bit when she came to Ned Monsey, and for a second the sea-green gaze intensified, making her heart beat faster in case she had displeased him. But then she was off again. 'And I was up there, on the stage, and it was lovely! Oh, it was—and they all clapped and I knew I was good, and then—and then——' Her face fell and she stared at him accusingly. 'And then you pulled me off and brought me here, and I dunno why, and—and——'

'And you're a very lucky girl that I was there to do so. If I hadn't got you out you'd be in the nick by now—you and Monsey, and all the rest of them.'

'The nick? But why? We didn't do nothing wrong. . .'

His face was set again, cold and hard, the brilliant gaze suddenly fierce. 'Because the place was being raided, you stupid chit. No licence, see? Penny gaffs are only run under licence, and Monsey is the kind of fly-by-night who doesn't bother with legalities. So, when I heard the rozzers arrive, I grabbed you—and all I got was a couple of hefty kicks on the shin. Now, there's gratitude. . .' He smiled mockingly, and Essie's heart nearly burst.

How wonderful he was, how knowledgeable and clever. Above all, how kind—to save her, to buy her cake and tea, to spend his valuable time talking to her.

'I'm ever so sorry,' she whispered, ashamed now of such terrible behaviour. 'I didn't know—I thought you was Shifty-face, trying to get me again.'

'Shifty-face?' The low voice deepened ominously, and she shivered, for no reason she could name.

'Monsey. Mr Monsey. He——' She looked down at the table, at her empty plate, and began picking up the last cake crumbs to avoid having to explain about Monsey.

'Don't bother to tell me. I can guess.' There was a pause, while she swallowed a crumb and felt herself burning all over at the memory of Shifty-face pawing her dress.

'Well, now, Estrellita. . .'

She looked up, hearing the reassurance in his voice. He smiled, regarding her over locked fingers. Bemused, she stared at those capable, miraculous fingers that had performed such marvels at the gaff. Her thoughts flew.

'Was it *really* there?' she whispered, hardly daring to ask.

'What?'

'The rabbit. Up your sleeve.'

Suddenly he was laughing, filling the warm, steamy tavern with richly infectious laughter, his hands reaching over the table to grasp hers, still sticky from the cake. 'Oh, Estrellita! What an innocent you are! No, of course it wasn't there—look, see for yourself. . .'

She smiled as he bared his forearm. It was pale and muscular, and she sensed its power, longing to stroke the wealth of fine black hair that crowned the rippling muscles.

'Nothing there, Estrellita. Agreed?'

She nodded doubtfully. 'Yes. No!'

Again his hands gathered hers, and he looked very deep into her wondering eyes. She was too entranced to see the thoughtful expression that abruptly appeared on his face. 'You're almost too good to be true,

Estrellita. A child out of the gutter who'll believe anything—a skivvy with stars in her eyes and a natural talent for the boards... I wonder...'

The quiet words were full of something that sent thrills through her. Almost mesmerised by the impact of his brilliant gaze, she could only stare and wait for what he would say next.

Luke looked into the wide brown eyes, and felt new hope surge inside him. What a find! Pretty and talented—surely just the girl to train up into the act, to help him return to London... Instinctively, he touched the silver star in his left ear, remembering the stardom he had lost and still longed for. Then he looked a little closer at the anxious face opposite, and his natural gentleness asserted itself. She was such a little innocent—in fact, hardly more than a child. He would have to protect her; make sure there was no repetition of the trouble with Harry, last year. Luke frowned, as memory clawed, and his mouth tightened.

Then he saw the brown eyes cloud uneasily, and smiled again. This little mouse was timid, for all her vitality and talent. He must treat her very kindly.

His hands were warm and strong, and Essie felt secure—at ease for perhaps the first time in her life. The sensation gave her back her vanished self-confidence. Now she dared to break the silence enclosing them.

'What do you wonder?' Once or twice in the scullery she had managed to coax unwilling Grace into jobs she wasn't supposed to do—now she put that urgent longing into her voice and face, smiling at him with all the charm she could find within herself. 'Tell me, then— go on—oh, please do.'

His eyes changed colour, and excitement flooded her mind. Thoughtfully he stroked her hands. 'Well, now that we've met again, maybe we ought to stay together—what do you think?' His voice was low and intimate, impossible to resist. 'Would you like to work for a magician, Estrellita?'

'With you? In your act? Oh—not half I wouldn't!'

He laughed at her pleasure, released her hands and then deftly produced a china egg from her right ear. 'Good! Splendid! So keep this egg as a token of my goodwill towards you. We won't have any contracts, Estrellita—just an understanding that I'll teach you all you need to know. . .' He paused, narrowed his eyes. 'As long as you promise to work well and not get above yourself.'

The egg was shiny, warm from his touch, wherever it had been hidden. It seemed like a bit of himself that he was giving into her safe-keeping. She cradled it between her small red hands and loved it. Over the table she smiled, joyous in the knowledge that he had become part of her dream and that, somehow, together they would make it all come true.

CHAPTER TWO

'COME down to earth, Estrellita. We must make plans.' Luke was heady with excitement as thoughts fell into place. To get back to London, to the West End—to rebuild the act! To be a star again. . . His hand flew superstitiously to the silver earring.

Watching him, Essie saw a man with the blazing light of ambition in his crystalline eyes, a light that shone as vividly as the star in his ear. Abruptly, it dawned on her that she knew nothing about him, not even his name. 'Who *are* you?' she whispered.

Dark brows winged upwards in surprise to fall again immediately. 'I'd forgotten,' he said wryly. 'Of course, I'm only the bear-boy to you. My name is Luke Grimwade, and my act is a mixture of conjuring and illusion. I've been working at it for the past ten years, and I plan to become the greatest magician in the history of the theatre.'

He looked so sure of himself that she asked nervously, 'And me? Will I be the greatest assistant, then?'

He didn't reply at once. When he did, she saw that the bear-boy had gone, the magician's face becoming pensive and assessing. If she hadn't been flying so high with excitement, she might well have been alarmed.

'You, Estrellita,' he said at last, his voice low and resonant, 'are, as yet, an unknown quality, save what my instinct tells me. I have a strong suspicion that you might well rise quite fast in the profession, but where your pretty wings will take you is something I can't truthfully forecast—it all depends on you. I just hope they won't get singed—remember Monsey? But don't worry, I'll look after you.'

That brought her down with a bump. She sat back fearfully. 'I'll never forget Monsey—never. But he won't be there, will he? Not where you are?'

Luke's mouth was grim. 'There's a Monsey in every show. You'll have to learn how to handle them.' A fleeting expression of scorn gleamed in his eyes. 'It shouldn't be hard—women soon learn.' And then, again, he became the bear-boy, smiling at her. 'But don't let's get too far ahead. We must talk about now. Where do you live?'

She gave a great gasp and her spirits fell. 'Oh, lawks! I'd forgotten—what's the time? It must be ever so late.'

His hand slid a silver hunter from an inner pocket and swung it in front of her.

'I'll never get in, not now! Mrs Grindle'll have locked the door—what shall I do? And me clothes— can I get them back? I can't go home like this. . .' Near to tears, she looked beseechingly at him. For if Mrs Grindle had bolted the door and gone to bed— and of course she had—that meant she was locked out. And she couldn't go back to Aunt B. and explain what she'd done, could she? Despairingly she stared at Luke, who was watching her so intently. 'Oh, what'll I do?' she whispered wretchedly.

'Forget the old life, Estrellita.' His eyes glowed, warm and deep, sending prickles down her back. 'Leave it all behind you. Yes, I mean it,' he continued as she opened her mouth to argue. 'You've said the door's been locked on you—well, think of it as providential.'

'Provi—what?'

His mouth twitched, but only for a second. 'An opportunity sent by Providence. It would be ungracious, not to say foolish, to turn it away.' Rapidly he got up to step behind her chair, drawing the heavy coat more closely about her shoulders and throat. Then, leaning down, he said quietly into the tangle of her wind-blown hair, 'Come with me, Estrellita. I'll see that you're safe. Forget about your job and your old clothes—after tonight everything is going to be new for you.'

A strange enthralment forced her to rise to her feet, unable to deny him anything. The power he'd shown on the makeshift stage at the gaff was working again, and she had no wish to break the spell that made her feel warm, special, and able to do whatever she wanted. His friendliness, his nearness, and the music of his voice banished all her doubts.

Smiling down, he said quietly, 'Come along.'

Halfway to the door, though, her churning mind centred and, suddenly afraid, she stopped in mid-step, making him bump into her. 'But I can't spend the night with you!' She stared up into his face, looking for the reassurance he had shown earlier, but seeing now only cold impatience and irritability.

He took her by the shoulder, roughly pushing her on. 'Oh, come on, girl! We'll argue about morals when we get there. Out of the door with you—maybe we'll be lucky enough to find a cab to take us home. . .'

Home. The word contained enough promise of an unfamiliar security to quieten her anxieties and so, docilely, she obeyed. As he had hoped, a cab clattered up Fore Street hill within moments, and he hustled her into it, saying wryly, 'No hope of finding something more modern, I suppose, in this benighted part of the country—well, this will have to do.'

By now she was exhausted, both emotionally and physically. The old hansom smelled of worn leather and stale cigar smoke, and its gently rhythmic creaking lulled her into drowsiness. Her head began to swim, and almost at once she fell asleep against Luke's side.

Minutes later she was awoken by the sensation of being carried through the windy darkness into the shelter of a dimly lit house in a silent street. She bumped against his arms as he climbed the stairs, and was then unceremoniously dumped on her feet while he searched in his pocket for a key.

Bewildered, she watched him open the door, and then stumbled into the shadowy room before her. In the middle of the dark space, alone and half asleep, she felt utterly confused by all that had happened since she'd done the washing-up with Grace earlier in the evening.

She clutched the china egg more tightly. It was the only thing that appeared to hold any reality—and yet even that had been produced from her right ear. . . Wide-eyed, she watched Luke lighting a gas mantle on the far wall. He was muttering something about electricity taking its time to reach the provinces, but she paid no attention, slowly looking around her, taking in the drab curtains revealed by the spluttering light, the heavy furniture and the worn, patchy carpet underfoot. So this is what he had called home, was it?

Unaware that he watched, her face uninhibitedly registered her disapproval, and she was jolted back to the realisation of his presence beside her when he said crisply, 'Not exactly the Ritz, I know. But we'll get there one day, you and I.' With a vivid smile he removed the heavy coat still draped around Essie's shoulders, and she shivered, looking at him with an expression so childlike and helpless that a quick smile lifted his set features.

'That's worth a thousand pounds on stage, all that innocence and despair—but perhaps you might change it to something more cheerful for now? After all, you've got a roof over your head and a new job—so do brighten up, Estrellita, or I shall think I've bought a pig in a poke.'

'A pig? In a p—p——?'

'Poke. A bad bargain.' His light tone brought reassurance as he pushed her towards the fireplace, where a few charred coals still held the promise of warmth. 'See if you can mend the fire, will you? There's kindling behind the scuttle. I'll go and find something more appropriate for you to wear.'

Obediently, she knelt down in her usual skivvying attitude on the hearth, feeding reluctant flames with small, dry sticks. When he came back he said kindly, 'Splendid. Now we can get warm and have a nightcap before we go to bed. Put this around you—at least it'll hide that ghastly red satin monstrosity.' He turned away again, going towards a closed cupboard on the wall, and she slipped into the dark, richly patterned Paisley dressing-gown without demur, her tired wits trying in vain to cope with the extraordinary and alarming situation she now found herself in.

Returning with glasses and a bottle of brandy, he looked at her searchingly as she sat in a large, uncomfortable armchair beside the crackling fire. 'That's better,' he remarked critically. 'Except that purple clashes with your hair—now drink this and don't look as if the end of the world were nigh. Yes, I'm sure you're tired—*and* anxious—but you're also extremely lucky, Estrellita. Fortune has smiled on you tonight. You have me to look after you now. Me to work for. Me to help you learn the ropes of the business and push you up the ladder to success—so smile, for heaven's sake!'

Sitting opposite, he sipped the brandy, and she watched his eyes glitter in the firelight. She took a mouthful from her glass, and the raw spirit made her body tingle as it went down, but it brought clearer thought and a fresh wave of courage. She sat up straighter. 'I know you're trying to help me, but—but——'

Luke sighed, slumped deeper into his chair, and crossed one elegant knee over the other. He looked forbidding. 'What now?'

She pushed a straggling curl behind her ear nervously and said, 'I mean—well, I'm grateful to you for saving me, down there at the gaff. And for the cake and the tea. And——' she gulped as again the brandy trickled down her throat like fire '—and for bringing me here, where it's warm—and safe. But. . .' Bravery, bolstered by uneasiness and brandy, swelled. 'But I'm not that sort of a girl, see?'

He was silent for a long moment, and she longed to take back the words. Then his lips twitched and he looked at her with a very straight face. 'I certainly see a poor exhausted creature wrapped in my one and only dressing-gown. She's drinking my brandy. She's got a red nose and bare feet. . .'

Alarmed, Essie shuffled her toes deeper into the gown.

'But—well, I'm damned if I know what *sort* of a girl I'm looking at. For heaven's sake, say what you mean. And hurry up, because I'm ready for my bed.'

Panic made her squawk. 'But that's just it! B-bed! An' babies! I mean, I'm not going to—to—oh, lawks!'

'I *see*!'

Now Luke, the bear-boy she remembered, was grinning across at her. 'So you thought I'd brought you here purely for my wicked pleasure? To have my way with you? What a laugh!' And laugh he did, loudly, enjoyably, until she hung her head and wished herself anywhere else, even banging on the back door, about to face Mrs Grindle's rage, but not here, with Luke laughing so cruelly at her.

At last his mirth subsided, and his voice grew lower, kindlier, as he said, 'You silly little goose! Ours will be a working partnership, Estrellita, never more than that. Anything else would be a hindrance, so don't worry—what you fear is an impossibility. I suppose you don't know the meaning of Platonic friendship, you poor little unschooled scrap?'

Despite the mockery, she heard a warmth beneath the hard words that enabled her to meet his gaze, slowly shaking her head.

'Well, it means companionship, with none of the

shackles and burdens that a more intimate relationship inevitably brings.'

Not completely understanding, she sensed what he meant. 'Like in a marriage? When a man knocks a woman about?' Briefly, she recalled Uncle Tom on Friday nights, coming home from the pub.

Luke stared, nodded his head, then drained his glass. 'Yes, Estrellita. Like in a marriage. Or a love-affair. When a woman betrays a man. . .' The brilliant eyes grew suddenly dark, and the last words died away into an uncomfortable silence. He brooded for a moment, remembering.

Such reasoning was beyond her, but he'd said he wouldn't harm her, and so she brightened up, wriggled inside the dressing-gown, and said, more hopefully, 'That's all right, then. So can I go to bed? This stuff's made me all woozy. . .'

She hadn't expected further laughter, but again it filled the quiet room, and then he was on his feet, pulling her up, lifting her, his hands warm, making her flesh tingle beneath the thin material of the gown, carrying her across the room and putting her down on the narrow bed in the corner, where she quickly slid down between the cold covers. 'There you are, Estrellita. Sleep well, and have no fear. Remember how lucky you've been tonight, and dream of the day when we're both stars. . .'

'Stars, Luke?' Already her eyes were closing. She suppressed a huge yawn and gave herself to the seducing comfort of the bed. But she couldn't resist murmuring the two magical words—his name, and the other word that meant the dawning of a rosy future.

'Yes, stars, Estrellita—if my instinct tells me true. . .' He bent down quickly, as if on impulse, and kissed her on the mouth.

It felt like a moth's wings, fluttering against her sleepy, relaxed face. His rich, low voice came to her like soft music. 'I hope you don't snore. Now go to sleep like a good girl, and tomorrow we'll start our new life together.'

She sighed, turned her face on the pillow, and, even as she smiled her reply, fell asleep.

Backstage at the Theatre Royal was a confusing new world for Essie. She followed Luke as faithfully as a pet dog when they arrived there on Monday morning, alternately tripping over ropes and bits of properties, or bumping into scene-shifters and fellow artists busy rehearsing. It was like nothing she had ever imagined, not even in the darkest days of childhood, when dreams were all she'd had to help her face the stark reality of life with Aunt B. at Tan Court.

But, for all its strangeness, the theatre and its atmosphere of bustling companionship pleased her. The smells of size and paint, of hot bodies, of stale food and tobacco, seemed to her to be what the perfume advertisements said about Araby's most exotic fragrances. She came to a halt in a tiny room to which Luke had led her, and stopped in the doorway, gazing back, taking in everything—forgetting, for a moment, that he had told her to keep her eyes on him and not be distracted by the things that went on all around her.

And then she heard his voice, within the room, saying quietly, 'What do you think then, Mr Rivers? An asset to my act, wouldn't you say? I used to have an assistant in London, but——' She heard him cut off the words, and stored the fact in her mind to ponder later on. Guiltily, she realised that she had failed to obey his orders. Turning, she stared anxiously into the room.

'I'm sorry, Luke—I was just. . .' Then she was tongue-tied, for two pairs of eyes were steadily regarding her as she hovered uncertainly in the doorway.

Luke was half smiling, that lazy expression which did not quite thaw the customary ice in his gaze, although it held promise of a sudden guffaw of loud laughter. The man behind the cluttered desk merely stared with dull, assessing eyes. For a moment Essie felt she might just as well be a cow in the livestock market, so cold and calculating was his expression.

'Bit thin,' he said dourly. 'But I s'pose she can pad her costume. Legs any good?'

'Excellent. Hitch up your skirt, Estrellita.'

'I won't!' she squawked, affronted. 'What do you think I am?' Stiffly her hands went down to the sides of the blue woollen dress which Luke had recovered from the gaff before she awoke this morning. In the pocket she felt Ma's photograph. It calmed her, but she still wasn't ready to give in without a fight. She glared across the room. Then Luke was at her side, his quick smile for her alone, his hand warm on hers.

'Don't be silly, Estrellita. Mr Rivers is the manager of the theatre—I can't take you on stage with me unless he agrees. Every new girl has to audition for him, so show him your legs, quick—just an inch or two.'

It was far worse than appearing on the makeshift stage at the gaff with completely bare legs last night. There she had felt at home, but here, with that cynical, leering face staring so carelessly at her, she felt as if she was about to do something indecent. For a few seconds longer she hesitated, looking at Luke and then seeing in his face the reassurance she so badly needed. He smiled more deeply, more encouragingly. Well, if he thought she should show that horrid old man her legs then she supposed she must, but. . .

'For me, Estrellita?'

Clearly, he had read her thoughts. Her fears vanished. Grinning saucily with relief, she tweaked up her dress and without further anxiety stood in such a pose that her thin, black-cotton-clad legs became more elegant and attractive.

'Not bad. Well, Grimwade, if you're sure you can train her in time for the first performance tonight——'

'I can. I will.' Luke's voice was firm. 'She'll have to work hard, but I can guarantee that she'll do it.'

'All right. Now then—see here; the terms of your contract say nothing about an assistant, so I can't pay...'

Essie backed out of the room as Luke sent her a silent message to take herself off. She had no interest in the money side of things—she trusted him so completely. He had said he would look after her and the memory of his words last night echoed inside her head like a well-loved tune. To be looked after! To become a singer, a dancer, a magician's assistant, handling Chinese rings and silk scarves, maybe even a lovely white rabbit!

'Mind yer back.' Two stage-hands forced her into a dark corner, and the dream shattered, to be instantly replaced by the even more thrilling reality of the situation. Tonight, he'd said—that nasty Mr Rivers. The first performance was tonight, and already it was mid-morning, and she didn't know what she had to do, or where to go, or——

'Estrellita.'

Like a homing pigeon, she turned, her panic suddenly calmed as she ran down the passage to where Luke stood. But even as she started to gabble out her fears she sensed she was being a fool. Luke, in the theatre, was no longer the bear-boy.

'Stop your chatter. That's lesson one. I can't do with noise while I'm concentrating. Here's our dressing-room—in you go. Now, listen to what I'm going to tell you, and remember it all. We haven't got a lot of time, and if—*if*, I say—you're going to work with me you must learn the business very fast. Do you understand me, Estrellita?'

Standing close to him in the stuffy, dark little cell of a room, she nodded her head vigorously. If this was what he was like as a performer, then she'd just have to accept the unsmiling, set face and impersonal manner, because those words 'if you're going to work with me' were abruptly all-important. She would learn and remember and do whatever he asked of her. For already she knew she couldn't bear it if he ever said, 'Go away, Estrellita.'

And so they started to work. She watched, amazed and breathless with admiration, as he flexed supple fingers, produced coins from his pocket and ran through a series of deft palming movements. First the coins were there—and then they weren't. He tweaked one from the end of her nose, the hem of her skirt, even from the wispy red curls that framed her astounded face.

'Oh, Luke!' she giggled.

'Dexterity,' he told her severely, 'must be practised daily—you'll see me doing this for hours on end. But other tricks are my secret, and even you, Estrellita—although you're part of the act, standing close enough to touch me, seeing every move I make—even you can't be allowed to know how I do the really mysterious things.'

'Mysterious?' Her eyes became saucers.

'Magical things,' he said softly, and she heard his voice deepening. 'Illusions. Near-miracles. . .'

She was unsure if he was being serious or just trying to amuse her. She opened her mouth to answer cockily that she'd find out his secrets in the end, but his eyes took fire and blazed a warning. She stepped away warily. 'All right. I'll just have to guess, I s'pose—like the audience.'

He nodded and looked less alarming. 'That's it, Estrellita. You, like the audience, won't be let into the secrets. Now—let's try that scarf movement again. . .' With that quick change of mood that confused her so much, he was smiling, approving and friendly. She completed the trick with him and was rewarded with a 'well done' which restored her natural confidence. But in her head she stored a newly learned fact: Luke had secrets, and she wasn't to be allowed to know them, come what may.

And then, almost before she realised it, the day had grown into late afternoon and backstage had become quite different. Following Luke as he walked towards the stage door, she sensed a hidden excitement in the air, a feeling that everyone she met and passed, or even saw in the distance, was getting ready for a wonderful, important event. A woman carrying an armful of spangled costumes unexpectedly smiled as Essie brushed past her. The carpenter's mate, small, roly-poly and quite bald, raised a straggly eyebrow at Luke. 'Not long now, eh, mate?'

And even Luke had something different about him. Scuttling along after him into the chilly March evening, Essie wondered if he knew he had wound himself up like a tight spring. For a moment she wanted to ask him, but already experience was guiding her. The long day's work had shown her what a close relationship there must be between them if the act was to succeed, and so she held her tongue, remembering he disliked too much chatter.

But once out in the street, the tension of the theatre left behind, she dared to slip her fingers into the fold of his arm. 'Where are we going? To eat? Lawks, I aren't half hungry!'

With a quick stab of hurt pride, she realised then that he had actually forgotten she was there, for, at her touch, he looked down sharply, pulling his arm away from her touch. Abruptly, surprise filled his face and he stopped in mid-step.

He'd been deep in thought, remembering London, busily planning for the future, and now, suddenly, here was this scrap of a girl at his side. . .

A vivid smile softened his lean face, and amusement rang in his voice as, impulsively, he put an arm around her in a warm, reassuring hug. 'Good heavens! It's

Estrellita! I was miles away—I'd forgotten you; forgive me?'

'Forgotten? But you said as how you'd look after me...'

'So I did. So I will.' Grinning, he patted her hand, pressing it to his side, then adjusted his steps to her shorter stride. 'How remiss of me not to keep my word. I'm afraid that's how I am when I'm working, but you'll get used to it. Well——' he pushed open the door of a brightly lit café, full of people '—you've been a good girl, Estrellita. So tonight you may have some supper. In you go.'

They ate steak and kidney pie and a mound of potatoes, washed down with mugs of steaming, strong tea. Essie sat, replete with food and warmth and weariness, looking dreamily at the other occupants of the café. Luke's fingers drummed lightly on the table, and it was some seconds before she realised he was watching her. She caught her breath. Was it the stern magician or the friendly bear-boy who regarded her so steadily?

He said intently, 'I sent a message to your employer today, saying you had found a new position. Why didn't you think of doing it yourself?'

Colour swamped her throat and face. Neither the magician nor the bear-boy, but someone finding fault with her, just like Aunt B. and Mrs Grindle had done. 'I—I——'

'You're thoughtless. Self-centred. I'm surprised at you.'

'They wouldn't have cared what I did!' She tried to justify herself. Her voice rose and her cheeks sported red patches.

Luke stared coldly. Irritably, he said, 'They might have started an enquiry. Things could have become very difficult for me. For Mr Rivers. For you, too— you must learn to think things out for yourself, Estrellita.'

'Yes, Luke.' She bowed her head. He was right, of course. It dawned on her painfully that she had more to learn than merely how to hand him properties on a brightly lit stage and then curtsy prettily as they took their bow. Her colour died, and she looked up at him timidly. 'You think of everything. You're wonderful.'

Luke's smile flashed out. 'Of course I am! Every performer is—you, too, Estrellita. Believe me, you'll soon become as vain and conceited as I am! Oh, yes, a good performance makes one ready to jump over the moon. And then it all goes wrong, so it's long faces and bad tempers and gloominess. . .it's something you'll have to get used to, little star.'

She caught her breath. He was so handsome, such an obvious master of his craft, that the possibility of seeing him gloomy and cross made no impression on her. 'Yes, Luke,' she breathed adoringly.

He was watching her very closely, seeing in her rapt expression all the feeling and vitality that filled her. His good humour grew. Such a talent this little scrap had—together they would surely rebuild the act to even greater success than before.

'Have you had enough to eat?' he asked kindly, and she nodded, words suddenly gushing out, as she tried to express her gratitude and excitement.

'Oh, Luke, I'll do whatever you say, and I won't ever be bad-tempered, and—and——'

His mood changed abruptly. Yes, she had all that was needed, except for one important thing. Rising from his chair, he silenced her tirade with a masterful look. 'Be quiet, Estrellita. It's time we went back to the theatre. I must have some peace and quiet before we go on.'

Miserably she trailed after him, suddenly afraid. Did she really want to become a star? It had been dull and wearisome being a skivvy, but at least she hadn't felt as nervous as this. Yet, as soon as the stage door shut behind them, she felt a return of that marvellous anticipation which made her forget everything else. How right Luke had been just now! Soon they would be out there, before the audience...soon, soon!

From then on the moments of excitement mounted rapidly. There was a bustle of backstage activity, a ripple of voices as the audience started to claim their seats. The orchestra tuned up. Essie, playing truant for a moment, was kindly smiled upon by a passing girl dressed in sequins and feathers, who took her into the shadowy wings and pointed out a peep-hole in the heavy curtains bordering the stage. 'Go on, love, have a look. Anyone you know out there?'

Daringly, Essie put one eye to the tiny hole. At first, all she saw was a dazzle of bright movement, but then the blur broke into individual faces. A lady in a lovely pink flower-trimmed hat, a man whose pomaded hair gleamed like satin beneath the lights. The audience. *Her* audience! Essie caught her breath, feeling excitement start to tingle through her body. She turned to the girl at her side. 'Oh, it's marvellous! I can't wait to start!'

Blue eyes stared into hers, and a pert, pretty smile warmed her. 'New to it, aren't you?' asked a blunt, northern voice. 'First time tonight?'

Essie nodded.

'Once you get out there, love, you'll never want to do anything else. But how did you get this job with Luke? He's known to be a fussy one, all right...'

There was curiosity in the girl's face, and Essie said proudly, 'We're old friends,' as her memories grew near and comforting.

'That sounds nice. Tell me all about it some time, eh? I'm Alice Tomkins, by the way—me and Albert are the Francarti Twins, song and dance and acrobatics...'

'And I'm Estrellita Dart.'

'Eee! What a mouthful!' Alice's pretty smile glowed. Then she pulled Essie back from the curtain. 'Come on, we'll get shot if we're found here. The stage manager's a fanatic about being where you shouldn't be. . . Go back to your dressing-room and wait for your call. I'll see you later. Nice to have another girl on the bill—most of the acts are men or old hags, see? We'll have a cup of tea at the café tomorrow, shall we?'

'Oh, yes—but I'll have to ask Luke first. . .' Essie's words faded as she watched Alice trip away down the passage, only pausing to glance back and wave, before disappearing into her own dressing-room doorway. In a frenzy of joy, Essie ran back to find Luke.

'It's filling up! Lots of people. Oh, Luke——' Abruptly she stopped, meeting his reflected eyes in the long mirror that hung above the shelf behind which he sat. He was putting something on his face, making it pale, almost ghostly. His raven-dark hair had been carefully brushed so that, neater than usual, it shone with a bright, elegant gloss. He looked so handsome— but unfamiliar, slightly unreal.

Stupidly, Essie said, 'Oh—you look all different,' and he seemed to see her for the first time.

'Where've you been? Never mind. Hurry up and get changed, then I'll do your face.' His voice was impersonal.

Obediently she went behind the screen, where the costume which had so delighted her when the wardrobe mistress had tried it on was hanging. A silver sheath of tight satin, it enclosed her like a glove and made her look like a fairy-tale princess. She wore silk stockings and absurd shoes with heels that lifted her nearly to Luke's height. A cluster of sequins at the high neck of the dress brought an answering sparkle to her eyes as she stared into the mirror before stepping out from behind the screen to meet Luke's critical gaze.

He stood there, surely taller even than usual, dressed in a black frock-coat with a scarlet cloak hanging from his broad shoulders. The silver earring shone like a star, emphasising the crystalline brilliance of his light eyes. Essie let out her breath in a gasp of admiration. 'Oh!' she cooed.

'Turn around,' said Luke curtly. 'That's it. Remember, you must keep that skirt close to your body. I don't want you hiding anything that I do, or handle. . . Hold your head up. Stand straight. Yes. Now, come and sit down.' And then, because she still stared mindlessly at him, 'Be quick, Estrellita.'

In the smudged mirror she watched as deftly he painted and powdered her surprised face until she looked good enough to eat, like a rosy apple on top of a highly decorated silver bowl. Some dark stuff on her long eyelashes, the exotic jewelled and be-feathered head-dress fitted over her unruly hair, and . . .

'You're ready. Stand up. Let me look at you. Yes, you'll do.' He stared, from the topmost bespangled feathers to the small silver shoes.

'Five minutes, Mr Grimwade.' There was a hurried rap on the door, the call-boy's voice penetrating her suddenly heaving emotions.

'Oh, Luke! I'm scared!'

Suddenly her legs were jelly, her stomach full of butterflies. She stared piteously at him, ready to run back to Mrs Grindle and whatever punishment awaited her there. 'I can't go on! I can't! Not on that great big stage—not in front of all those people. . .'

She expected him to be merciless, to say in that cold and distant voice, which already she feared so much, that he knew she would be no good, that she had better leave at once, that he never wanted to see her again. . .

Instead, amazingly, he looked down thoughtfully at her for a long, terrifying moment, before reaching out to put his hands on her trembling shoulders, gently to draw her into his arms, cradling her, and whispering, with a bear-boy friendliness that made the quick tears rush into her eyes, 'Little goose! It's only stage fright, and every good artist has it. You'll be all right. I'll see you through. The first night is always terrible. Trust me, Estrellita—just trust me.'

He bent and brushed her lips with his own, smiling as he did so, and it was as if a current of something powerful, magical, entered into her. Essie could only gape.

But the moment was past. Luke stepped away and, reaching behind him, produced from the cluttered shelf the china egg, which had become her talisman. 'Here you are,' he said indulgently, his smile turning her legs to jelly, 'your lucky charm. Every performer has a charm of some sort—a rabbit's foot in his make-up box, a special ring, or a necklace. . . You, Estrellita, are the very first to put your trust in a china egg. But then, you're a very special girl, aren't you? A star in the making!'

She clasped the egg to her bosom, and looked at him with glowing relief. 'Really, Luke? Really and truly?'

'I think so, Estrellita. If you do as I tell you. If you think hard, and behave well. If you. . .' He paused, and touched her hot face with one long, powerful finger. 'If you stay as you are: sweet, young and—innocent. . .'

Then he stepped away from her. 'Time to go on,' he said crisply, adjusting the heavy, scarlet-lined cloak. 'Make sure your head-dress is firmly fixed. Don't turn your back on the audience, not ever—and, for God's sake, Estrellita, smile! Try and remember all I've taught you. Now come along.'

She followed him along the passage as in a dream, stood beside him in the hot, dark wings, listened unthinkingly to the applause greeting the last duet the Francarti Twins sang, and then, without realising what she was doing, stepped out on to the stage to feel the lights, searingly hot, embrace her, to sense the expectation of the waiting audience.

This, thought Essie, with a shock that sent a shiver tingling down her back, was the moment she had been waiting for all her life.

CHAPTER THREE

THE heavy dark red curtains lifted with a hiss and an accompanying scurry of dust around Essie's feet. Luke's hand reached out and held hers. It was cool and firm, and seemed to be controlling her. As the first reaction of fright swept through her, his finges pressed harder, and then she was no longer the new Estrellita, on stage for the very first time, but merely Essie in her old blue woollen dress, learning the act in the dressing-room that smelt of fish and chips and even older mustiness.

Watching Luke, she suddenly grew cool and quick-thinking. He looked magnificent, so masterful and strong. He smiled at her, his brilliant eyes sending a message. The scarves. The Chinese rings. The box with the see-through panels. The coins. The wand, hovering up there, without any visible support. . .handkerchiefs slipping through her fingers as if she had always been able to handle them so easily. And already the finale was here—she produced the old tin kettle, handed it to Luke, and listened, her smile never faltering, as he asked the audience to request their favourite drinks.

He poured out glasses of whisky, tea, lemonade. Obediently she ran down the steps at the side of the stage to deliver the glasses to the hands that were held up. She waited while the varied liquids went down hot throats, while faces lit up with amazement and pleasure, returning to Luke's side in time to watch him turn the full kettle upside-down, with never a drop of liquid appearing, before finally throwing it into the cheering audience.

The act had ended. Time now to take their bow.

The theatre rang with fervent applause. As Luke dropped his hands to his side, he stepped forward, smiling first at the bright faces down in the stalls and then, slowly, all around the shadowy auditorium, while the plaudits thundered even louder.

Essie stood motionless, as she had been instructed, at the side of the stage, eyes riveted to Luke's radiant face. Inside her, wild emotion swelled until she thought she must burst from sheer excitement and happiness, but Luke's insistence on discipline at all times on stage remained in her churning mind.

Not until he turned and came to her side, reaching for her hand, pulling her with him back centre stage, did she dare to look away from him. For his smile still bore a message, and she knew now was the time when she, also, must thank the audience which applauded so freely.

Her eyes went slowly around the theatre, as his had done, and her smile grew. Luke released her hand, stepped back, bowed to her, and she was alone. Shyly she curtsied, until the short silver dress brushed the dusty boards. 'Smile,' Luke had said, 'whatever happens. . .' Again, she let her luminous smile embrace the cheering crowds.

And then his hand was around hers again, sweeping her off stage as the curtains billowed down behind them. In the airless, dark wings, he pulled her close, so that she was crushed against his chest, his resonant voice vibrating through her body, the joy in his words making her gasp with delight. 'Marvellous! Well done, my little love—I knew you could do it. Ah, here we go, let's take another bow. . .'

She was pushed ahead of him through the gap in the closed curtains, and again the lights, the heat and the voices engulfed her. Then back into the shadows, down the long, shabby passage dotted with numbered doors, back to the dressing-room where reality awaited.

Running ahead of him, Essie immediately found

what she looked for—with the china egg in her hands she whirled around as he entered, closed the door and stood, looking down at her.

'It *is* lucky!' she crowed. 'As you said, it's my lucky charm! Oh, Luke, weren't we good? Wasn't it just wonderful?'

She expected smiles and further praise. Instead, Luke turned away wearily. 'No,' he said flatly, 'it wasn't. You were late handing me the box and you nearly dropped one of the rings. We'll go over it all again tomorrow—over and over until you could do it in your sleep.' He took off the cloak and hung it on a peg then sat down heavily before the long mirror, avoiding her hurt eyes. 'Go and change, Estrellita— and be quiet, will you? I've told you I can't stand too much chatter. A performance drains me. . .'

She stood transfixed, not believing that he could switch so fast from sheer enthusiasm to such critical condemnation. 'But—you said—just now, when we came off, that I—I was. . .'

Wretchedly, she watched as he began wiping off the pale, thick make-up. Curtly, he said, 'Yes, yes, I know—you think I'm being hard on you. But one mediocre show won't take our act into London's West End—and that's where we've got to go.' Suddenly, his eyes found hers reflected in the mirror. 'You have a lot to learn still, my girl,' he said wryly. 'So—you weren't too bad tonight, but tomorrow you must be better. Understand?'

Tears threatened, but she kept her head. It wouldn't do to cross him, not when he was like this: tired, unfriendly and full of criticism. She began unfastening her head-dress, and from her trembling fingers drew a new strength. Damn him, he wouldn't get her down, whatever he said or did. 'You're worse than Mrs Grindle, you are,' she exploded. 'Couldn't do nothing for her. . .'

'Your grammer is atrocious, Estrellita.' He glowered

at her from beneath thunderous brows, but she was beyond caring.

'All right, Mr Know-all, couldn't do *anything*, then—and it's the same with you, Luke Grimwade! Out there you said I'd done well, and called me your little love, and now——' The flood of words ended abruptly. *My little love.* Had he really said it? She bit her lip, remembering. One tear ran down her hot cheek and she brushed it away furiously.

Luke was on his feet, standing beside her, looking at her with a strange expression on his face that made her start with alarm. She'd seen him mocking and friendly, hard and distant, but this was a new side to him. He looked passionate and eager—something she'd never hoped to see.

His gaze took in her hair, her swimming eyes, and her drooping mouth. 'And now?' he asked, very low, fingers suddenly cool on her feverish cheek.

Something new and fervent in his voice, the caress in his fingers, made her tremble, caused the brimming tears to spill over. 'And now it's all spoilt!' Emotion burst out with fierce relief.

'Because I told you the truth? That you'd done well enough for a first night, but that you'd made mistakes which mustn't ever be there again? Surely not just because of that, Estrellita? Even an innocent scrap like you knows about discipline and obedience. . .so tell me why, suddenly, it's all spoilt?'

His nearness, his unexpected understanding, the warmth of his hands reaching for hers, made it impossible to say why. How could she remind him of those three wonderful words which had made her heart sing louder than all the applause of the audience? If he didn't know what he'd said and done, well, she'd die rather than tell him.

But he did know. 'My little love,' he murmured, bending his head to kiss her pulsing throat, her pink cheeks, and then putting his lips on hers in a sweet, light kiss that left her trembling.

'Oh, Luke!' She clung to him, hardly daring to believe what was happening. So he did care, after all. He wasn't cold any more, he. . .

'Estrellita, little Star, little love, you have so much to learn—and not just about our act.' Carefully, then, smiling tolerantly, her pushed her away towards the screen at the end of the room. 'But we'll talk about that later. Hurry up and change, and then we'll go home.'

'But, Luke——'

'Do as I say.' The quiet authority calmed her, and she undressed without another word, her mind taken over completely with the memory of his kiss. The few minutes it took her to change into her woollen dress and old coat, re-dress her hair and wipe the make-up from her face, gave her time to decide what to do next. She would show him she could be quiet, could perform better tomorrow, be the well-behaved girl he wanted, if only he would. . .

Just as she was ready to come out from behind the screen, however, there was a rap on the door, and a man entered, stepping into the dressing-room as triumphantly as if he were making an entrance on stage.

'Well—didn't think I'd find you in a one-eyed dump like this, Luke! Not after that splendid season in London last year.'

The voice was jolly, but something in Essie shrank from it. Ned Monsey had sound jolly at first, and instinct now told her that this newcomer's jollity was also only a cover-up for something far less pleasant. Yet he seemed friendly enough. She stood behind the screen, watching him take off his hat, smiling broadly at Luke. She saw Luke's face freeze, heard his voice suddenly erupt, curt and defensive.

'Harry! Good God, where've you come from?'

Essie quivered at the unwelcoming tone. Carefully,

she inched towards the edge of the screen, where she could see better. The man standing beside Luke was of the same height and build, but there any resemblance ended, for his face was weak and fleshy, his hair a nondescript greying brown and, despite his actorish manner, he lacked the star presence that Luke possessed. Essie disliked him on sight, and waited for Luke to get rid of him in that same distant manner he occasionally used towards her.

Slowly the surprise on his face died. Essie watched an expression of chill suspicion settle, saw how his lips tightened and his eyes glittered dangerously. Leaning back against the make-up shelf, he looked at Harry's outstretched hand and studiously ignored it.

'So!' he said, at last, and his voice was cold enough to cut the heavy atmosphere. 'The bad penny turns up again. What in hell do you want, Harry?'

'Heard you were down here in the West Country. Couldn't seem to settle into another act without you, Luke, old man—kept thinking how good we'd been. How good we could be again. . .'

Essie thought the stranger's voice was full of false bonhomie.

Luke's gaze grew thoughtful. 'You feel we should forget our differences, Harry? Team up once more?'

'I do, indeed, Luke.' Harry threw his jaunty felt Homburg on to the shelf alongside Luke, where it fell among the greasepaint and empty mugs, and, uninvited, came into the centre of the little room, looking around, smiling as if he felt at home there. He stood with legs apart, hands in the pockets of his smart single-breasted tweed jacket, unblinking, pale eyes finally smiling confidently into Luke's guarded gaze.

'Watched you tonight. Of course, the old magic's there—but not like it was.' Leaning forward, jovially he punched Luke's shoulder, and the smile grew sly. 'After all,' he went on, 'you need me. Can't do it without me, can you, old man?' His throaty laugh made Essie wince. 'I'm what's known as indispensable, eh? Well, your luck's returned, Luke, old friend—here I am again!'

Luke was still staring, eyes chill, a frown setting his face in rigid lines. Essie watched the newcomer's confidence fade, then heard the almost pleading note in the thick voice, as he cajoled, 'We could build up the act again—think about it, eh? Said I was sorry, didn't I? Well, then. . .'

Luke stood motionless, eyes fixed on the soft, smiling face. Essie held her breath, instinctively aware of a crisis, and one that would affect her as much as Luke. 'You're saying I can't do without you, Harry. You know my ambition, and you're playing on it.' His voice was reflective and quiet, but Essie, knowing him, felt the coiled spring within him slowly tightening.

'I'm thinking of that contract we were chasing in the West End, old man—the one you'd set your heart on. Well, it's still possible, you know. London audiences are going mad over magic shows these days, I can tell you. Saw Houdini last week; what a genius! But nothing to what *you* could do, Luke. I mean—what *we* could do—together. . .'

The words mystified Essie. Luke had never said his previous assistant was a man, and she couldn't believe this wheedling Harry would look as good on stage as she did. She frowned. Why was he saying all these things? What was he trying to get Luke to do?

Silence lapped the hot little room, and Essie, in her growing uneasiness, moved clumsily. The screen tumbled sideways and she stood revealed, cheeks very red and eyes anxiously watching Luke's face, awaiting his rebuke.

But his smile was full of humour, and the charged atmosphere abruptly collapsed. 'As usual, your timing is immaculate,' he murmured, and then, louder, 'Estrellita, allow me to introduce Harry Whitman, an erstwhile colleague of mine. Harry, this is my new assistant, Miss Estrellita Dart.'

Essie blushed, but held out her hand proudly. She didn't know much about social graces, but she realised that Luke was introducing her as grandly as if she'd lived in a palace and not Tan Court. 'Pleased to meet you,' she said brightly, hiding her dislike of the man whose smile sent prickles down her back. She gave Luke a rapid, sidelong, adoring glance.

Harry Whitman's fingers were limp and moist. He replied ingratiatingly, 'Lovely performance, Miss Dart,' and his eyes flickered up and down her body in a rapid, sensual sweep.

Casually, Luke said, 'Pretty, isn't she, Harry? Talented, too. She and I are going places together. Without you.' And then, taking his coat from the peg, he opened the door, stretching out his hand to take Essie's. 'Come along. It's time we were off home. Goodbye, Harry.'

'But Luke—don't be like this! I came all the way down from town...you're a fool! You'll regret not taking up my offer...' There was a hint of violence in the words that made Essie cling all the closer to Luke's arm as they left the dressing-room and walked quickly towards the stage door.

'Don't look back. Don't say anything,' Luke ordered, hurrying her along.

The cold air outside the theatre was a slap in the face to Essie's wrung emotions. She tried hard to keep up with Luke's long strides. 'Who was he, that Harry? I didn't like him. Why did he say all that about the act not going well without him?'

Abruptly, Luke stopped in mid-step, looking down at her with a fierceness that made her catch her breath. 'Do all women chatter as much as you, Estrellita?'

She stood her ground. 'I wasn't chattering, I just wanna know about him. After all——' She hardly dared say it, but found the courage as she recalled the enthusiastic audience's reception of their performance.

'I *am* part of the act now. I—I have a right to know. Don't I?'

The street was crowded with theatre-goers shouting for cabs and waiting for omnibuses. Jostled by passers-by, Essie waited with trepidation for Luke to answer. Had she gone too far? Would he curtly tell her to mind her own business?

Beneath the lamplight, she saw irritation cross his face, followed by a certain grudging glint of quickly hidden amusement. He grabbed her hand, and once again led her on, saying sharply, but without the coldness she feared, 'Women! Heaven preserve me from them!'

'But you can't do without *me*, can you, Luke?' she asked pertly, reassured by that flash of humour.

Once more he stopped, so abruptly that she nearly lost her balance. He stared at her and his voice rasped, 'Don't ever say that again, Estrellita, or I'll throw you back where I found you.' His tone grew loud and angry. 'I can live quite well without your company, let me assure you. . .'

'But I only meant you needed me. In the act. . .' Dismayed, she watched his eyes thaw, then grow deep and sad. For a moment he stood there, still staring, and she sensed the uncertainty filling his mind. Instinctively, she smiled. 'Let's go home, Luke,' she pleaded softly. 'It's cold, and I'm tired. . .'

And this time it was her hand that found his, leading him away from the city lights into the shadowy sidestreet where they lodged.

She was awoken by Luke muttering in his sleep. Quickly she slid out of bed, tiptoeing across the room to where he slept on a mattress before the lingering fire. She knelt, and dared to put her hand on his forehead. 'It's all right, Luke—just a dream, I expect.'

He didn't awaken, but restlessly twitched his head away from her light touch. 'Damn you, Harry, you know me too well. You know what I want. But I'll get there on my own—somehow. . .'

And then he was still again, breathing quietly and regularly. Essie sat back on her heels, staring wistfully at his pale, haunted face. Something strong and urgent arose inside her, and before she knew what she was doing she was leaning down, kissing the straight mouth, conscious of the harsh prickle of unshaven stubble, wondering at such outrageous behaviour, yet consumed with a burning need.

He slept on, as peaceful now as a small child, but Essie, returning to her own bed, lay awake for a long time, aghast at the thoughts and longings that raged inside her.

Next morning they rehearsed, as Luke had ordered. Again and again Essie went through the movements required of her until repetition grew tedious. She ventured a question as the hours slid past and her stomach began to complain. 'Aren't we stopping for dinner?' Suddenly Luke dropped the coin he was palming, and she stepped back as he bent to pick it up. 'Oh, lawks! I'm sorry. I didn't mean to—to——'

His face was set and brooding, its leanness accentuated by the heavy shadows beneath his eyes. Essie forgot her fear of his anger as anxiety flew through her. 'You're tired. Didn't you sleep?'

Wearily, he turned away, going to the fireplace, where he leaned against the mantelpiece, head in hands. Essie hesitated, unsure what to do or say. Then she remembered the quarter-full bottle of brandy, and ran to the cupboard to find it. She poured a full glass and offered it to him. 'Drink this, and I'll go out and buy some bread and cheese.'

Luke straightened up, stared at the glass, and then at her. Slowly he nodded, the beginnings of a smile easing the strain on his face.

'You're a good girl, Estrellita,' he told her huskily.

'Kind and thoughtful. And I know I'm difficult—I don't deserve someone like you. But—well—thank you. . .' Now the smile was in full flower, its strength and charm having a weakening effect on Essie's legs. 'No,' he added, sighing a little, 'I didn't sleep very well. I was too busy thinking. . .'

She watched his left hand rise to finger the silver star in his ear. It was on the tip of her facile tongue to mention the nightmare, but wisdom was slowly growing within her. Instead, 'Let's have a tanner, then,' she said brightly, holding out her hand. 'I'll be back before you've finished that drink,' and, grabbing her hat and coat, scurried down the stairs and out towards the shops.

She had no intention of being longer than the errand took, but fate decided otherwise. First, she bumped into Alice Tomkins, looking into the window of the smart draper's shop in the High Street, and couldn't resist saying hello.

Alice beamed. 'Oh, shopping, are you? Just look at that dress—lovely, isn't it? One of the new tea-gowns. . .' Wistfully, she turned back to the window, and together they stared at the peacock-blue concoction of sweeping silk that had caught their eyes.

'One day,' said Alice determinedly, 'when Albie an' me is rich, I'll have a dress like that. Ee, think how it'll feel—how it'll sound, all those pleats swishing and crackling. . .'

Essie handled the solitary coin in her pocket, remembered her dream, and tossed her head. 'I'll have one, too,' she said earnestly. 'Only I'll get mine before you do—I'm going to be famous *very* soon.' For a moment they looked into each other's covetous eyes, and then giggled.

'You did all right last night,' Alice told her warmly. 'Maybe some manager or producer'll be in the audience soon, and pick us both out for a new show in London. . .'

Essie caught her breath. 'Is that how it'll happen? Like that?'

'Of course. Only you've got to be *really* good to be picked. Got to have an act that catches their eye, see? Here, I'll tell you what——' Alice's pert face took on an impish expression '—you want to do a little twirl—all on your own, see—when Luke's not looking—in case someone grand's out there watching. So that they'll see you've got extra special talent. . .'

'Oh, I couldn't!' Essie was shocked. 'I only do what Luke says. He'd be so angry——'

'Pooh!' Alice shrugged her shoulders and marched off down the street so that Essie had to run to catch her up. 'You'll never be famous, never have a lovely dress like that if you let *him* take over your life.' She looked at Essie sharply. 'Where are you going?'

'To buy our dinner.'

'Huh! Fish an' chips? Or p'raps *caviare*?' Alice pronounced the strange word in a way that made Essie laugh aloud.

'Bread an' cheese!' she exploded. 'Or maybe a nice bit of eel. . .'

'Me too.' Alice linked her arm through Essie's, and together they approached the fish café. They were talking so hard as they went that at first Essie didn't hear the thin voice calling her name.

'Essie? Essie Dart! Well, I never——'

She looked around, stopped, gasped. 'Grace! What are you doing out here?'

Grace's downturned mouth pursed tightly, and she pulled her unbecoming black hat more firmly on her head as the bleak March wind sneaked around the corner on which they stood. 'I might ask the same of you, Essie. *I'm* doing an errand for the mistress.' She held up a library book, and stared disapprovingly at both girls.

'I'm——' Essie felt the old rebellion surfacing in spite of her new-found wisdom. She met Grace's glare with a bright smile. 'I'm shopping with my friend. We're both showgirls, you know, Alice an' me. . .'

Grace's obvious horror was added fuel to the wicked fire now burning steadily inside Essie. She gave her imagination free rein. 'The Theatre Royal this week,' she boasted airily, 'London next, and after that we're off to Paris. Paris in France, you know, Grace——'

'I know where it is,' said Grace, shocked. 'And I know what goes on there, too. Why, Paris is the place where the King goes to meet Mrs Keppel—respectable girls should never go there!'

Essie slid a sly grin at Alice, and they both swallowed their mirth. 'It's only for a week or two, Grace.' Essie couldn't stop her story once she'd started it. 'An' then I'll be back with Luke, as I am now. Luke Grimwade, the magician, you know. I shall be famous an' rich, an'——'

'Luke who? Eh?' Grace's eyes were huge.

Essie graciously explained. 'My employer. The man I work for. He teaches me the act, you see, and looks after me. . .'

'He's your protector?' squawked Grace in horror. 'You mean you live with him? You wicked slut. . .!'

Essie's delight collapsed. She scowled. 'Course I live with him—where else would I go? Not back at Aunt B.'s, thanks very much. An' Mrs Grindle wouldn't want me no more—any more—would she?'

Grace sniffed and pulled herself up very straight. 'You're past all hope, Essie Dart. Living in sin with one of those stagey rogues and vagabonds. . . Well, I'll pray for you, but you'll go to hell, the way you're going, and that's all I can say.' She drew away as if both girls had the plague, and went quickly down the busy street, leaving them looking at each other doubtfully.

Alice's hearty laughter was infectious, and as they went home with their papers of hot fish Essie finally laughed too, but inside she felt anxious and guilty. Was it true that sharing a room with Luke was really living in sin? She couldn't wait to ask him.

The opportunity came very soon. After the fishy newspaper had been cleared away, and mugs of tea made on the gas ring in the corner, Luke sat by the little fireplace and smiled companionably at Essie.

She knew she must pick her moment. Incessant chatter made him cross, so, seeing his smile, she slid out of her chair and settled herself on the hearthrug, looking dreamily into the flames as she chose her words. 'Luke, can I ask you something?'

'Mm.' He sounded genial, and looked relaxed. Clearly, the food and the warmth of the fire had done him good.

She took a deep breath. 'We're living in sin, aren't we?' Suddenly she looked up at him, tense and wide-eyed. 'Oh, Luke.'

She watched anxiously as he put down the empty mug and leaned forward until his face was close to hers. Amused and lazy, he asked, 'Who's been telling you that?'

'Someone. Luke—is it really wicked, our being together like this?'

He sat back, regarding her very intently. 'For heaven's sake, Estrellita! We're not living with old Victorian morals any longer! This is a new century, a new age. Why, the King himself is showing us how to live—with elegance and laughter. Glamour, if you understand the word. So stop thinking about your Puritan-minded Aunt Beattie and her righteous, narrow ideas. Enjoy yourself!'

'But Grace said. . .' She bit her lip, avoiding his laughing eyes. How could she say it while he looked at her like that?

'I can't imagine what. But tell me. Go on.'

Grabbing at her dying courage, she muttered, 'That we'll go—to—to hell. . .'

Luke's explosion of mirth held a hint of anger, and she looked back at him warily. 'It's not funny!'

'Of course it is, you little idiot!' Taking her by the shoulders, he gave her a shake, but she saw good humour replace the annoyance she had feared. 'When will you learn that the Graces of this world live in the past? What's sin to them has become a way of life now.'

She wasn't convinced. 'But, Luke——'

He let her go, his gaze burning into her confused thoughts. 'No,' he said at last. 'We're not wicked. Because we're not really living together, are we?' A dark brow quirked upwards, and she blushed.

'I see.' She stared awkwardly into the fire's leaping flames. 'So it's just—just sleeping together, is it? I mean, we don't—but if we did, would that be wicked?'

Luke stroked her hair, and she turned quickly, meeting his deep-set eyes, full now of a sadness that touched her heart. 'No,' he replied flatly. 'Not if we loved each other.' Then he frowned, as if clearing his mind of something painful. 'Estrellita,' he asked quietly, 'have you ever loved anyone?'

Her eyes widened with surprise. 'Of course I have. My cousin Will, who was kind, and played games with me when I was little.'

The corners of Luke's mouth twitched. 'I meant since you grew up. How old are you, Estrellita? Seventeen?' She nodded, and he added, 'Since you became a woman. . .'

Something in his voice, his mesmeric gaze—or was it perhaps the sheer excitement of knowing herself to be a grown woman now, no longer a foolish creature?—struck deep chords within her. She thought hard. As a woman, who did she love? The answer came swiftly, too fast and truthful to be carefully considered. 'Just you, Luke.' And then, even as the words flew out, the new-born woman inside her knew they would have been better left unsaid.

She blustered unsuccessfully. 'I mean, you've been kind—given me this chance—looking after me. . .' Her voice quivered, for she could see by his expression that she had said too much. He disliked hearing her chatter on like this. He was always telling her so.

She tensed, all her contentment abruptly gone. He must be thinking her stupid. She dared to meet his eyes again, and saw with a new glow of hope that his face was full of something she could not identify. Not mockery. Not anger. Not even the pain he had shown her once or twice. A softer, warmer expression. He said nothing, but reached out his hand again, curling powerful fingers delicately around the curve of her throat.

'So you love me, Estrellita? How strange.'

The music of his low voice made her blood sing. She sat entranced, conscious only of his touch and of the unbounded joy rising within her.

Then he removed his hand and his voice grew firmer. 'No, no. You think of me as a father, or a brother—an employer who will feed you, keep you safe from the Monseys of this world,' he told her authoritatively. 'You know nothing of love, little star.'

'Oh, but I do! I do, Luke! I know that I love *you*. . .' She was torn between happiness and tears, her words husky with emotion, hands instinctively reaching out in a bid to make him understand.

Irritably, Luke shook his head, and slowly her hands fell. She turned away to the fire, shoulders drooping and her heart full of a misery that she knew nothing could ever relieve.

Until, after a long silent moment, he got to his feet, pulling her up beside him and looking deep into her swimming eyes, saying harshly, 'You don't realise what you're saying. Love is trust and faith and commitment—and what do you know of all that?'

With every ounce of strength she could muster, she whispered, 'I just l-love you. . .' as if it was a charm that would remove the brooding, cynical expression from his face.

'Love!' He sounded doubtful.

'I won't—won't ever ask you for anything, Luke, but let me stay—oh, please let me stay. . .' Her shaking voice trembled into silence, and she could only watch his eyes registering his thoughts. Disbelief. Anger. Was it memory? Certainly sadness. And then, the wonderful miracle she had forgotten—the quick change back to amusement.

Luke's thoughts were legion. This little scrap he'd picked out of the gutter was so vulnerable—so lovable. At first, he'd only thought of the help she'd be in rebuilding the act, in aiding his ambitious return to London. But now her sweetness had made him realise he had a responsibility towards her. She would always attract men—and some of them the worst kind, like old Monsey. So surely the least he could do would be to offer his protection, see that she came to no harm in this dangerous world of theatre?

The decision was swiftly made. Throwing aside his former moodiness, he dropped a kiss on the end of her nose, and smiled lightly, as if the bear-boy had pushed aside the shadows and come out into the open once more.

'Well,' he said, almost matter-of-factly, 'if you feel that way, Estrellita—if you're afraid of hellfire—I suppose we must do something about it.' He took her hands and smiled reassuringly into her anxious eyes. 'Would you like to take my name? How about becoming Mrs Luke Grimwade?'

CHAPTER FOUR

'MRS LUKE GRIMWADE!' Essie's most fantastic dreams had never gone this far. Foolishly she gaped at Luke, eyes wide in disbelief, and watched his face soften into a tender, amused smile. His strong fingers stroked her trembling hands.

'Is it such a terrible idea?' he asked lightly, and she gulped back her surprise before she could reply.

'No! Course not! I mean—well—oh, Luke...' Amazement lessened, and her thoughts began to fly out in all directions. Mrs Luke Grimwade! His wife! *Marry him*... Why, that meant she'd be with him for the rest of their lives! The act would—surely it must?—become famous, and they'd be rich and happy ever after. Suddenly, she saw her entire life mapped out, the childish dream a miraculous reality.

'Yes, I'll be Mrs Grimwade—not 'alf I won't!' Now she was beaming, her whole being vibrating with excitement and joy. Pulling her hands from his grasp, she flung them around his neck, forcing his head down to meet her ecstatic kiss.

Taken completely unawares, Luke's response was merely brotherly—until his arms met around her warm body, and he pressed her closer, closer. And instinctively Essie responded.

Their kiss seemed timeless, growing in fervour until, abruptly, he drew back, staring down with eyes so full of haunted intensity that her rapturous smile died.

'What is it? Why do you look like that?' And then, as the old inferiority once again rushed in, 'What've I done wrong? What've I said?'

She realised, watching his face set into heavy lines, that for some reason his wrought emotions made it impossible for him to reply. Then, sensing his need, bravely she put her hands against his chest, smiling up at him. 'It's all right, Luke,' she coaxed huskily, thinking that he must be regretting his offer of marriage. 'I won't be no trouble—honest, I won't. I'll do what you say, and I won't chatter, and—and. . .'

She didn't understand then why he grabbed her hands, fondling them almost roughly, or why his expression changed so fast—why his low voice hovered between pain and mirth, as he said unevenly, 'You funny little scrap! Oh, God, am I doing right in taking you on, I wonder?'

'Yes,' she assured him earnestly. 'Yes, you are. Two can live as cheap as one, and I'm good at penny-pinching, always had to be——'

'I don't mean the money, Estrellita.'

'Oh.' She watched his eyes, deep greeny grey pools of regret that quickly mingled with uncertainty and only half-hidden wry amusement. 'What, then?'

'Us,' he told her bluntly, still holding her hands close to his chest, so that she felt the steady thump of his heart. 'You and me, being together. You're so vital, so young. I'm older. And more experienced, more ambitious——'

'But I'm ambitious, too, Luke. I wanna be a big star.' Her voice faded into dreaminess, and he shook his head, a reluctant smile chasing away the shadows that bedevilled his face.

'You're incorrigible!'

Not knowing the word, she decided it was a compliment. 'Thanks! An' you are too—honest, you are!'

'Estrellita, we must be very serious about this.' He moved away, her hands still in his, sitting her down on the far side of the hearth, and then standing with his back to the fire, looking intently at her bemused face. 'After all, sharing my name is a sort of contract, you see.'

Essie listened tolerantly. He was so tall and so

handsome, she didn't care how boring he was being about the old contract. If he wanted to go on, then she'd let him—just for a bit. But not too long. She yearned to jump out of her chair and fling her arms around him, go on kissing him for ever and ever. That first long, demanding kiss just now had been so wonderful, awakening such extraordinary feelings and sensations inside her—well, if that was what marriage was like, then she could hardly wait for their wedding day.

He talked again about the contract—whatever that might be—as they walked to the theatre, and Essie nodded docilely, and kept saying, 'Yes, Luke,' without really hearing a single word, for her mind was filled with just one glorious fact—she was going to marry him!

But, back in the dressing-room, her dreamy mind began to focus on reality once more, for Luke was in a chatty mood, one that she had not encountered before, and insisted on talking to her as they both changed and prepared for the evening performance.

'Tell me about your childhood, little star,' he invited, sitting down and reaching for the greasepaint-stick. 'We must get to know each other better.'

Behind the screen, her fingers suddenly ceased fiddling with the many hooks and eyes that fastened the silver sheath. Memory abruptly came alive. 'I lived with my aunt Beattie and uncle Tom——' Tan Court seemed a million miles away now.

'And your nice kind cousin Will. . .'

She peeped around the side of the screen suspiciously. Was he making fun of her? No. She saw only curiosity in the blue-green eyes that looked up, twinkling at her, before she disappeared again. 'That's right; Cousin Will.' She smelt the spice and snuff on his grocer's assistant's white coat. Could almost feel the handful of raisins that he'd always hidden in his pocket for her.

Luke's quiet voice made her blink. 'Were you happy, Estrellita?'

'No. I've never been happy. Not till now.' In the small, square, tarnished mirror on the wall behind the screen, she watched her face flower into a wide, rapturous smile.

'Tell me.'

Instinctively, her hand reached out to feel the pocket of the blue woollen dress, hanging over the back of the screen. 'My ma left me with Aunt B. when she went back on the stage, when I was born.'

'In the business, was she? What did she do?'

Essie pulled out the photograph and stared at it. 'She was a dancer, my ma was—a singer, too. She ran off with an ice-cream man, Aunt B. said.' Pride made Essie's eyes glow. 'She had to go back on the stage, see.'

'Mm. Didn't that make you sad?'

'Course not.' Then she frowned, and thought about it. 'Well, just a bit—but I know how she felt, 'cos I feel the same.'

She heard Luke's chair scrape back. Warmth and excitement filled her. Pulling aside the screen, she found him beside her, looking down, his eyes thoughtful. 'In the blood, I suppose,' he said slowly, almost to himself. Then he frowned, dark brows menacing her new happiness. 'You're a little fool, and so was your mother,' he told her sharply. 'There's no lasting happiness in this business.'

'But *I'm* happy...' Essie looked up pleadingly, thinking how extra-handsome he seemed in his magical make-up, the brows pencilled even blacker than normal, eyes cleverly widened and deepened, and a great curling moustache emphasising the lean angles of his thin face. She shuddered for no reason she could think of, and hastily produced the small photograph for him to see. 'My ma.' She smiled down at the oval print in the frail gilt frame. 'Pretty, isn't she?'

Luke took it from her. 'She reminds me of someone,' he mused. 'But, of course, it's you—she's not as pretty as you. But you've got her nose. Her hair.' Suddenly the frame broke into two parts, one falling at their feet.

'You've broken it! Here, give it to me. . .' Essie bent, trying to snatch it up, but Luke was there before her, turning the two pieces over in his fingers.

Carefully he removed the photograph from the remainder of the broken frame. 'I'll mend it for you. This piece chipped off, that's all.' He handed her the small oval piece of faded board with the photo pasted on to it, and Essie turned it over curiously. She had never seen it out of the frame before.

She caught her breath. 'Look! There's an address.'

Narrowing his eyes, Luke read the brown, spidery writing aloud. 'Mrs Isabel de Carle, 57 Middle Brimley, Teignmouth, South Devon.' He laughed, amused. 'Didn't go very far, did she? Not much scope for a small-time dancer and ice-cream man at Teignmouth, I would think—unless they lived near the pier. . .'

Essie was instantly incensed. 'Don't you make fun of my ma, Luke Grimwade!'

'I'm not,' he told her, straight-faced. 'Simply pointing out the reality of the situation. Here, give me the photo——' Looking down at the broken frame, he held out a hand, but Essie clutched the precious photo to her breast.

'Don't be silly, little star. I'm only trying to mend it for you.' And then, because no photograph was forthcoming, he looked up and saw the hurt in her eyes, sensed the tension that filled her small body, and realised just what this one memento of Ma meant. 'Estrellita?'

She blinked, suddenly vulnerable because of the sympathy in the quiet word. 'What?'

'I promise to mend it for you. Go and sit down and do your face, and don't be so upset.'

By the time she had made up her face—and it looked rather blotchy, she thought anxiously, because she'd never done it before—his capable hands had made whole what was broken. He stood behind her chair, smiling gravely into her reflected face, as if restoring a precious toy to a distressed child. 'There you are, all mended.'

'Thank you.' Lovingly, she held it in her cupped hands.

They looked at each other in the mirror and he ran a finger down one bare shoulder. 'One day,' he said, very low, 'I'll tell you about *my* past. But not now. It's nearly time to go on.'

Essie jumped up, giving him a dazzling smile. He seemed so agreeable that suddenly she knew what she must do, now—now, before they went on stage, because—who knew?—Luke could be funny and changeable at times, and suppose the act went wrong, and he said he didn't want to marry her after all, when they came off?

'I'm going to see Alice,' she said rapidly. 'Just for a moment. About—about being Mrs Grimwade. . . Let me go, Luke? I'll be back in time, honest. . .'

'You child!' But he grinned, calling out to her, and swinging his silver watch emphatically as she turned. 'Eight minutes, and if you're late I'll eat you for supper!' But he was smiling good-humouredly, and she ran down the passage, bursting into Alice and Albie's dressing-room with only a quick rap to announce her arrival. She had pictures in her head, voices in her ears. There would be flowers, a new dress, music, Alice and Albert, all dolled up in their best, and she and Luke walking solemnly down the aisle of that huge, shadow-filled cathedral, side by side. . .

The dressing-room smelt of hot hair and stale costumes. Essie leaned against the door, and said breathlessly, 'Luke an' me's going to be married—will you be my bridesmaid?'

Alice, busy with curling tongs, giggled. 'Will I? Heck! You bet I will. Popped the question, then, did he? You clever lass! Here, sit down, love, tell me all about it. . . Albie, take your lionskin and put it on over there. Go on, we won't look.' Her eyes sparkled, and she held the tongs so long in a ringlet that her hair began to smoke. 'Oh, Lor! Set the place on fire, I will! Give me that glass o'water, quick—ow! Stings, not half it don't. There, that's all right. Well? Go on, love, tell me.'

But Essie had had time to think things over. Luke was a man of secrets, and they weren't hers to tell, not even if she knew them. Not yet. So, with a wisdom that surprised herself, she merely said rapidly, 'Will your Albie give me away? Haven't got a father, see. . .'

A disembodied voice from the far end of the room muttered something about not having a dark suit for a wedding, but Alice frowned, and said firmly, 'I'll see to it, love. Got a ring, have you?'

Essie looked at her work-hardened hands and frowned, abruptly unhappy. Luke hadn't said anything about a ring, although everyone knew it was the most important thing. An engaged girl always sported her ring to show how clever she'd been, how happy she was going to be. She avoided Alice's gimlet gaze, saying hastily, 'Going to get it tomorrow. No time this afternoon.'

'Lovely.' Very carefully, Alice powdered down her pink face. 'What sort o' ring?'

Essie's dreams took flight. 'A ruby. Blood-red. Big as a doorknob.'

'Set in brass?' They exploded into laughter. As Alice dried her eyes, she asked, 'What about the dress, then? White silk and a bookay o' orange blossom?'

'No,' said Essie primly, with a new-born sense of duty. 'Luke can't spend too much; we've got to think of our future. But——' she allowed herself the smallest indulgence '—p'raps something cheap. Or free. Aunt B. used to get nice things left over from church bazaars, or the Ragged Market.'

'I know!' Alice tidied away the cooling tongs, and critically assessed her make-up and crimped hair. 'Ask Mrs Taylor to lend you something out of Wardrobe. She wouldn't say no, not if you slipped her a shilling.'

'I will. Oh, I will!' Overcome with excitement, Essie hugged her friend. 'Got to go now. Mustn't miss our call. See you later.'

'Aye. An' remind Master Luke about the ring, love. The brass doorknob one. . .'

Essie was still smiling when she got back to their own dressing-room, where Luke paced restlessly up and down the tiny space. His eyes were brighter than ever, and enthusiasm lightened his thin face. He swung round as she entered. 'About time! How you women love to gossip. . . Now, listen, Estrellita, I've got it all worked out——'

'Five minutes, Mr Grimwade.' The call-boy's voice brought a swift expression of impatience to Luke's glowing face.

During the last twenty-four hours he had thought hard and deeply about Harry's return. Despite the disaster last year in London, they had been together too long to split up for ever. He knew all too well what Harry was like—unreliable, devious, and a womaniser, but he was still Harry of the shared childhood, and the success of last year's West End stardom. So—wasn't this a second chance that mustn't be turned down? Wouldn't it be unlucky to disregard it? He touched his earring—a new girl, a new act, and a reformed Harry to help build it up once more?

He chuckled to himself, even as his mind cleared. Harry Whitman, reformed? Hardly likely! But—the laugh died, and his eyes glittered as the vision of a London theatre with the name of The Great Grimwade sparkling outside filled his mind. Suddenly he knew.

He'd take the chance and damn the doubts to hell—he and Harry together again, last year's hard lesson learned, and Estrellita to put the final gloss on the act. . . Yes. *Yes*! He had decided.

He stopped his pacing, and looked at Estrellita very intently, talking fast, eyes alight with enthusiasm. 'I've decided to team up with Harry again. After all, he's come looking for me; I'd be a fool to say no. . .' For a second the exuberance paled, and a frown narrowed his hooded eyes. His gaze seemed to bore through Estrellita into a region she could not imagine. 'We've got to forget last year,' he went on, almost to himself. 'Both of us. Oh, I know he's a bit of a rogue—an opportunist, one for the girls. . .but we've been together so long. We've learned it all by long, slogging years of effort, so, yes. . .' Then again he was smiling, and now he seemed to Essie a radiant, god-like figure who could excel at anything he tried to do.

'We'll get there! We'll be stars again—and you too this time, Estrellita!'

Abruptly she was swept off her feet and whirled around the dressing-room. Luke planted a kiss on the end of her nose, and then she was back on the ground, a little dizzy, but so happy that her words tumbled out like a stream in spate.

'It all sounds wonderful! Stars! And me being Mrs Grimwade, too. . . Oh, Luke, what about my ring? I've got to have a ring. . .' Her voice tailed off, for Luke had taken her hand and was pulling her after him, out into the passage, closing the door behind him.

'That can wait. If we get a suspicious landlady you can always wear a curtain-ring. Come on, little star, put your mind on what we're doing *now*. . .' He released her, slapped playfully at her bottom, and sent her running into the hot, dark wings, confused about her precious ring and wondering whyever a landlady should be suspicious.

But then the magic of performance took over, and

as she followed Luke on to the stage she forgot everything but this exhilarating moment. His voice rang in her ears—'put your mind on what we're doing *now*'—and she did her utmost to obey the order.

Essie couldn't believe it—not a proper marriage? No church, no flowers, no choirboys singing 'Oh, Love Divine'? No Alice and Albie, all decked out in their best?

'I—I don't understand...oh, Luke, but you said——' Her handkerchief was rolled into a soggy ball, which she clutched with shaking hands, crouching miserably in the chair by the dying fire, home again after the performance, not wanting Luke to see her like this, but unable to contain her heartbroken disappointment.

He was pacing, like a caged animal, face set, and eyes dark with what she thought could only be annoyance. 'For heaven's sake, girl, stop your wailing! Why, you'd think the whole world had come to an end, the way you're carrying on...'

Pausing for a second, he flashed a look at her, realised how deep was her misery, and immediately resumed his restless steps, angry with himself for inflicting such hurt, but irritated, too, by her naïveté. 'You must have realised what I meant,' he growled. 'I offered you my name and my protection, that's all—I couldn't have made it clearer, surely? How was I to know your foolish, romantic little mind thought I meant a *real* marriage? Great heavens, we've only known each other for about five minutes!'

'T-ten days,' she hiccuped wretchedly.

Luke stopped abruptly, and darted a scowl at her. 'Trust you to have got it all worked out. Like the wedding. I suppose you've even been to the cathedral and booked next Saturday morning, have you?'

He sounded so exasperated that Essie's tears stopped flowing. Sniffing hard, she put the wet handkerchief back in her pocket and managed to return his scowl. 'No, I haven't. An' don't make fun of me, Luke Grimwade, else I'll—I'll. . .' She chewed her bottom lip and tried to stop herself shaking so stupidly. She'd made a fool of herself all right, but she'd get over it, she supposed dully.

Luke watched the struggle going on inside her, and suddenly all his irritation fled, as he acknowledged wryly to himself that it was engendered by his own guilt. Kneeling by her chair, gently he smoothed back the wiry red tendrils running down her wet cheeks, and looked deep into her still swimming eyes. 'Look, little star,' he said apologetically, with a hint of amusement in his low voice, 'it's just a misunderstanding. I meant one thing, and you another. No harm's done, so can't we forget it? Kiss and make up, perhaps?'

Essie sniffed and gravely bowed her head. 'I'm s-sorry,' she whispered, with great dignity. 'I got the wrong idea. But I understand now. And th-thank you. . .'

Luke's amusement died, and for a moment he felt humbled. 'I'll look after you, Estrellita,' he assured her, his low voice very gentle. 'You may call yourself Mrs Luke Grimwade, and we'll share a room in digs, because that's cheaper, but. . .'

Her eyes stared straight into his, and suddenly he was embarrassed. Surely she hadn't really imagined they would sleep together? Ridiculous! But then he remembered the few kisses they had shared, and something warm and lovely moved deep within him. Then he read the expression on her face, and felt guilty all over again. Had he led her on? Made her expect too much? Of course she was a desirable and lovely scrap, and he would enjoy teaching her how to love, but. . .no. He got up from his knees and stiffly walked as far away from her as he could get. He had sworn never to love, or even trust, another woman. So little Estrellita must remain a virgin, make-believe wife.

'Well, you'll be Mrs Grimwade from now on, little star!' He forced a note of sham gaiety into his voice. 'There'll be no more Monseys bothering you, and if, when we go down to Plymouth next week, we find our landlady is looking at your left hand, I'll get you a ring to wear.'

Silence. Turning, he saw she was out of her chair, coming over to stand before him. She had a new expression on her face, one that surprised him. He hadn't realised little Estrellita could look so independent.

'Thank you, Luke.' Her tone was as light as his had been. 'You've made it quite clear. So let's. . .' for a second she paused, and a fleeting expression of vulnerability crossed her upturned face '. . .kiss and make up, the way you said, shall we?'

Bemused, he nodded, and bent his head towards hers. Her lips tasted of salt tears and were as gentle as a summer breeze's light caress. Then she turned from him, and Luke felt once more that stirring within him, a sensation he had prayed never to feel again. She was so lovely, so honest—so truly good. He watched her getting ready to go to bed with a mixture of irascibility and genuine regret.

But within minutes he was able to remind himself of the fact that this was a sham marriage, of convenience only. And he would do well to remember it.

Harry Whitman came the next morning, recalled by a message from Luke, and Essie saw the look on his soft, weak face—a sort of I've-been-waiting-for-this-moment look. He pumped Luke's hand at once, and started reminiscing about the London season last year.

'Can't forget it, can you, old man? Stars on our dressing-room doors, those crazy reviews, cheering fans waiting at the stage door as we left—oh, yes, and all those pretty girls wanting our autographs!' His eyes gleamed slyly. 'Believe me, Luke, we'll do it again—and we'll be even more successful this time!'

Luke's reaction was equally volatile, and for a while they shared the happy memories. Then Luke grew more practical, and he turned in his chair to look at Estrellita, sitting near by, busy with some mending. He flung out a hand, impulsive, caressing, and stroked the top of her head. 'Harry—something you should know. . .'

'What's that, old man?'

'Estrellita and I are—well, not married, but sharing my name.'

Essie sensed a note of awkwardness in his words, and came to the rescue, smiling across at Harry with a friendliness she didn't feel. 'My new name is Mrs Luke Grimwade. It's cheaper to share a room, see? And. . .' her eyes sparked suddenly '. . .and it'll keep me safe from nasty old men.'

'Very wise. You're a beautiful bride, my dear.'

There was enough prurience in Harry's smile to make her shudder, and, instinctively turning to Luke for reassurance, she was alarmed to see quick anger rise in his eyes.

He got to his feet in a sinuous, almost sinister movement, towering over Harry as he stared down at him and said, very softly, but with deliberate menace, 'Hands off this time, Harry. I'm having no repetition of last year—understand?'

There was a brief, awkward silence. Essie quivered, sensing the suddenly charged atmosphere. Then Harry's hand fingered his weak chin, and he shook his head, smirking unattractively.

'Of course not, old man! As I said, that's all over. Forgotten.' The sly, pale eyes glanced quickly in Essie's direction. 'Just my way of complimenting the little lady—no harm meant. . .' The blustering words tailed off.

Essie's eyes, riveted to Luke's face, saw with

immense relief that he had accepted the devious apology. His face was stern, and a nerve twitched at the side of one cheek, but he nodded, and sat down again. 'That's all right, then. But—just watch your step, Harry.'

The two men stared at each other, Luke with suspicion still plain in his narrowed eyes, Harry grinning fatuously in his effort to heal the breach.

And then, once again, things were back to normal, and Essie let out the breath she had been holding for what seemed hours.

'So—where were we?' Luke's taut question brought a wordy answer from Harry, and, while he gabbled facts and figures, and mentioned names she'd never heard before, she began to understand a little more of Luke's past—and a conflict about a woman, which had involved Harry. And now Harry was here, smarmily trying to make up for whatever had gone wrong before.

Darkly, she wondered if Luke really knew about Harry's slyness, and his animal passions, but she would never dare to ask. Better to ignore him. Never let him come too near, though—another Ned Monsey, was Harry Whitman.

Now, suddenly, she realised the benefit of having Luke's protection, and felt doubly grateful. Turning her head, she met his brilliant eyes, watching her, even as Harry went on talking, and was surprised at the emotion she saw in them.

They talked long and deeply until it was time to leave for the theatre. And again, after the show, Harry came back to the lodgings. Plans were discussed and discarded, new ideas debated. Their voices rose and fell until Essie was almost lulled to sleep.

She felt exhausted, what with the performances, and the shock of knowing her fairy-tale wedding had turned out to be just a dream. If only Harry would leave. . .

She yawned loudly, and tried to catch Luke's absorbed eye.

At last the two men stood up, shook hands and seemed ready to part. Essie woke herself up and managed a chilly smile in Harry's direction. He grinned back, clasped her hand moistly, and said, 'Sleep well, Mrs Grimwade,' in a knowing whisper that wasn't meant for Luke's ears.

She ground her teeth, until the door closed behind him, and then burst out, 'I can't stand that Harry Whitman! All oily and—oh, I dunno—but he's just *nasty*. . .' Too late, she realised how foolish she was to show her feelings.

Luke turned, in the act of damping down the few remaining coals, and stared at her. 'Then you'd better find another job,' he said wearily. 'Harry's part of our act. For God's sake, girl, try to be friends, can't you?'

'I just—don't like him. . .' Hastily, she tried to make amends. 'But I will try, honest, I will. . .' She paused. 'Luke?'

His name seemed torn out of her. She wanted to run into his arms, to explain how tired and disappointed she was, to ask if he couldn't find it within himself to take her on as a proper wife, so that her loneliness and sense of fear would disappear, but, bitterly, she knew that it was no good. He was—had been, would be again—a big star, and she was only a jumped-up skivvy, an inexperienced part of the act.

And he'd made it absolutely plain that she was Mrs Luke Grimwade in name alone. Looking away from his watchful gaze, she said, in a tiny, dismayed voice, 'I'm going to bed now.'

'Yes. Very well. Goodnight, Estrellita.'

They stared at each other until the silence seemed about to explode. 'But—not alone? Oh, Luke—please—not alone?'

He moved fast then, one hand heavy on her shoulder, forcing her over to her bed beside the far wall. 'You're tired. Overwrought. It's been quite a day. Hop in and you'll be asleep in two shakes. Go on; do as you're told. . .' Again he met her pleading eyes, and she saw his expression grow hard and wretched.

'I told you,' he said, in a fierce, low voice, 'I told you it was a sort of contract. Just a business proposition. Giving you my name to keep you safe. To make sure I had a good, trained assistant. And nothing more. *Nothing*. . . I told you, and you didn't say no, did you?'

She remembered that walk to the theatre. Her, bouncing along in a dream-world, and Luke's voice going on about the rotten old contract. This was what he had meant.

Dismay and pain surged together. Suddenly, she screamed at him, 'I hate you! All you think about is the act! The damn old act! Well, I want more than that. I—I. . .'

He was about to walk away, to leave her, but before he turned she caught a glimpse of erupting passion in his deeply hooded eyes, and knew that, beneath his frozen mask, he too raged. That he, too, was lost and yearning. Instinct told her, startled, that he wanted her as deeply as she longed for him. But he would not—could not—allow himself to show that need. Or that love. . .

Silent and miserable, she got into her cold bed, and heard him doing the same. It was a bitter end to a strangely chilling few days, and for a long while she lay sleepless, going over all the events and conversations leading up to this disastrous climax. And then, just before sleep finally overtook her churning mind, a face swam before her eyes.

Ma. Not sideways on any longer, like the photograph, but looking at her now, smiling, saying something she couldn't quite hear. . .

Essie's last waking thought was that, in spite of Luke's rejection, she wasn't really alone after all, for

Ma had certainly been through all this. This lack of loving, this boring matter of the business always being so much more important than people. If only I could find her, she thought drowsily. Talk to her. Wonder how we'd get on?

She dreamed of looking for Ma. Of knocking on doors and at last being welcomed into warmth and homeliness. And in the morning, when the growing light awoke her, she heard Luke's steady, regular breathing, and came to an important decision, born out of his coldness to her, and her own urgent longing for love.

She would find Ma. She had the address on the back of the photo. One day she'd go there—one day soon. Finding Ma! Just think of it—having a family again, trying to forget Luke's harsh words, talking to someone who would understand, comfort and perhaps advise. . .

Yes. Very soon she would go and find Ma.

CHAPTER FIVE

PLYMOUTH was no better than Exeter, thought Essie crossly, worse, actually, for it rained all the time and, the day after they arrived, while walking on the Hoe, a gale-force wind had blown away her violet-trimmed hat. She'd had to coax Luke into giving her money for a new one.

'Don't be extravagant,' he warned her. 'We need every penny. Why didn't you run after it and save it?'

''Cos it blew into the sea,' Essie snapped. 'And I'm sorry, but I can't swim. Didn't think you'd be pleased if I drowned and you had to train a new girl. . .'

'Drowned, not drownded,' he corrected automatically, and then looked at her suspiciously. 'Estrellita, you're getting above yourself—answering me back.'

Blandly she smiled into his disapproving, curious eyes. 'I'm your wife. I can say what I like now.'

'I suppose so.' But he didn't sound pleased.

They shared an even seedier room than before, and Luke slept on an ancient chesterfield that wasn't quite long enough. His bare feet, white and strangely vulnerable, hung limply over its edge and were the first things Estrellita saw in the mornings when she awoke. In an odd way they emphasised her loneliness. She longed to creep out of bed and go over and caress those pale, slim feet—so cold, so open to whatever life and the relentless Plymouth weather sent their way.

The strength of her longing grew uncontrollable, and one morning she found herself actually kneeling on the threadbare carpet beside Luke, staring down at his relaxed, sleeping face. More than anything in the world at that moment she wished she had the courage to pull back the blanket, slip in beside him, and wind her arms around his warm, yielding body. She longed for warmth and human contact. Oh, dear Lord—if only he would love her. . .

He awoke, looking directly into her wistful face, shook his head, yawned mightily, and then turned over, so that all she could see was the back of his thinning, striped nightshirt.

'Put the kettle on, there's a love.'

His voice was husky with sleep, unguarded and gentle, and made her heart race, her hands hanker to stroke his ruffled black hair. But, even only half awake, his power over her was still strong, and so she whispered, 'Yes, Luke,' angry and lost with disappointment, but still his to command.

It was the same at the theatre. As the days passed she missed Alice's chatty company more and more. Sometimes she slumped into despondency, and the only bright spot was being on stage with Luke. But the joy she had experienced of working with him in Exeter was gone. For now Harry Whitman was here, and the act was no longer a happy partnership.

Harry lodged a few streets away from them. 'Old friend,' he told her with a knowing grin. 'I was born and bred in these parts. Always find a friend when I need one. It's wise to keep in contact. . .'

He was constantly at Luke's side, suggesting this, arguing about that. Essie watched and listened, her awareness growing daily. She noticed that where the performance was concerned even Harry was not allowed to interfere. On stage Luke came into his own, magnetic as ever, dominating the act.

'We'll try out Leda and the Swan at the end of this run,' he told her one morning, his face vital and his smile warm. 'The last night, maybe—see how rehearsals go. I've got it all worked out with the stage manager.'

They had gone into the empty theatre directly after breakfast on the Monday of their second week in

Plymouth, Luke's eyes burning with inner fire as he planned ahead. 'Estrellita,' he called, beckoning her from the shadowy auditorium, where she wandered among the empty plush-covered seats, staring upwards at the gilt cupids and swags of opulent decoration. 'Come over here—quickly.'

'What is it? What are you going to do? A new act?' Recognising his excitement, she felt it entering her own mind. This, then, was the beginning of their return to London—the first illusion, aimed to be tried out on a provincial audience and then repeated as a show-stopper up-country.

'Leda was very popular last time we did it,' he told her, animation softening the hard lines of his thinly bearded jaw. 'There's no reason why we shouldn't repeat it.' He gave her a rapid, brief smile. 'A moment of glory for you in it, too.'

'What've I got to do?'

'Listen carefully, first of all, and remember everything I tell you. You'll have to learn the timing——'

Harry's thick voice cut in offensively. 'Suppose she can count, can she?'

'Course I can!' Essie was enraged, and turned to glare back at him. 'I'm not an ig—ig——'

'No, you're not an ignoramus, Estrellita.' Luke's eyes glowed kindly at her. 'Take no notice of Harry. I'm sorry, little star.'

Essie's fury died in the knowledge of his understanding, and she listened obediently to the list of instructions, finally asking, a little bewildered, 'Who was this Leda?'

Luke paused. 'The wife of the King of Sparta.'

'King of *what*?'

Harry's unkind guffaw made her flinch. For a second she feared Luke's reaction, but he lowered his voice, smiling patiently. 'She was an ancient Greek, Estrellita. A queen. And she took a lover—actually the god Zeus, who came to her in the form of a swan.'

'A swan? A lover? Lawks, I'm not having anything to do with that. . .' Her face flamed and, like Harry, Luke laughed, but the expression on his face was gentle, and slowly she calmed down.

'It's just a tableau, Estrellita—a picture, a scene. No need to get worried. Here, come and sit down and I'll tell you exactly what happens.'

Beside him in the front row of the stalls, the quietness of the dark theatre emphasising their closeness, Essie was slightly mollified by the fact that he was taking the trouble to explain everything in simple words she could understand. She listened intently as Luke's musical voice painted the picture for her.

'We show a studio on stage. You know the sort of thing—a garret, with an attic window, and a sculptor—that's me—busy shaping a lump of clay into a statue of Leda and her swan lover.'

'But, Luke—I'm not clay. . .'

'No, Estrellita. You're a warm, responsive woman.' He turned, looking deep into her eyes, and her heart fluttered. 'And it's because of what I know you can put over to the audience that I'm deciding to repeat Leda and her swan. The other girl I used. . .' for a second his face grew cold, his voice distant '. . .hadn't your talent for showing true emotion. You'll be better. Well——'

The doubtful compliment chased away the last of Essie's uneasiness. 'So there's the clay,' continued Luke, using his hands in demonstration, 'formed into a swan, and another lump that looks vaguely like a human form. And then——' He stopped suddenly, and she saw a rare satisfaction fill his shadowed face. It lighted up his sombre features, made the deep-set eyes glow more vividly, and allowed her own spirits to soar. Now she would do anything he asked—anything—just to see him so happy.

'And then?' she prompted timidly.

His smile caressed her. 'And then I magic you into

the clay, little star, and you're there with the swan, and you'll show the audience that you're truly a woman in love. Easy, isn't it?'

'Yes. Oh, yes, I can do that all right. . .' She bit her lip. Would he realise what she meant? That she knew all about being in love? Or would he argue, rebuke her, remind her once again that they were merely a working partnership and it was wrong of her to say such foolish things?

But Luke smiled. She felt his steady gaze almost mesmerising her. Involuntarily she made a sound—was it pleasure, or pain?—and he took her hands in his, bending close, whispering, as he said, 'Will you do this for me, Estrellita? I know it's not singing, or dancing, which you love—not even handing me scarves or boxes. No, it's something quite different. It's acting. And I believe you can do it very well. Will you try—please?'

Unable to speak she nodded, and encouragingly he pulled her up with him as he rose. 'So, let's see how it goes, shall we? Come along, on stage with you. . .'

Following him, she heard Harry's voice in her ear, and wondered quickly where he had been sitting, how much he had heard. 'Wind you round his little finger, can't he, eh? Trust old Luke! Always knows how to work a woman up. . . Tell you something, shall I?' He edged nearer, his breath moist and warm on the side of her averted face. 'In London, last year, we went to parties where the women were all over him—couldn't keep their hands off him. That's what stardom does for you! He had the pick of London society, and old Luke knows how to choose—I'll say he does!'

Bewildered and abruptly apprehensive, Essie allowed herself to be placed on a wooden plinth. 'We'll make it marble by the end of the week,' Luke told her merrily, his hands arranging her body in an artistic pose. She lay immediately behind lumps of dirty-looking, brownish-beige clay, which Mr Pascoe, the stage manager, brought out on to the empty stage and dumped without even looking at her, his big red hands fully occupied with the setting up of the properties.

Harry stood in front of the pit, centre stage, watching Luke's every move with unblinking concentration. 'Nothing attractive about that,' he shouted up to Luke, nodding in Essie's direction. 'Can't see a single line of her body through that thick dress.'

Luke's brows rose. 'She'll look better without her clothes,' he called back over his shoulder, and then winked at Essie's shocked face. 'Don't be worried. You'll be wearing a tightly fitted pale pink tunic—I'm not having the Watch Committee making complaints. Now, are you comfortable? Sure?'

She nodded, even though feeling stiff and awkward, and hating the fact that Harry's eyes were on her.

'Stop worrying,' scolded Luke. 'Don't be so tense. Be yourself. Forget everyone out there. . .'

Was he telling her that Harry didn't matter? She managed a stiff smile, and Luke turned away, shouting for Mr Pascoe, who then came and rigged up some thick gauze drop-curtains an inch from her nose. 'Don't 'ee move,' his deep voice warned, still not looking at her. 'Don't want my gauzes ripped. Just stay nice and still. Remember you'm a statue—and don't 'ee sneeze whatever happens. Gauzes cost money. . .'

Luke took up his position beside the lumps of ugly clay. 'Now, Estrellita, you can see what I'm doing. Watch my hands out of the corner of your eye, but don't let the audience see that you do so. Start counting. And *don't move*. . .'

'That's what Mr Pascoe said. Well, of course I won't move.' She felt disgruntled and stupid. Singing and being Luke's right hand, ready with rings and scarves, had been child's play compared with this business of having to try to act.

He came nearer, smiling into her defiant eyes. 'Acting is only being someone else, little star. You know what it is—you do it all the time, although you don't think you do. So now you've got to be a queen who's in love with someone else.'

'A bloomin' swan. . .' There was ridicule in her voice, and he shook his head good-humouredly.

'Easy. Forget it's a swan. Imagine it's actually a god—Zeus himself, with a straight Greek nose, curling hair, and a wonderful body. And a love for you that's greater than heaven and hell put together!' He paused, then bent lower so that his face was only inches from hers. 'Feel it, Estrellita,' he begged. 'Let it come out. Try, please try. . .look, I'm shaping the clay—see my hands? Making the curves of Leda's body, her arms, her legs, going up again to form the arch of her back, her long, beautiful throat, her face. Eyes, nose, mouth, soft sensual lips. . .go on, little love, act—for me—please. . .?'

Imperceptibly the gauze curtain rolled up, and Essie started acting. Easily, and with a degree of pleasure that made her forget the restriction of the hard plinth on which she lay. Suddenly she was no longer Essie feeling stupid and awkward on an unlit stage, with the carpenter ogling from behind the flats and Harry Whitman unashamedly devouring her with his prurient eyes from the front of the pit below. No, she was another being, a woman in love, and although, smiling wistfully at the lumpy plaster swan beside her, obediently she tried to imagine Zeus, the Greek god, as Luke had suggested, of course it was Luke himself she thought of.

Luke in her embrace. Luke sharing her love. Oh, yes, it was easy enough to portray on her face and in the softening of her body and her limbs the semblance of a woman in love—she just did it.

A silence spread throughout the stage and its billowing, drab curtains, broken only as Luke's beaming face shattered her daydreaming. 'I knew you could do it. Marvellous! You're a born actress. . .' Pulling her up from the plinth, he hugged her joyfully. 'If that doesn't catch the West End by the throat, then I don't know what will! We'll try it out before we go—that still gives us a full week of rehearsal. . .not bad, though, on the whole. Now, Pascoe—Pascoe—we need to do something about that clay; it's too hard to use. . .'

Essie, forgotten, watched him chase after the stage manager, cornering him in animated conversation, and sighed. Standing disconsolately in the middle of the empty stage, feeling herself and her new achievement instantly cast aside, she became aware of Harry coming through the wings towards her.

He grinned unpleasantly. 'Mustn't let old Luke get you down; he's uncaring with women, a moody, selfish chap, most of the time, I'm afraid. Not like me, eh?' He touched her arm, making her look reluctantly at him. 'Always got a smile, I have—see?'

He stood very close, and she couldn't stop herself responding to the cheeriness in his voice. Looking up, she watched the promised smile flash out on his almost chinless, fleshy face, and let a little hiccuping sigh of unhappiness betray her disturbed emotions.

'I don't care. It doesn't matter.' She saw a sly knowledge deepen his pale blue eyes, and added defiantly, with a touch of the old snappiness that always came to her when he was near, 'I don't know what you mean, anyway.'

'Yes, you do. I've seen the way you look at him. Pretty girl like you shouldn't bother with a cold fish like Luke. Come on, now, Essie. . .' His arm went around her shoulder, and she pulled away.

'My name's Estrellita.' The familiarity, added to his personal comments about Luke, was too much. Tossing her head, she marched away from him, but Harry clung, like a shadow.

'Not to me it isn't, darlin'. You may be a cold old mouthful to *him*——' jerking his head sideways

'—but to me you're warm little Essie, with lots of love waiting for the lucky man.'

Halting, she stared. His logic was undeniable. And something else raced through her mind. She disliked his loose, full mouth, and the knowing expression in his slightly protruding eyes, but he resembled Luke in some other, mysterious way.

Her silence seemed only to encourage him. Taking her hand, he slid it into the crook of his arm. Then, winking, he led her off stage, down the passage towards the stage door, talking persuasively as he did so. 'You an' me could get on very well. Lots to talk about, I dare say.' Again he slid a quick glance at her. 'Like to know about old Luke, wouldn't you? His past and so on? After all, you are Mrs Grimwade. . .' The easy laugh, full of insinuation, turned the knife in her festering wound. Dumbly she nodded, and felt his arm pressing her hand closer to his side.

His warmth and understanding, sly as it was, over-rode her inherent dislike of him. Desperately, she needed company. She longed to talk, to be with someone who would listen, sympathise, and perhaps even advise. And Harry was an old friend of Luke's. Maybe he could tell her something that would help her accept the complexity of Luke's mercurial character.

Her indecision and need must have been plain on her face. Harry smiled into her distressed eyes, nudging her hand even closer. 'Tell you what; we'll go for a drive. Like that, wouldn't you? Girls always go mad over motor-cars, and mine's a Rover 8—bought it with last year's money. It's beautiful as a woman—well, almost. . .'

Again, the laugh. Then a knowing glance. 'No need to tell Luke, of course. Not that he'd mind, but—well—know what he's like, don't you?'

'I couldn't do that!' She was shocked by his duplicity. Luke's friend, but playing games behind his back? Sticking out her chin, she glared disapprovingly and pulled her hand away. 'You've got a nerve, Harry Whitman!'

'You're right, darlin'! And it works wonders! Come on, don't be so stuffy!' His smile was very broad. 'Just a drive up the road in a motor-car? Nothing wrong there. Why, the way you're looking you'd think I wanted something more...'

Essie blushed and was furious with herself. Pale eyes glinted mockingly. 'You're a rotter, you are! Don't know why Luke bothers with you——'

'Can't do without me, that's why.' Harry edged closer. 'You look magnificent when you're angry—like a lion ready to pounce...'

Infuriatingly, a giggle escaped her tight lips, proving her downfall. 'I'll pounce on *you*, if you go on any more...'

He laughed delightedly, and she couldn't resist joining in.

'Tell you what,' murmured Harry, never taking his eyes off her face, 'you come for a drive, and I'll let you into old Luke's secret past—what do you say, eh? Come on, darlin', give me a break.'

'Oh—well—all right, then.' She knew she should have said no. He *was* a rotter, and she was failing Luke by agreeing, but, oh, dear, the temptation of finding out secrets was too much.

Harry stepped back, eyes flickering up and down her body. 'Good,' he said smugly. 'Meet me tomorrow, then—two o'clock, eh? I'll be down the side-road, out of sight of the theatre, just in case Luke should see. We'll have a drive around, and I'll tell you all the old chap's secrets.' His eyes darkened and his thick voice lowered slightly. 'I'm looking forward to having you all to myself, Essie...'

Shame and dismay rose within her like a swamping wave, but it was too late to change her mind. Abruptly she turned, heading for the dressing-room where her coat hung. Quickly she shut the door, but not before

Harry's echoing, throaty laugh set off warning bells in her guilty mind.

'Hop in,' called Harry, not bothering to get out of the driving seat of the shining green Rover 8 with the dark hood and gleaming wheel-trims. He was dressed in a hideous check suit that made him look like a bookie, thought Essie, stifling a giggle. Yet in some way she could not fathom the resemblance to Luke seemed even more marked. Not his face, she told herself, covertly studying him as they slowly began to drive out of the crowded city streets towards the sea, but the shape and build of his body. Yes, that was it—those powerful shoulders, slender hands and, most of all—she nodded, discovering the secret of the likeness—the graceful set of his head on his body.

Sitting there beside him, if she hadn't known it was Harry Whitman, and not looking too closely at his fleshy profile, which lacked the clean-cut lines and wholesomeness of Luke's, it might well have been Luke himself driving the motor-car. Indeed, once or twice she almost expected his hands to leave the wheel and automatically go through the palming movements that Luke constantly practised.

Harry parked along the road overlooking the shimmering, sunlit waters of the Sound, and turned in his seat to look at her. 'Glad you came?'

Essie nodded, a reluctant smile hovering on her lips.

'Thought you needed cheering up a bit. Come on, darlin', give us a proper smile—I'm not such a bad chap once you get to know me.'

The answering chuckle stuck in her throat, but he winked at her approvingly. 'That's it. We're friends now, aren't we? Well—suppose you want to hear all about old Luke, eh?'

'Yes, please,' said Essie brightly. She sat up straighter.

'Where do I start? Don't tell me—at the beginning. . .' The usual annoying laugh, then Harry inched nearer to her. 'You see, poor old Luke was fished out of the sea when he was a baby. The ship he was on with his mother was wrecked on the coast, off Gurnards Head. Down in Cornwall, that is. Near where I lived in an orphanage. Dumped by my mother, I was. . .' He gave her a sideways look, as if asking for sympathy. She nodded gravely, remembering her own lonely childhood. 'Well,' he went on, 'me an' Luke grew up together—ran away together. . .'

She watched memory give his unremarkable face a deeper quality. Then it was gone, and the familiar easy brashness returned. 'Near-brothers, we were, I can tell you. . .close as peas in a pod. What he did I did. Taught me a thing or two. . .'

Shrewdly, Essie considered. So Luke had always been the leader, ever since that shared experience of leaving the orphanage. And he was still the dominant one, although Harry tried hard to bolster up his own importance. Now she guessed that the bear-boy had found Harry a minion's job in the travelling circus—something lowly, something that didn't entail wearing bizarre clothes and being master to a wild animal. Something that maybe fed Harry's envy, even in those past days, making him the smarmy, false friend he now seemed to be.

Warily, she asked, 'Were you in the circus, with Luke?'

Harry's smile died. 'Yes,' he replied shortly, staring straight ahead. 'I ran errands for the nobs—fetching and carrying, getting the tobacco and the beer. . .'

Essie watched his fingers splay out around the steering-wheel, and instinctively realised that here lay another reason for Harry's jealousy of Luke. He had never attained the conjuring skills that had lifted the bear-boy out of the grime and baseness of the circus.

Watching how the powerful fingers whitened with

their grasp on the wheel, she changed the subject, asking quickly, 'And what else happened?'

Harry relaxed, his left hand edging along the back of her seat until it rested on her shoulders. He turned and beamed at her nostalgically. 'We got into music hall then—those were the days! We did all the provincial theatres, up and down the country. Then it was off to America. Paris, too. . .' He paused, eyeing her expectantly.

Essie put him down at once. 'Luke told me about going to Paris.'

'Did he? And what else did he tell you?' An intimation of roughness sounded in his voice, and the unblinking pale eyes grew cold.

'Not much,' said Essie, suddenly wary. 'Just that he—I mean, you and he—were doing well in London before going to Paris. Luke was beginning to do illusions as well as conjuring, he said.'

'We were. We were doing wonderful things. God save us, we certainly were. . .'

She couldn't stand the look of pride that now covered his face. It had been Luke who'd done all the tricks, not Harry, so why must he take all the praise? 'Until the act broke up,' she snapped, and then bit her lip, wondering if she had gone too far.

Harry's fingers reached up, stroking the back of her neck, and the hairs rose in protest. Trying not to move for fear of annoying him, she sat straight and still, wondering how one man's touch could send shivers of alarm through her body, while another's mere smile had the power to set her soaring on wings of sheer joy.

Abruptly, Harry's hand returned to his side. 'That's it,' he said, and she heard displeasure and uneasiness mingle in the two words. 'Not my fault, of course.' Essie felt him looking at her set profile, and turned to meet the staring eyes. 'Well, let's be frank. . .' He was smiling again, an unnerving smile she didn't like.

'There was a girl involved,' he went on. 'Always a girl, isn't there? Mind you, it was Luke's doing. . .'

Bending nearer, he put his hand over hers, lying clasped on her lap. 'Old Luke's too ambitious to keep a woman. Well, found that out, haven't you? The truth is, Essie, that he fell for his assistant. Nice little thing she was—but she got other ideas.' Hot fingers pressed down on Essie's tight hands. Harry's face was too near, the look in his eyes too revealing, and she knew that in a moment she must escape—but not yet. She must find out what exactly had gone wrong in London. Had the girl run off? Was Luke still in love with her?

'Tell me, Harry.' She managed to smile encouragingly, even as her body rebelled against his increasing nearness.

'We went off together—her and me. I was warmer, more a man than Luke, see? She couldn't stand his jealousy when she looked at other chaps. . .well, I know how to treat a woman, how to make her happy. . .'

Essie watched his face grow red, saw dark pupils split the pallor of the blue eyes, and knew the time for action had come. Pulling herself away, she snatched at the door, unlatching it and climbing down in one swift movement. 'I'm going for a walk,' she called back, as she marched away quickly along the pavement.

'Hey, come back!' He sounded furious, and she increased her pace.

'No. I'll walk home, thanks.'

'You silly little bitch—what the hell's the matter, eh?'

The penetrating words echoed in her head as she walked on. Passers-by stared, and she couldn't release herself from the fear his physical nearness had caused. She must escape. . .

After a while she had relaxed enough to stop and look back. There were other motor-cars and a few carriages where Harry had stopped, but the green Rover was not among them. He had gone.

A great wave of relief ran through her, and for a moment she braced herself against the sea wall, allowing strength and reassurance to fill the quaking void of her instinctive fear. How good it was to be safe and alone again.

She smiled at the view of the sea with its scallops of creamy lace, listened to the shushing murmurs of the waters stretching endlessly at her feet. The sun's caressing warmth on her face brought happier thoughts. If only Luke were here. . .

She sighed, and in that moment knew life would always be incomplete without him. It was important now to go and find him, to somehow let him know that she understood a little of what lay between him and Harry, and, understanding, also accepted it.

Ten minutes later she was walking briskly down the road beside the theatre, her body suffused with enjoyable warmth, cheeks rosied by exercise and sea air, mind intent on only one thing—finding Luke.

Seconds later, as if called forth by her need of him, he walked around the corner, the sight of him filling her with a glorious sense of rightness. She started to run, eager eyes never leaving his black-suited, charismatic form. He seemed a figure of darkness, yet, as they drew nearer one another, she saw only the lightness of his vivid eyes, the shining star in his ear, and the pallor of his gleaming skin, so deeply emphasised by the close-cut beard and falling raven-black hair.

'Luke! Luke!' Her voice was full of love and innocent happiness. An old woman, passing with a laden basket on her hip, stopped to stare as Essie ran past. On the opposite side of the busy street, a young boy grinned, an acute expression of envy plain on his spotty face.

'Where've you been?' Luke's quick anger didn't immediately alarm her. She would tell him how she disliked and distrusted Harry, and with what good reason. Would ask him to walk with her—perhaps the sea would remind him of Cornwall and his past. He would tell her all about it, about the girl, how it all happened. . .

'Harry took me out in his motor-car,' she said gaily. 'We drove down the road and stopped at a look-out place. Oh, Luke, the sea is so lovely with the sun shining on it, and the birds, and——'

'Damn the sea. Damn Harry. Damn you, too, Estrellita—dear God, what a fool I am! I might have known. Trust Harry to try his luck with you—and you, playing up to him. . .'

'What? Luke, don't look at me like that!' She pulled at his arm as he turned, walking away from her with long, urgent strides. The words he had used, the fury in his voice, the expression of pain on his face, made her heart ache. Her own words rose shrill. 'I haven't done nothing—anything—wrong. Honest, I haven't.'

He scowled down at her. 'You've been with Harry.'

'Yes, but——' She had to run to keep pace with him. 'But only in the motor—and not for very long. . .'

Luke's fury grew. 'Harry's always scheming,' he exploded. 'Always manipulating someone. I was a fool to think we could work together again.'

Essie, trotting along beside him, felt her bright new world splitting asunder. In vain she tried to keep up with his furious pace. 'Wait for me,' she pleaded. 'You're going too fast——'

'Then stay behind!' he snapped over his shoulder. 'Stay with Harry if you want to—I'll work the act on my own, be damned if I won't. I don't need him—and I certainly don't need a girl who runs after him the moment he appears in his blasted motor——'

He stopped abruptly, staring down at her with a passion that made her tremble. 'Keep away from me,' he warned, his voice shaking with emotion. 'I swore I'd never fall for a woman again, so stop looking at me as if you were Leda—oh, yes, I know what a fine actress you are, but don't act with me, Estrellita. Just leave me alone, do you hear? I won't go through it all again—I'll take the act to London on my own—somehow... I don't need you, or Harry...' He swung away, and she reeled in dismay.

'But Luke——' Her voice was full of such pitiful intensity that he paused and stared back at her, his frown hard and purposeful.

'Well?'

'Luke...' Unevenly, she repeated his name timorously, holding out her arms, not knowing any other way of showing him her love, and quite unable to put into words all the misery she felt.

He stared into her swimming eyes, suddenly realising how harshly he had treated her. But she'd been out with that bounder, Harry... 'Look,' he muttered, already ashamed of his outburst, 'I know what he's like. And you don't. But if you want him—well, go back to him. I don't care a damn...'

Essie snatched at her breath. 'But I don't! I don't—it's you I want, Luke——'

'That's what *she* said, and then she went off—with Harry.' Essie could only just make out his last words, for he spoke quietly, as if to himself. And then he walked away, the set of his back and his bowed head telling her she was, indeed, unwanted.

People jostled her as she stood alone on the busy street, but she saw nothing, heard nothing, so vivid were her thoughts, so deep her humiliation. But out of the wretchedness truth emerged, as if to console and comfort, a small nugget of honesty that she took to her heart as she considered it. She had been curious about his last assistant ever since she met him—well, now she knew. Luke was still in love with the girl who had been in the act in London. Harry had wheedled her away because of his envy of Luke, just as he had tried to wheedle her, Essie, and so Luke was left wounded, and for evermore vulnerable.

Her recent memories of the lulling sea she had been watching with such content sank without trace, and she became aware of that other sea, the powerful monster that could wreck ships and drown passengers and crew. A sea that, twisting between carelessness and compassion, had washed up an infant on to a foreign shore, decreeing that his life be lived among strangers, establishing him in circumstances that must be for ever filled with emptiness and insecurity.

Yes, now she understood so well Luke's mercurial disposition, his quick changes from humour to melancholy, from pain to affection. Still lost in her thoughts, Essie wandered aimlessly, finally finding a streetlight and, leaning against it, weeping noisily. No one approached to offer help. Indeed, whereas minutes before her radiant face had attracted many eyes, now the passers-by seemed to turn away their heads as they approached. When the hot tears stopped, she mopped her face and slowly started walking again. Around the corner. Over the road, dodging carts and carriages and bicycles. Along the next street. It didn't matter where she went. Luke didn't want her.

And then, gradually, the pain turned to anger. . .

When a loud and unfamiliar noise caused her to look up, startled, it took her withdrawn wits a few seconds to realise she was standing outside the railway-station entrance. A train had just come puffing in, disgorging hurrying passengers, its doors banging, and the guard's voice echoing down the platform.

'Hurry along, please—all stations to Exeter.'

Essie's fingers sought and found the photograph of Ma that she always carried in her pocket. Suddenly she thought of Ma, and her own desperate need of love. Then she was standing in front of the booking office, clutching the coins Luke had given her for the new, as yet unbought hat. Surprised, but resolute, she heard herself say, 'A single ticket to Teignmouth, please.'

CHAPTER SIX

WITH Ma's photograph clasped in her right hand, Essie ran out of the station entrance at Teignmouth, shouting at a nearby porter who was wheeling away his trolley from a departing hansom.

'Where's Middle Brimley Street?'

The man halted, gaped, then said disapprovingly, 'Turn left, up over the hill, then left again.' He continued to stare as she called back her thanks, and it came to her that she probably looked as strange as she felt—no hat, her hair streaming in the slapping April wind, and all her anxieties plain to see on her distraught face. But she ran on, for nothing mattered except finding Ma.

Number fifty-seven was a gaunt, tall villa that had clearly seen better days. Essie stopped at the gate, her heart thudding and her breathing noisy. For an instant she wondered if she was right to come—to present herself so unexpectedly to the mother who had willingly left her behind seventeen years ago. But the thought was quickly dispelled by her desperate need. Opening the gate, she walked briskly to the front door and tugged at the bell-pull. Once, twice, three times she heard the lonely sound clanging through the lower regions of the house, and then bit her lip as disappointment flooded through her.

Clearly she'd come at a bad time. Perhaps Ma was out—or ill in bed, unable to come to the door. Even—Essie swallowed the fearful lump that came into her throat—dead? No! Certainly not. She wouldn't allow Ma to die without letting her know. What sort of a mother would do such a thing when her child needed her so badly?

Essie forced a smile on to her downcast face as the absurdity of the thought became clear to her. Well, she'd just have to try next door. Neighbours would know where Ma was. Nothing should stop her from finding Ma. . .

As she closed the gate behind her, a figure emerged from the side of a large, yellow-flowered forsythia bush in the next garden.

'Empty,' said the old man, who gazed at her with rheumy eyes. 'Fifty-seven's empty. Gone away, the Brownings have.'

'Brownings? Is that who lives there?' Essie pounced with such vigour that the man shrank back towards his hiding place.

He shook his head emphatically. 'No, them's gone. I just told 'ee.'

'But—I thought—I mean, I'm looking for Mrs de Carle. She lived here once. A long time ago.' Essie's confidence faded. There was no sign of recognition on the suspicious old face watching her so closely.

'De Carle? Never 'eard of no one o' that name.'

'Isobel,' persisted Essie, with a break in her voice. 'Isobel de Carle. Belle, they all called her. She was a dancer and a singer. . .' A great sigh burst from her, and as the breath flowed out she felt all her hope going with it. To have left Luke and the act, to have gambled so much on the certainty of finding Ma—and she wasn't here. Tears pricked in Essie's eyes, and at first she didn't see the old man's expression change.

'Belle?' he mused, and was silent for a moment. Then, with a toothless grin, 'Belle! Why didn't you say as it were Belle you wanted? Everyone knows Belle— lives down by the back beach, she do. Puts up them pierrots every Easter. Now, if you'd only said as it were *Belle* you was looking for——'

Essie cut him short, her voice soaring as joy filled her. 'What's the address? What road is it? Tell me— quickly.' She couldn't stand still for another second, but danced impatiently around him, wanting to shake him out of his slowness. Why couldn't he understand that she must go now—*now*—this instant?

'Number three. White cottage backing on the river beach. . .'

His wheezing voice just reached her as she left him, running back the way she'd come. 'Thank you, oh, thank you!' The words rang out with renewed strength, and, when she reached the corner of the road where she turned back towards the station, she glanced over her shoulder to wave at the watching figure, only half visible beside the shining bush.

She ran fast, instinct guiding her towards the distant sea. In the town centre, unerringly she headed for the long, curving promenade, following it to the point where the wide river flowed strongly out into the sea. The back beach he'd said—did he mean that strip of sand bordering the river, running back towards the town? Where the row of fishermen's boat-houses ended, a road began, leading her ever on. Yes, there were the cottages, their fronts facing the road, so surely their back doors must lead out on to the continuing sandy river beach?

She paused briefly, when a sudden run of people erupted into the road, calling, laughing as they came. She gasped with delight. Pierrots! Just as the old man had said. Three of them, running out of an open cottage door—bulky figures, grotesque in loose white ruffled blouses and oversized pantaloons.

Essie smiled as she saw bobbled pierrot hats, perched like ridiculous pimples on three black-scarfed heads. Blown on the wind, she heard tambourines and happy voices that made her own excitement grow.

'The pierrots! It's the pierrots. . .'

Now they had reached her—small groups of people following the white-suited, leaping figures as they danced down the road. Women in wide-brimmed straw hats topped with nodding flowers, ribbons and dangling fruit. Dark skirts and open, bright parasols, since the sinking sun's rays were still warm and brilliant. There was a child with a hoop, another pulling a clumsy wooden animal, and they were as entranced by the pierrots as their mothers seemed to be. Essie stepped aside quickly as a man near by collided with her.

Clutching his straw boater, he smiled sheepishly and called back over his shoulder, 'So sorry! But it's the pierrots—we always follow them down to the pier when they come at Easter. . .' And then he was gone, one hand gripping his little boy, and his wife's parasol bobbing as the three of them disappeared around the corner of the road.

Essie took a deep breath. The pierrots and their admirers had all gone. Now she could go to the cottage they had come from, and find Belle. Find Ma. . .

'Looking for someone?' asked a voice. Essie stopped, stared into the familiar brown eyes of a small woman standing outside her open door, then took in the overwashed, overworn print dress and dull grey shawl that hung loosely on the little woman's sloping shoulders.

It took her a long moment to know. Then, 'Yes,' she whispered, 'I'm looking for you, Ma. I'm Estrellita. You know—your daughter—the baby you left with Aunt Beattie. . .'

They stared into each other's eyes in taut silence, and all Essie's hopes of happiness and security diminished as slowly she realised the truth.

Ma was no longer pretty, no more a fellow-dreamer. She was hardly recognisable from the photograph. She was too thin, too small, too old to be the Ma Essie had expected to see—and so badly needed to see. But, for all that, she was still Ma. . . Essie, somehow, shrugged off her surprise and disappointment. Bravely she acknowledged that this little old woman looked as if *she* was the one who wanted looking after.

Squaring her shoulders, Essie opened her hands in a welcoming gesture. 'Can I come in, Ma?' she asked gently. 'I wouldn't half love a cuppa tea. . .'

Silently Ma looked at her, before nodding doubtfully. She turned away into the cottage doorway, and Essie's reviving spirits were dashed yet again when she saw her mother limp heavily as she went indoors.

'Well, you've grown into a real big girl.' Ma was busy at the range at the far side of the small, dark room, her voice so husky that Essie could hardly catch the words. A kettle hummed, the caddy was reached down the from the tall mantel, and in the slow ritual of tea-making Essie found strength to curb her aroused feelings.

She longed to put her arms around Ma, to hug her and say yes, she was a big girl, a strong girl who would look after her mother. That they were together again now, and Ma need never worry for money or for loving company. She wanted to ask what had happened to make the dancer limp, to cause the singer's throat to become so husky. But Ma's back, small as it was, had a rigidity about it that defied such overflowing emotion. So Essie sat down on a hard kitchen chair, and recalled Luke's first lesson. Don't chatter so much. No doubt Ma felt the same. All right, then, she'd just sit here and wait for things to happen.

The tea was comforting and hot, and when Ma finally sat herself down on an equally straight, hard chair on the opposite side of the range Essie was able to smile companionably and hold her tongue. Wisely, she knew that the first move towards friendship must come from Ma.

It did. 'I dessay you wondered why I up and left.' Ma wouldn't look at her, but kept unblinking eyes on the rag rug beneath their feet.

Essie swallowed, thought hard, then answered carefully, 'Well, couldn't take a new baby on stage, could you?'

Slowly Ma raised her eyes. 'No. Wouldn't have done.' Another silence. 'Missed me, did you, then?'

It was the last straw on the camel's overloaded back—to have to lie and stoutly say no. Essie's heart fluttered, and suddenly she was on her knees, head bowed into Ma's lap, unable to check the noisy sobs that came from deep inside, expressing all the pain and longing she had fought back for most of her seventeen years. 'Yes. Oh, yes, Ma. I missed you so much! I can't tell you—and—and now I've found you, and. . .'

'And I'm not what you thought to find.'

Sniffing, Essie knelt back on her heels, staring into her mother's ravaged face. Again, the truth was undeniable.

'No,' she muttered baldly, and saw a shadow of pain deepen Ma's eyes. 'I thought you'd still be on the stage.' Wildly she tried to explain, to excuse her bluntness. 'You know, singing and dancing. . .'

'Not with this knee.' Ma hitched up her dark serge skirt, and Essie stared in horror at the swollen, misplaced joint.

'How did you do it?'

'Fell off into the pit.' Ma cleared her throat, paused, and then grudgingly chuckled. 'Silly of me, eh? Put paid to my career for good, that did.'

'But—you can still sing?'

'Get on with you, maid—hear this voice, can't you? Strained me larynx, that's what the doctor said. Never been right since.'

'But that's awful! So how do you make a living, if you're not on the stage? Is—is *he* still here?' Essie shrank as Ma's prematurely lined face contorted into plain contempt.

'Him? You mean Vittorio? Huh! Walked out on me two months after we came here. Went on the bottle, he did. Said as how he'd sell more ice-creams upcountry than in a seasonal place like this. Don't talk no more about that Vittorio.' Putting down her cup,

Ma drew herself up, and in that small, resolute move Essie saw her own attitude to the hardships of life reflected.

Warmly, she smiled, tears forgotten. 'So what do you live on, Ma?'

'Lodgers, that's what. Pierrots at Easter, concert parties all summer, then a few posh holiday-makers in the autumn. And in the winter I do the washing for one of the big houses.' She paused, face suddenly grim, looking at Essie as if wondering whether to confide further. Then the grimness faded, replaced by a growing enthusiasm. Slowly, she added, 'And another thing—I belong to the Army. The Salvation Army. I'm saved, that's what—*saved*. . .' Her eyes glowed, and for an instant Essie saw the vitality and attraction that must have given the younger Ma the ability to entrance an audience.

'You mean prayers out of doors? Tambourines and hymns?' Essie frowned. She wasn't sure if she liked the idea of Ma dressing up in dull dark blue with one of those old-fashioned poke bonnets. But the expression on Ma's face sent her fears flying.

'I mean being part of something that helps poor people; the world's full of those who can't help themselves, and the lucky ones don't care, do they? Well, once you join the Sally Army, you're doing something worthwhile. You're in the Lord's hands—you'll go anywhere, do anything. You're *saved*! I tell you, my gel. . .' Ma's husky voice grew in strength and her wan cheeks flooded with colour '. . .it's time things changed! We had a procession here last week, and I was in it. Marching through the town. Oh, it was wonderful!'

'But what good does that do, Ma? A procession?'

'Shows the world that love works miracles! Yes, love's a marvellous thing—and it helps turn men from the drink. Oh, I just wish my Vittorio had heard the message—been saved. . .' Ma looked wistful, but only for a second, and Essie's lips tightened, as she warily left unsaid all that came rushing into her mind.

If Ma had become a do-gooder, it would be best to ignore the fact—for the moment at least, until she knew whether she was here to stay or not. And then amusement came out of nowhere, softening her mouth, making it twitch, as she thought she should at least be thankful that Ma wasn't one of those interfering suffragettes—what did they call them? Shrieking Sisters!—that she'd heard about, for ever in trouble with the Police, and making such a nuisance of themselves. . .

Quietly, she changed the subject. 'Well, Ma, I'm here now, even if *he* isn't, and I'll do all I can to help you.'

'Going to stay, are you?'

Curiosity, tinged with alarm, widened Ma's eyes, and Essie replied wryly, suddenly hurt, 'Don't worry, I won't get in your way. . .' Her voice tailed off, as memory assailed her. *Was* she going to stay? But wouldn't Luke come, looking for her? And, if she did stay, would she ever go back to him? To the act? Did he really need her—or not?

Sighing, fingering the brass curtain-ring on her third finger that Luke had given her, because of the crotchety stares of the Plymouth landlady, she looked very directly at her mother. 'Ma,' she said bleakly, 'I've got a lot to tell you. I need your advice. You see, I'm not really sure if I've done the right thing, coming here. . .'

'Men!' sniffed Ma, at the end of Essie's story. 'All alike. On'y ever think of themselves. And your chappie don't seem no different.' Suddenly she frowned, her eyes glinting at Essie in the shadows of the darkening room. 'Luke, was he called? A magician, starred in the West End? Hmm. . .'

'That's right.' Essie's heart raced. 'Don't know him, do you?'

'Knew a lot of people, course I did.' Clearly, Ma

wasn't going to be drawn into reminiscence, and Essie nodded, accepting the fact that much of Ma's life would always remain a closed book to her.

They stared warily at each other across the room. 'Mind you——' Ma's mouth turned down at the edges '—you been proper silly. A job's a job, and from what you say this Luke'll be back in London soon, and then think of the chance you've missed. Ah, but you'm like me, maid, I can see it plainly—yes, just like I was, before the Lord took me. Never one to stop and think, always chasing that old ambition.'

'That dream.'

For the first time, they smiled openly at each other, and Essie's despondency began to fade. 'You're right, Ma. And my dream's still there, strong—oh, so strong. . .'

Ma rose, limped to the coal bucket to put a shovelful on the glowing ashes before Essie could reach her. 'Ma! Let me do it! Oh, your poor leg——'

'Look here, maid, let's get this straight.' Ma was a good inch and a half shorter than Essie, but her dominance was enough to make Essie feel a child again. 'I lives my life and you gets on with yours. I don't need no help, see.'

'But you do! Ma, please understand. . . I've come specially to find you, because I need you—just like you need me. You need a daughter to—well, to help, to—to love you. . . And I want a home. Security.' She paused, before continuing, very low, very humble, 'Someone to love me.'

If she had expected Ma's salvationist training to result in inviting maternal arms held wide, she was quickly disappointed.

'Got a husband, haven't you?' asked Ma shortly, turning away. 'Then get on back to him. You've made your bed; well, now you must lie on it. Same as me.'

'But—but you did say love was important. Just now. . .'

Ma limped to the sink, tidying cups as she went. Pointedly she glanced back at the clock ticking away over the mantel. 'My lodgers'll be back soon, wanting their supper.' Her hard face suddenly cracked into a grudging smile. 'There's love an' love,' she said bluntly. 'I don't say as you're not welcome, maid, but it can't go no further than that. Not after all that's been missed out between us, over the years.'

'Oh, Ma!' Wretchedly, Essie looked blindly into the shadows of the small, shabby room. Let down by such cruel rejection, she felt at the lowest ebb possible. Surely a mother must feel something other than casual interest for the child who had come running in need? Essie bowed her head and fought the swamping tide of emotions. Momentarily, anger pushed aside the pain, and she muttered fiercely, into her handkerchief, 'So it's all right to love all the boozers and roughs that you pray for in your silly old Sally Army—but not to love *me*?'

She heard the bitterness in her voice, and was unashamed. It seemed wrong that Ma should be like this. Looking up, she stared across at her mother's thin back. 'Wish I hadn't come!' she shouted harshly, and the words hung around the quiet room.

Slowly, Ma turned, her eyes deep and wary. 'So do I, maid, so do I. There's some things in life that it's best to forget—like the mistake I made with Vittorio, and giving you over to Beattie. . .' Just for a moment her face contorted, and in that glimpse of regret and vulnerability Essie learned all she needed to know.

'So you do love me! You do! Oh, Ma. . .' She leapt to her feet and ran across the kitchen until she was close to her mother. 'Say you do?' she pleaded. 'Just once—it. . .it means so much to me. . .'

Ma shrank back. 'Leave me alone, maid,' she said quickly, 'I need to do things slowly; no good to rush like this. Maybe in time—well, we'll have to see.' They stared at each other, and Essie gradually realised she had met a worthy adversary in Ma. Sighing deeply, she returned to her chair by the fire, while Ma busied herself with the dishes.

Luke's face suddenly swam before her eyes, then Harry's, and finally Ma's, as she remembered her in the photograph. Reality dawned painfully, slowly, and she stared across at her small, crippled, yet indomitable mother, and nodded in acceptance. 'All right,' she agreed weakly, 'I s'pose we'll just have to wait and see. . .'

Ma came and stood above her. 'That's right, maid. That's the way to do it. Now—you'd better call me Belle, then. I don't like this Ma business. Gilda never called me Ma.'

'Gilda?' Essie's head shot up, and her mother said swiftly, with a note of pride that roused a stab of unfamiliar jealousy inside Essie,

'My other daughter. Born before you was. In America she is. Part of an acrobatic act. Coming home soon—had a letter last month. She calls me Belle, so you can too.'

'My—sister?'

Belle thought deeply, pausing as she returned to the sink to dry the cups. 'Half-sister,' she said at last. 'Her dad weren't yours. Yours was——'

'I know. Vittorio, the ice-cream man!' Essie's vitality could no longer be constrained. She grinned impishly across the room, and was rewarded by an answering brief smile. Belle turned away to find bread in the stone crock on the larder floor.

'You can stay the night, if you want,' she said casually, 'but after that you must go.' She glanced back and nodded over her shoulder, face firmly set, and Essie's heart suddenly plummeted into her boots. She had counted on too much. Ma—Belle—wasn't the loving, welcoming mother she had imagined. A raging pain enveloped her, and it was all she could do to prevent the tears that pricked behind her eyelids from falling in a great, hot flood.

* * *

Leaving Belle to prepare her lodgers' cocoa and sandwiches, Essie strolled down the road to the promenade, taking unexpected pleasure in the vivid palette of the sunset, and the raucous screaming of the gulls following a fishing boat into the harbour at the river's mouth.

Although still despondent at Ma's unloving attitude, she felt a little more relaxed now, as if she'd done a hard day's housework and could at last rest. As a skivvy, such weariness had been purely physical, but for the first time Essie realised how exhausting emotional experience could be. Once more, Luke's voice sang in her ears, quiet and wry. 'You have so much to learn about life, little star. . .' and she knew, feeling humble as never before, that he was right. Well, she *was* learning—and fast.

Suddenly, with an ache that caused her to moan aloud, she yearned for him to be with her, his magnetic, warm personality sheltering her fears and ignorance, giving her the renewal of strength and hope she so badly needed.

Her thoughts were restless. Why had she taken this ridiculous, impulsive step of running away from him? From the man whom she loved and always would? For a moment, with all her heart, she wished herself back in Plymouth, on stage with Luke, hot and flushed from lights and happiness, basking in his approval, in the audience's applause—then going home together, quiet and companionable, sharing their dingy room as they undressed and went to their separate beds.

'Seeing his poor, cold feet when I wake up. . .' She muttered the words aloud, and made herself smile, even though inside she still felt confused and wretched. For it was Luke himself who had told her to go— 'Keep away from me.' Again she heard the anguish in his voice, saw haunting despair in his narrowed, darkened eyes.

For a long while she sat in a covered shelter, staring out at the ocean as the colours of the sun-stained sky reflected their glory in the swelling waves. But, even as she appreciated the beauty around her, her thoughts continued to chase each other in a foolish circle of doubt and dismay. Half of her knew she'd been a fool to come here, while the other half argued irritably that she would never have found Ma—Belle—if she hadn't run from Luke.

The conflicting images went around her head until, unable to resolve them, abruptly she got up, and walked towards the pier. She needed something else to think about, people to watch, to talk to.

Groups of smiling, chattering families were strolling towards her, the children sleepy-eyed and slow now. It became evident, as she drew nearer the pier, that the evening's entertainment had ended. Her spirits revived slightly as she recalled the pierrots and the gaiety they had shared with the following crowds earlier that afternoon. She felt a sudden comradeship with them—professionals who worked so hard to amuse and entertain—and again she was thrown back on her memories of Luke and the act. Yearning filled her. To be on stage again, hearing the applause, smiling down at the watching, happy faces. . .

Almost without knowing what she did, and guided purely by her need, she walked briskly into the entrance of the long pier, looking around. . .for what, she wasn't quite sure—a friendly face, an opportunity to do—what?

She heard voices inside a small pavilion ahead of her, and followed them instinctively. A familiar smell made her pause. She smiled, remembering the only two theatres she had as yet known, and suddenly realising that here was a third. The pavilion was newly painted, but nothing could hide the fact that it was a weather-ravaged old building. Briefly, she thought of winter gales and wind-flung spray, and accepted all the only half-hidden tell-tale stains of damp and rot. It was still a theatre, and that was all that mattered. . .

She went, fleet-footed, towards the voices, slid behind a wavering flat, and abruptly found herself face to face with two of the pierrots whom she had seen dancing down the road from Belle's cottage.

'I want a job! I'm used to being on stage—I can dance, and—and sing, and handle properties, and...' She flung the gabbled words at the older man, who looked up in surprise and then watched her shrewdly, with none of the innocence she had naïvely imagined pierrots to possess.

'How do you know we need a new girl?' Accusingly he stared into her bewildered eyes.

'I don't! I only know I want a job—need one, badly.'

'In the business, are you?'

'Y-yes.' Confusion filled her. It wouldn't do to mention Luke. No one would think much of her letting him down. Lightly she said, almost holding her breath, 'Between jobs, actually,' and watched the man nod, pursing his lips and wiping his glistening face free of the thick white make-up that covered it.

'Well, now, you couldn't have come at a better time. Our girl's just wrenched her ankle. Had to send her home in a cab. Told the manager he'd have to do something about those old boards this year—blooming danger-traps, they are. Well, now, I'm Charlie Griggs. What's your name?'

'Er——' For once, she was flummoxed. Estrellita was too much of a give-away, Essie could still be traced. Belle's husky voice came out of the blue. She smiled brightly. 'Gilda. Yes, Gilda—er—er—Smith.'

'Gilda Smith. Let's see what you can do, then. Show us a step or two. Frank, come and look at this...'

From the back of the darkening, airless backstage area, a younger man appeared, his face already cleaned of make-up, hands busily undoing the voluminous white blouse that made him look so large, despite the gradual appearance of a slightly built, be-shirted body from beneath the costume.

'What is it, Charlie?'

'New girl. Just come in. Well, now, answer to prayer, I'd say—if she's any good, of course——'

'I *am* good!' Essie's pride could stand no more of this impersonal assessment. Her nervousness fled, and she pranced across the uneven floor with her usual abandon, lifting her skirt to reveal a saucy inch or two of shapely ankle, and smiling as she had learned to do, a smile that warmed the heart of all who watched, and brought hands clapping in prompt applause.

'Not bad. Sing, can you?'

In reply, Essie trilled out a verse of 'Villia', last year's hit by Lily Elsie, and had the satisfaction of seeing the older man's heavy face slide into an approving smile. 'All right, that's enough. You've got it all, I can see that. Well, now, you'll have to start working at once. First thing tomorrow morning, down here. Can't pay you much, but I'll fix a standard wage with the manager when I know how bad Judy's injury is. All right, then, Gilda Smith?'

Essie's eyes shone. Breathlessly she said, 'Oh, yes, yes, that's wonderful.'

The two men watching smiled at her enthusiasm, then Charlie stepped away, continuing to remove his make-up, but the other boy went on looking at her, his face expressing open admiration. Essie was elated, but suddenly uneasy. She had a request to make, an idea that had suddenly filled her mind and was all-important, but was unsure how it would be received.

The boy called Frank came a step nearer, and seemed to read her thoughts. He grinned knowingly. 'You want to try on the costume, don't you, love? You girls are all the same—only interested in what you'll look like. See here, I'll tell you this. . .' He paused. 'Never done this work before, have you?'

Dumbly, Essie shook her head.

'Well, you won't become famous for your face,

love—not with all this white lard and zinc on it. And no one'll admire those neat ankles you just showed us—here, take this home and get used to looking like a big white balloon!' He grinned, friendly but ironic. 'It'll take the gilt off the gingerbread, I dare say, but you'll feel more at ease by tomorrow, when the show goes on. Here you are—these should fit you all right. . .' He laughed as he handed over a pile of shapeless white garments. 'And don't forget the lard— it'll complete your disguise properly, that white face will!'

'Thank you.' Essie's bravado had left her now, and she stood with her arms full of clothes, topped by a small, greasy tin, which contained the white make-up. Frank turned his back on her as he stepped out of the voluminous pantaloons, and she made her escape out of the hot, sweaty, salty pavilion into the welcome coolness of the April evening, with one thought only stabbing into her already fading excitement.

A disguise, he'd said, that Frank—exactly what she needed, didn't she? A disguise to stop Luke, or Harry—or even a policeman—her face blanched at the idea—from finding her, if any of them came searching for her.

Very slowly she walked back to Belle's cottage, wrestling with her innermost feelings. Impulsively she had thrown herself into this convenient, timely new job—she even had a disguise to shelter behind. And yet she couldn't stop thinking of Luke, wanting him, even imagining every man she saw walking down the promenade was Luke, looking for her. . .

Too late she realised now the foolhardiness of her thoughtless, impulsive action. Luke hadn't really meant it when he'd said, 'Go.' Oh, she was a fool; no doubt about it. Estrellita, Essie, and now Gilda Smith—how stupid she was to give herself such names, when all that mattered, deep inside, was that she was truly, and for evermore, Mrs Luke Grimwade.

CHAPTER SEVEN

EASTER week, a tang of salt in the air, and a summer-blue sky dotted with fluffy puff-balls of drifting cloud. If it hadn't been for the unresolved need to be loved forever niggling in her mind, Essie could have been happy.

Staying overnight with Belle—would she ever get used to the unfamiliar name? wondered Essie wistfully, pining for the comfort of 'Ma'—had been uncomfortable yet enlightening. For she had seen Belle with her pierrot lodgers, heard her talking to them as equals, and had winced at the realisation that Belle was more at home with her professional friends than with her own newly acquired daughter. The lesson had been painful, but Essie had thought hard and, as a consequence, had learned much.

Belle might seem brisk and offhand where family feelings were concerned, but clearly her heart was warm. She had shown sympathy for Judy and her wrenched ankle, offering at once to make a knitbone poultice. And then, when told that the girl was in good hands, staying with a relative who lived near by, had turned to Essie with a knowing look.

'Take her place, eh? Just for a few days. . .' The meaning was plain, and Essie had nodded, reassured that Belle would allow her to stay until the job ended.

Just for a few days. The phrase lingered in her head, tautening her indecision even as, next morning, obediently she tried on the sloppy white costume and, grimacing, larded her face before putting her mind to learning the new act.

'My word, but you're a quick study—where've you worked before?' Frank was attentive in his boyish way, smile full of appreciation and something else, too, a warmer message that Essie saw but could not bring herself to respond to. She didn't want this lank, immature lad ogling her, and adroitly changed the subject. Silently, she cried out Luke's name, and heard it echoing, unanswered, through the emptiness of her uneasy heart.

The afternoon came, and with it the first daily performance on the pier. Now Essie found herself part of the traditional run down the crowded prom. She knew she ought to be enjoying it, but pleasure was far from her thoughts. Even the usual joyful anticipation of performing, of being up on a stage, with an entranced audience watching, felt sadly lacking in some vital ingredient.

For the life of her, she couldn't recapture the spontaneity and excitement which, she knew instinctively, had been the original spark that had attracted Luke to her, that night at Monsey's squalid penny gaff, beside the river in Exeter.

Luke. Everything came back to Luke. Her whole life was centred on him. And yet she had left him. . . She shook her head in confusion.

Once inside the tiny dressing-room behind the stage, she inspected her zinc and larded white face, listening as she did so to the voices humming outside the frail matchboarding of the little pavilion theatre, situated at the head of the long pier, jutting out into the sun-swept ocean.

She had the usual butterflies in her stomach. Staring at her white reflection in the fly-blown, blotchy mirror that was the best the pier manager had been able to find, she thought how silly it was to feel nervous, yet Luke had said every good artiste had nerves. Luke, again. . . She caught her breath, and then was aware of Frank coming close to her. Beneath his own white make-up she recognised familiar tension to her own, and couldn't stop herself asking, 'Are you all right?' as the camaraderie of the profession abruptly blocked out her pain.

Frank's hazel eyes focused on hers. Briefly he nodded, pushing a few sandy hairs further beneath his black head-scarf. 'Should be—house filling up nicely, sky's clear, weather forecast's good, piano's as steady as we can get it on the sand——' He stopped, stared, leaned nearer. 'Give us a kiss for luck, Gilda?'

She drew back, unnerved even further by the strange name, but his clumsy lips were warm on hers, and she laughed as their white faces touched. 'Butterflies?' she asked shakily.

'Course. All get them, don't we, never mind how often we go on? You look lovely, Gilda. Go out and knock 'em cold, love. . .'

Charlie Griggs edged his huge frame through the doorway, and looked at his two companions without speaking. Ageing, experienced eyes ran over their costumes—black silk scarves beneath white cone-shaped hats, perched at a jaunty angle on each head.

'You'll do.' His wheezy voice rumbled through the airless, confined space. Rummaging under his blouse, he produced a battered watch. 'Two minutes and we're on. Good luck.'

Essie's and Frank's faces cracked into brief, tight smiles. 'Good luck, Charlie.' There was a moment of silence, of nerve-racking waiting, of three minds gauging the number of paying bodies whose voices they heard chattering only a stone's throw away. Eyes glanced keenly around the tiny room, making sure all props were in the right, handy places. Then, 'We're on.'

Charlie led them out, around the corner of the boarded structure that was to be their makeshift theatre for the season, and suddenly the butterflies inside Essie took wing and flew, leaving her excited and full of elation, ready to get on with the show.

A strange idea flickered through her busy mind: if

Luke could only see her now, he'd still be proud of her, even though she was working with strangers and no longer with him. She wouldn't let him—or Charlie—down.

The thought was a consolation, a strength. Easily now, she slipped into the rehearsed routine of bright, introductory chatter, following Charlie and Frank on to the rectangular little stage space, turning a couple of nimble cartwheels over the bare boards, and picking up the cues they threw her with a relaxed yet sure confidence.

'Here we are, here we are, full of fun and joys!

The pierrot troupe of Teignmouth—three lovely, handsome boys!'

The first ripple of laughter swept in from the sun-baked sands, where deckchairs in neat rows supported the audience, laughter that was music to the ears of the three people on stage above them.

'Boys? You flatter yourselves, chaps. *I'm* the only *boy* among you. . .' Charlie, fat and ugly, struck a comic pose which brought the laughter surging again, and Essie, running around the stage, knocked his knees from under him so that he fell in a seemingly broken heap, miming his bad leg, his arm, his back. Again, the laughs soared.

Essie, a slim, bright-eyed imposter of a boy in her concealing, sexless costume, looked innocently out at the audience, winked at them and started juggling nonchalantly with oranges produced from a hidden pocket.

Oh, yes, it was good to be back on the boards— even without Luke. Slowly her pain faded as the stimulation of the performance took over. Finishing her purposely bungled juggling, she sank down, cross-legged, while Frank sang his first solo, the hit of the year, 'Shine on, Shine on, Harvest Moon'. Listening to his sweet, pure tenor voice telling of unrequited love, she watched his homely face with interest. A nice boy, Frank, ordinary but with in-built generosity and affection. Unsought, another face danced before her eyes for a second—that of Harry Whitman, and instinctively, inside her concealing costume, she shuddered.

The song was over. Applause fluttered around the beach, and Essie hurriedly focused her mind on what came next. Time for the dance. Frank's slim hands were cooler than hers, and it was good to feel his innate sense of rhythm infiltrating her own body, as they whirled and swayed in the tiny space, feet tapping, arms swinging in time with the tinny music that somehow Charlie's fat fingers managed to coax out of the old, upright piano.

Essie smiled at Frank as he swung towards her. And then, as they had rehearsed, he gave her a smart slap on the bottom that sent her flying, to land, spread-eagled, across the stage, huge eyes innocently asking the audience what she'd done to deserve such unkind treatment.

Laughter rang in her ears, and she was up again, somersaulting over to the piano, where she grabbed the waiting tambourine, ready to join in a selection of popular songs of the day before leaving the stage, while Charlie started in on his joke routine.

Getting her breath back, she listened to yet another landlady story. '"The flies are a bit thick in here," I complained to my landlady,' said Charlie, in his rumbling voice. '"What do you think you'll get for a shilling a day?" she asked. "Educated ones?"'

Behind Essie, Frank slipped an arm around her waist, and she turned, startled, to stare into his smiling eyes. 'Going well,' he whispered. 'You're terrific, Gilda. Didn't slap you too hard, did I? Wouldn't want to hurt you, love. . .'

She shook her head, and together they continued listening to the familiar old chestnuts which brought spontaneous bursts of mirth from the audience. Frank's arm tightened. 'You an' me next,' he breathed into her ear. 'My favourite part of the act.'

Their duet went well, even although Essie was surprised by the feeling that Frank put into the words of the saucy number they shared. She was glad to join in another bout of slapstick comedy before Charlie's final comic monologue heralded the end of the show.

The finale was triumphantly patriotic, with all three of the cast loudly proclaiming love of country and respect for the King—'Good old Teddy,' said Charlie very seriously, doffing his white hat, and producing cheers from the audience, before turning the cheers to even louder laughter as a huge Union Jack unfolded from within the small space.

Taking her bow, Essie was uplifted by the feeling of warmth and approval that the audience projected, and, when Charlie nodded at her, indicating that it was time to go around with the hat, she left the stage willingly, anxious to mingle with the crowds who had shown such approval of her performance.

She was down, off the stage and among the people before Charlie had finished whispering instructions, smile as eye-catching as her appearance, which, had she been aware of its attraction, would have raised her effervescent spirits even higher. For a pierrot costume, so voluminous and seemingly shapeless, worked wonders on her slender figure, with every lissom movement giving the lie to the pretence of being a boy.

'Thank you, sir. Oh, thank you, ma'am—most kind. Enjoyed it, did you? Good. That's what we're here for. Come again, won't you?'

In the background of the reluctantly departing audience, Charlie's fingers tinkled a jolly tune at the weary piano, and Essie's thoughts were exuberant when unexpectedly she found herself staring at a figure she knew. Tall, broad-shouldered, dark-clad—a man with his back to her, a man who, clearly, had been in the audience and who was now leaving. A figure she recognised. . .

She came to an abrupt halt, clutching Charlie's battered old hat to her breast with both hands, as if in prayer. *Luke*. It must be Luke. . . So he'd come looking for her, after all. He'd watched the show. Seen her performing—her mind whirled—and now he was going, not bothering to search her out. Did it mean he hadn't known who the smallest pierrot was? But surely Luke must have known her, whatever disguise she wore. Or perhaps he didn't care to speak to her. Perhaps he was too angry, too embarrassed—she caught her breath—too ashamed of what she had become?

Essie's heart pounded as the unanswerable questions flung themselves around her mind. What was she to do? Run after him? The inclination was almost impossible to resist. Words rang in her head. Luke, Luke, come back. Oh, how I've missed you—take me home, Luke, please. Please?

But she did nothing. For, even as the deckchairs emptied all around her and the little groups of audience left the beach, Frank came on to the stage behind her, calling, 'Gilda? Come on, love. Let's see what the takings are. Can we eat tonight, or not? *Gilda*. . .'

He had raised his voice to call her, and the name rang out in a sudden lull in the chatter of the dispersing crowds. Essie's irritation flared. She had no time for a silly, mooning boy like Frank—after all, she was Mrs Luke Grimwade. She tossed her head and refused to look back at him. But the tall figure she was watching had heard also, and turned—and in that moment Luke's vivid eyes caught hers, and lingered.

'Luke! Luke!' Galvanised into instant movement, she raced across the space separating them to throw herself at him with such impetus that he rocked back on his heels, involuntarily raising his arms to hold her. He was smiling, but looked strangely nervous.

'You were going away!' she cried furiously. 'You must've known it was me, but—but you were leaving! Without saying anything! Oh, how could you? You're cruel, heartless——' She beat her fists against his chest in a red-hot rage which was partly real, but also compounded of her secret delight at seeing him again. She was back in his arms, close to him. So close that she didn't notice his expression change from curiosity and uncertainty to relief and intense warmth.

For a second he pressed her to him, looked down into her uplifted, bewildered face as if finding what he had always sought, and then his quietly amused voice sounded in her ears, wonderfully reassuring and calm, through the flurry of her emotional outburst.

'Well, you're a nice one to talk! Cruel? Heartless? And yet *you* ran away from *me*. . . Dry your eyes, you wicked girl. I suppose you don't care a damn that half the population of Teignmouth is gaping at your performance? Who ever saw a pierrot sobbing in a stranger's arms? And now I've got lard all over me. . .'

He released her, searching for a handkerchief to wipe the smeared make-up off his cheek. Essie couldn't believe it. He was laughing at her! Yet he had just held her so close that she had felt his heart thumping against her breast. And he wasn't angry, just making fun of her. Laughing. . .

'Luke?' Her eyes widened, and she took the handkerchief from him to mop her tears, still staring up at him uncertainly.

'Yes, Estrellita?' If she hadn't known differently, she might have thought he was actually fond of her—the two gentle words seemed to caress her sore spirit, and the strength of his presence displaced all the miserable insecurity that had haunted her since leaving him.

'How—how did you know where I was?'

He smiled, as if at a favourite child. 'I guessed you would run to your mother.'

Essie sniffed. It wasn't the time to tell him the truth—not yet. She tried again. 'But who told you I was here? With the pierrots?'

'Where else could you possibly be? In a theatre, of course.'

'Oh. . .' She hiccuped a last sob. 'Have you—forgiven me?'

For a long moment his vivid eyes probed hers, as if seeking out all her secrets. Then, 'You're asking the wrong question,' he answered, half smiling. 'Surely it's you who should forgive *me*? No, wait. . .' as she began to argue '. . .I said unforgivable things to you yesterday.' He shook his head, as if confused. 'Dear God, was it really only yesterday? It's been so long without you. . .'

Already she was recovering, his admission of guilt sending her volatile spirits soaring to new heights. 'Did you miss me, then?' She was too happy to realise how brash she sounded.

Momentarily, Luke's lean face lost its warmth, and he took a step back from her. 'You're incorrigible, Estrellita.'

'I know. You said so before.' She smiled with complete assurance, and watched his lips reluctantly twitch.

'It's not a compliment, little star.'

They stood, a few feet apart, smiling foolishly at each other, and Essie knew then, with a certainty that had never been so strong before, that she and Luke had, in some strange way, grown a little nearer, and all because of their parting. Now she felt on equal terms with him, no longer afraid of saying foolish things, or displeasing him. The knowledge made her feel very humble. Lowering her eyes, she shuffled her feet in the sand and said, in a low voice that he had to bend his head to hear, 'I'm sorry I ran away. I know I let you down. I was—angry. And hurt.' Quickly she looked up to meet the full force of his brilliant sea-

growing fond of her, the expression abruptly changed to one of subdued excitement.

Reading his face, Essie asked quickly, 'What is it? Something about the act? Oh, tell me—quickly!'

Luke fingered one of the buttons on her white blouse, and she saw his eyes deepen, rapidly brimming over with satisfaction. 'We have a contract in London,' he told her, casually and quietly, but with the vibrancy that always expressed the feelings he controlled so rigidly. 'The West End. We open in three weeks' time.'

'Luke! But that's wonderful!' She threw her arms around his neck, then remembered her white face, laughed in confusion and disentangled herself from his arms. 'Sorry! I keep forgetting this stupid old lard. Oh, Luke, isn't it exciting?'

He smiled down at her. His brilliant eyes were deep with feeling, and his resonant voice rang like a bell. 'It means a hell of a lot of hard work. Harry's gone up already, to prepare things—talk to the backers, find lodgings, and so on. You and I will join him at the end of the Plymouth run.'

She watched the brilliant eyes grow crystalline with a vision she could not share, and felt her heart growing bigger and bigger with her love for him. London. The West End. She and Luke. . .stars perhaps—the dream coming true!

She was overjoyed, so full of imaginings and happiness, that she quite failed to hear, behind her, Charlie's thick voice shouting, 'Gilda? Come on, gel, get a move on. We've got another show in less than an hour.'

The pupils of Luke's eyes contracted suddenly. 'What did he call you?' He frowned tensely, and Essie instinctively tried to change the subject.

'I don't know. I get called all sorts of names these days!' She smiled cheekily, and was rewarded by seeing his curiosity fade.

'I bet you do! I called you a few myself when I realised

you'd run off. . . Go on, then, little star, do as your new boss orders. And make sure you keep his act going for him.'

'I will, Luke. I promise.'

'Good girl.'

Abruptly awkward at the moment of parting, they looked at each other. Then Luke nodded, patted her shoulder, glanced at his watch, and said, rather too matter-of-factly, 'Time I went along to the station. Mustn't miss my train back. Mustn't let the customers down. . .well, goodbye, Estrellita.'

'Good—goodbye.' Her voice was small, all her effervescence suddenly quashed. She watched him turn and climb the steps leading up to the prom. Once he looked back and waved, a magnetic, handsome figure etched against the blue sky, and such was her terrible sense of loss that she stood on tiptoe, shouting, 'I'll be back soon, Luke. Honest I will. Very soon. . .'

He was gone. She blinked away the threatening tears and resolutely returned to the pavilion, where Charlie and Frank were drinking tea and stuffing themselves with hot pasties bought from a café lower down the pier. They looked up as she entered.

Frank's hazel eyes were wounded. 'Didn't know you had a gentleman friend,' he said thickly, through a mouthful of onion and turnip.

'There's a lot you don't know about me,' snapped Essie pertly. 'And you won't either—I shan't stay in this job for ever. Only until Judy comes back.'

Charlie's voice rumbled disapprovingly. 'Well, now, no one's asking you to, Miss High 'n Mighty—just do the job for as long as you're needed, and then you can be on your way. And a good thing, too. I don't want no temperamental tarts in *my* show. . .'

Grudgingly, he nodded to where a cup of cooling tea and an uneaten pasty lay on the cluttered make-up bench. 'Not too grand to eat your tea, are you? Long time to supper, you know.'

Ashamed of herself, Essie sat down, staring at the hard, thick pasty and the congealing tea. She longed to be alone with her thoughts, to savour those few recent, lovely moments when Luke's warm arms had enfolded her, when he had smiled with approval and what almost looked like affection—and to repeat to herself certain fond words and phrases which were already echoing through her head. If only she could leave this horrid little place and run out into the invigorating, cool evening air. But the sound of Frank slurping his tea, and Charlie's false teeth making heavy weather of the leathery pasty, reminded her of something else Luke had said, and, even more, of what he had implied. Something unromantic, but important. That, no matter how she had let him down, he expected her to complete her job here, regardless of personal feelings.

It was a hard lesson. But resolutely, and with a strength that she had not known she possessed, Essie steeled herself to sip the cold tea before turning to look apologetically at Charlie Griggs.

'I'm sorry, Charlie,' she said courageously. 'I didn't mean to say nasty things about the show. It's very good—and I like being in it with you.' She saw Charlie's shrewd old eyes narrow, and realised with a sinking feeling that all the polite little apologies in the world wouldn't change his bad opinion of her. Only the truth would do that. And the truth would lower her in her own eyes, which was much worse. . .

Bowing her head, she added humbly, 'I was in a rotten mood. I behaved very badly, taking it out on you. I—I won't ever do it again.' No, she certainly wouldn't. She imagined Luke's cold stare, had he known how she behaved, and winced inwardly.

There was a long, thoughtful pause, and Essie felt miserable. Charlie's teeth clicked on until he finally swallowed the last, lingering crumb of the pasty. Essie's eyes flickered towards Frank, sitting opposite, nursing his empty cup as he stared dolefully at her.

She wondered at what she had just said. At first it had seemed an awful come-down to have to admit she actually was the temperamental little 'Miss High 'n Mighty' Charlie had called her. But Luke's high standards and sense of responsibility had impressed themselves on her receptive mind deeper than she knew. Suddenly a feeling of satisfaction rose inside her, and she grinned across at Frank, who was still regarding her sourly.

'And if you really want to know all about me,' she said persuasively, 'well, I was a skivvy before I got my first job. You know, in service. Washing up, cleaning grates, and things.'

Instantly, the atmosphere lightened. Charlie scraped back his chair, heaved himself to his feet and, in passing, put a huge hand on her shoulder. 'All right, Gilda, gel, let's ferget it. We all gets a bit funny at times. You've got less than thirty minutes before curtain-up, so leave the next instalment of your wicked life-story till tomorrow. Well, now, it'll be something for us to look forward to. . . And you, Frank, stop gawping, lad, and give me a hand. That damn old piano lost one of its legs while you and Gilda were bouncing about on the boards. See if we can prop it up.'

Grudgingly, Frank rose, pausing as he passed Essie to say, in a low, quick aside, 'Friends again, Gilda?'

'You bet.' She gave him a beaming smile over her shoulder, and then, alone, looked thoughtfully at the uneaten pasty. A healthy hunger suddenly assailed her, and she ate it with keen enjoyment. So this was theatrical life. This was what Ma—no, Belle—and she shared, even if they could share nothing else. The pasty went down quickly, and inevitably her thoughts returned to Luke, on his way back to Plymouth and the evening performance. How would he manage without her?

She tempered the awful feeling of guilt by reminding

herself how proud of her he would have been, had he heard her recent unstinting apology to Charlie.

Later, getting ready for the second show, knotting the slippery scarf over her hair and making good the blurred make-up where Luke's hard cheek had pressed against hers, another thought came to her. By her own efforts she had, at last, become a proper professional. What was it Luke had said? 'A real trouper'. Well, now she was one. Essie smiled into the smudged mirror, and enjoyed a small but intense burgeoning of pleasure, as the truth grew in her mind, slowly becoming a new level of confidence and responsibility.

When she got back to Plymouth, she'd show Luke just how much more grown-up and sensible she had become. And maybe he would repay her by letting her love him. Please let him—oh, please. . .

She ran on to the stage with such stars in her eyes that Frank's and Charlie's performances both rose a degree higher to meet hers. The show was a stunner, and the bottling that evening provided them all with a splendid fish supper.

No wonder Essie returned to Belle's cottage with her weary head held high, to sleep the sleep of the blessed, even though her bed was a hard one in a tiny box-room smelling of mice and mould, and the tang of the nearby sea.

CHAPTER EIGHT

IT WAS an increasingly difficult time, staying with a mother who seemed to care more about her lodgers and her role as a soul-saving convert than making friends with a newly found daughter.

Belle made no bones about Essie's being in the way. 'When are you going, then?' she asked briskly. 'Said as how you could stay the night, that's all. I'm not made of money, you know.'

'But I can't leave the show, can I? I've got to be a trouper. . .'

Essie had used the term proudly, only to have her illusions shattered by Belle's, 'A *what*?'

'I mean I can't let Charlie down. And, anyway, I've got a sub from him. Here's five shillings for my keep.'

Belle pocketed the money absent-mindedly. 'Get on with you; Charlie can always find a girl if he wants to.' The dark eyes smouldered. 'Seems to me you only want to stay because you and that young Frank are all over each other.'

'Oh, we're not! We're just friends.'

'Huh. Reckon he don't think so. You mind out, my girl, or you'll have trouble on your hands. Men don't like being played with.' Belle limped off to immerse herself in a cloud of steam as she did the weekly wash at the stone sink, and Essie's quick rage evaporated.

Glumly she thought over the cutting words, and then wondered, dismayed, if perhaps Belle weren't right. Frank was for ever at her side. He was easy to talk to and, plainly, he admired her. And *that*, thought Essie with a grudging sense of truth that tore at her inborn vanity, was what was so nice about him.

Angrily she clenched her fists. Was Belle always

right? Did wisdom for ever have to be hard and hurtful? Idling her way around Teignmouth that morning, and shopping for the straw hat that Belle had ordered her to buy with the last of her sub—'No daughter of mine's going to go around without a hat'— she discovered there was no avoiding the nub of her deeply felt trouble.

All right, so she had found her mother, who wasn't prepared to give all the unstinting love Essie asked. Well, could it be that Essie herself was asking too much? And, if that was true, then maybe the same applied to Luke as well. Was she being selfish in asking for what he clearly could not give her? The answer came swiftly— a bleak yes. So, what if she tried harder and asked for less? Love, Belle had said, works miracles. . .

Frowning to herself, yet feeling a lightening of her downcast spirits, Essie planned a new campaign. Be patient with Belle. No more unthinking flirtatiousness with Frank. And—most important of all—when she returned to Luke, just love him. Quietly, and undemandingly. It would be very difficult, holding back all her fiery passions, but she would try.

Adjusting the new hat, she went back to Belle's laundry-filled cottage for the midday meal of bread and cheese, knowing that she had more to be thankful for than she truly deserved.

And then, as if her lesson in self-denial was being rewarded, that very evening Judy returned to the show, looking at Essie with an unfriendly scowl, and demanding that her costume be handed over for the second performance.

'Got it dirty, haven't you? What a mess.'

Stifling her excitement at the prospect of returning to Luke next day, Essie meekly offered tips for removing spilt tea stains and smudged lard, but was frowned at even further. Then, realising just how unwanted she was, she retreated resentfully from the stuffy little dressing-room, avoiding Frank's yearning gaze, to join the waiting audience seated on the beach below the curtained stage. There, as the show started, she understood the reason for Judy's unpleasantness. Frank had been praising Essie's dancing—Judy was clumsy with her feet, and her voice lacked beauty and tunefulness.

All Essie's despair faded as she watched the little show deteriorate into sheer amateurism, and humbly she realised that she had a true talent. It was painful to watch Charlie and Frank dragged down into a travesty of the performances they usually gave, and Essie left early. She had already said her goodbyes to them, thanking them sincerely for taking her into the act and giving so freely of their experience and friendship. Now she hurried home to hide away in her tiny room, before they came back half an hour later to have their cocoa and sandwiches while chatting by the fire with Belle.

She stared through the uncurtained window at the starlit sky, and went to sleep in the middle of a dream in which Luke welcomed her back, kissing her with a fondness that set her body shivering and trembling with anticipation.

The next morning she was unnaturally quiet—a characteristic which Belle commented on as Essie got ready to leave for the station. 'Something wrong? Not like you to have nothing to say.'

Essie looked at her mother and smiled wistfully. 'No. Nothing wrong. I'm just trying to—well, to be sensible.'

Belle sniffed, but her eyes were warm. 'You're learning, then, maid.'

'Trying to. Ma—I mean, Belle—it's been lovely being here with you. Do you think—well, can I come again? Later? Some time?'

Belle didn't reply at once, but looked at her daughter's shining smile. Then, briskly, she said, 'I've got a meeting this morning, down at the Triangle. You wait a minute and I'll walk along with you. Get my tambourine off the shelf, will you, maid?'

Essie wasn't sure if she was embarrassed or proud, walking through the town beside her navy-blue-clad mother, who carried a concertina strapped around her body, and the tinkling tambourine in one hand. She was unsure how to say goodbye when the moment came.

Facing her, Belle looked very directly into her daughter's hesitant eyes. 'Now, you go back to that magician of yours and behave properly. If you've got the talent, as Charlie says you have, then you should do well. But don't get above yourself—it never pays. . .'

'I won't. I mean, I'll try not to. . .goodbye, Ma.' The old, familiar term slipped out unnoticed. Belle's face twisted a little, and awkwardly she laid her free hand on Essie's arm.

'I'm glad you came,' she said hoarsely. 'Mebbe we'll see each other again—p'raps in London. . .' For a second her eyes glowed, but then the old, querulous expression returned. 'Mind you behave yourself, my gel—understand?'

Essie blinked back tears that she refused to allow Belle to see. 'Yes, all right. Well, here's the train. I'd better go. Good—goodbye. . .'

She would never forget leaving her mother, so small and dowdy, yet engrained upon her memory because of her indomitable strength and personality, standing on the platform and waving her tambourine as the train slowly puffed out of Teignmouth station.

It was, of course, raining in Plymouth. Essie smiled with joyful nostalgia, and rushed from the station to their lodgings, hoping and praying that Luke would still be there. Mrs Preston, the crotchety landlady, looked at her disapprovingly as she ran down the stairs, disappointed to find the door locked.

'O-ho! Come back, have you? Been on holiday, I suppose. . .'

Essie fought back the pert reply that flew into her mouth, and managed an unconvincing smile. 'No. A business trip, actually. Where's Luke—where's Mr Grimwade?'

The suspicious eyes gleamed. 'Gone to the theatre, I dessay. He's a hard worker, he is—no running off for him.'

Essie took exquisite pleasure in banging the door very loudly behind her, and ran all the way to the theatre, arriving out of breath and out of control of her excitement, despite a fierce determination to stay calm.

The stage-door keeper nodded affably towards the long, dark passage of dressing-rooms. 'He's in there—cor, in a hurry, aren't you?'

She threw open the dressing-room door, and there he was, sitting in his usual chair beside the mirror, hands moving effortlessly through the palming exercises, dark hair flopping over the high brow, lean face intent, body still and relaxed.

'Luke! I'm back!'

Light from the naked bulb hanging above shone suddenly on the silver star in his left ear as he turned to look at her, and momentarily distracted Essie's eyes from the expression on his face. Had she seen the clear relief, joy and glowing warmth that he registered in that brief second, she would have been the happiest creature on earth. But, by the time her gaze had focused on his brilliant eyes, all that was left was a friendly, welcoming smile—no more. 'So you've come home, Estrellita. . .' Rising, he opened wide his arms, and she flew into them. Luke held her close, for a long, wonderful moment, savouring her nearness and her warmth. Then, sighing, he let her go—ambition must always come before everything else, even though this little scrap of vitality and affection seemed to have forced herself deeply under his skin. . .

Yes, Essie told herself, she truly *was* home. Warm, secure, wanted. But there was something different about him. About the way he embraced her, kissing the tip of her nose, not her lips, and teasingly telling her that the Teignmouth sun had brought out her freckles. London, he went on, would be full of smuts, so she'd better make the best of such natural beauty.

He was so chatty and friendly that it took her a little time to realise where the difference lay. And only when he began talking about the new contract did she understand. It was ambition that was driving him, making him smile at her, put his arms around her. Ambition. Not love.

'The act's been impossible without you,' he told her briskly. 'I took on a girl who was quite useless. She slipped on stage last night, and let the rabbit wander all over the boards.' He grinned handsomely and, despite her disappointment, she tried to look pleased. 'Never mind, little star. You're back now. Everything will be all right again. I've heard from Harry today.' Turning to the bench below the mirror, he picked up a letter. 'He's found decent lodgings, and says the manager of the Irving Theatre is being very helpful. And another thing—the stage manager is Joe Colley, who I worked with before. That's splendid news—he's got an excellent carpenter, who's knowledgeable about trick machinery. . .'

Essie sat down in the empty chair, suddenly drained and low-spirited. Perhaps she had expected too much. But surely he might have kissed her properly, made a fuss of her, not treating her as just the girl who knew how to make the rotten old act run smoothly?

'What's the matter?' His voice broke into her glum thoughts, and for a moment she stared blankly into his abruptly anxious eyes. 'Not ill, are you?' He put a hand on her forehead.

'I'm never ill.' Somehow she kept all traces of her feelings out of her voice, even managed to sit up and attempt a nonchalant gaiety which was quite false. The plan—she must stick to the plan. . .

'I'm hungry, that's what. Had breakfast early this morning.' She smiled at him with all the coquetry she could muster, and was rewarded by his burst of relieved laughter.

'Of course! Always demanding to be fed, aren't you? Well, come along; we'll go and find a meal. Can't have my invaluable assistant fading away, just when our big chance is here.'

They went to an eating house up the road, and Essie watched his sparkling eyes as he told her of his plans for their rosy future. She felt exhausted afterwards. Acting was something she was becoming increasingly good at, but oh, lawks, it was hard work.

London, Essie decided ten days later, was a magical city. Dirty, beautiful, crowded, noisy—oh, yes, quite the most wonderful place she had ever seen.

'I'm going to like it here,' she told Luke cockily, as they travelled in a motorised taxi-cab from Paddington station, along Bayswater Road and Oxford Street, to their lodgings in Soho.

'You don't mind the hurry and bustle?' he asked teasingly. 'The size of the place? All these people, rushing about with intent faces?' Essie followed his gaze, staring out of the window.

It was like a new world, she thought excitedly, after the quiet, slow pace of the West Country. Here there was a throbbing atmosphere of activity and power that held her entranced. She stared first at the towering, weather-blackened buildings slipping past the cab window, and then at the people. Men and women of all ages, walking determinedly down the thronged pavements as if their very lives depended on how soon they reached their destinations. Where could they all be going? What were they doing?

Luke's voice broke into her busy thoughts. 'Women are freer up here,' he told her good-humouredly. 'They work in all sorts of positions nowadays—secretaries, shop-girls. . .of course you've heard of the Suffragette Movement?'

Unable to take her eyes off a particularly smart female, Essie nodded. As the cab passed she looked back, to stare at the vividly painted face and bright, feathery finery. 'Oh, what lovely clothes!' An image of herself, in the same old blue dress and limp coat, was soul-destroying.

And then Luke's hearty laugh made her jump. 'She's a tart, Estrellita—a street girl. Don't imagine all the women working in London can afford to dress like that!'

She flushed red, realising how ignorant she must seem. Once more, she sensed his worldly experience, so much greater than hers. Setting her lips, she said grimly, 'Well, I don't care what all the other women wear—*I'm* going to look smart and lovely, the way that tar—the way she did. One day.'

Silence. Essie slid a defiant sideways look at him, adding, 'One day *soon*,' and met his eyes. They were thoughtful and kind—not mocking, not even irritated, as she had feared. The moment, surprising as it was, engulfed her, releasing pent-up thoughts and words in a sudden torrent. Impulsively, she touched his arm.

'Can I have some new clothes, please, Luke? Just a dress, and p'raps a hat, and—well, my boots've got an awful hole in them. But I don't need a new coat. It's getting warmer every day now, so. . .' She tailed off, suddenly ashamed of the need to ask for what, even as a skivvy, she had been used to providing for herself. 'Those suffragettes—those Pankhurst ladies,' she muttered darkly, 'they've got a point, haven't they?

Women *should* be able to go about and do things. Have money. Just like men. . .'

'You awful little rebel!' Again Luke burst into laughter. Then, good-humouredly, he pulled her towards him on the shiny leather seat, and for a second she was in heaven. Close to him. Pleasing him. His free hand dived into his pocket, producing a leather wallet. Letting her go, he took out a banknote and fluttered its white crispness under her startled eyes. Then it disappeared to come out from beneath her coat sleeve, just as the china egg had been conjured from her ear, that night in Exeter. . .

'I've had a good payment in advance,' he told her lightly. 'It's a sort of sub. Solomon Kurtz is so sure we'll be a hit, he wrote me out a cheque to cover our fares and our living expenses. . .so there you are. All yours. Spend it wisely, now. Not too many feathers, and definitely no make-up, off stage. Can't have you being mistaken for a lady of the night, can we?'

'Lady of——?' Knowledge came in a rush, and she was furious with him. 'What a thing to say! I'll only buy something respectable. . .' Her voice dropped and her eyes shone as she began to plan her new wardrobe.

Behind the crowds were huge shops, plate-glass windows gleaming in the spring sunshine beneath linen awnings. She caught tantalising glimpses of wonderful hats, elegant suits and dresses. Turning to Luke, she smiled brilliantly. 'Oh, you are good to me! Thank you, Luke.'

Spontaneously, she reached out to aim a generous kiss on his pale face, but he was too quick for her, moving away, almost as if repulsed, so that her cheek merely brushed his shoulder. Abruptly, his eyes wore the old veiled, touch-me-not expression, and his voice was clipped as he said brusquely, 'Don't be ridiculous. It's no more than you deserve. You've worked well— apart from that stupid business of running off to

A CERTAIN MAGIC

Teignmouth. And you haven't asked for any wages before.'

Essie was speechless, reduced so clearly to a mere employee. Perhaps he understood her hurt silence, for the next moment he gave her a conciliatory stare, adding, 'Another thing. You're Mrs Luke Grimwade, and here in London that's going to mean something. We'll be seen together, meeting a lot of important people in the profession—impresarios, managers, and so on. You must look well-dressed. I don't want you to let me down.'

Vanquished by a pain almost too intense for her to control, she could only sit, staring blindly at the white note in her hand. So that was all he thought of her. Someone to help work the act. Someone to play the part of his wife.

Anger came then, hot and releasing, cauterising the awful wound his thoughtless words had caused. She turned on him, huge eyes blazing, words ripping off her tongue like the chattering of an enraged magpie. 'Well, thanks very much! Luke Grimwade's wife! At least I know what part I'm supposed to be playing. . .' She chuckled, loud and bitter. 'And I'll make a success of it, too—you see if I don't.'

'Of course you will.' He looked puzzled, suddenly even apologetic, but she was past caring. Rage brought a miraculous power with it.

'Right, then. My first scene, as Mrs Luke Grimwade. . .' pausing, she saw him frown '. . .is to say that I need a room to myself. No more seeing your white feet in the morning. No more sharing, see?'

'But, Estrellita, I can't afford that. . .' Suddenly he was scowling, his temper as high as hers, but more rigidly held in check. Even in anger, his voice was low and even.

'Oh, yes, you can!' she said triumphantly. 'You've got more fivers hidden away in your wallet—I saw them! Good for Solomon Whoever-he-is. . . Well, as your so-called wife, I deserve a bit spent on me. I'm like Mrs Pankhurst, you see—I want my rights, and I'm going to get them!' Glaring into his narrowed eyes, she felt heady with satisfaction. Now she knew for certain that the old Essie had been left behind in Devon, along with the battered hat that the sea had swept away. Here she was in London—Mrs Luke Grimwade—and, by definition of Luke's own words, a woman to be looked at and admired. A voice to be heard.

All right, then! Luke had made it absolutely clear that he had no personal feelings towards her. He needed her only as an assistant on stage, and a well-dressed, attractive girl playing the part of his wife afterwards. So be it, thought Essie, fuming. She would play the game his way, but her private life would be her own from now on, to do whatever she wanted with it. She felt the world was at her feet, and it was a wonderful sensation.

Harry Whitman was at the new lodgings in Garrett Street to meet them. Ignoring his ingratiating welcome, Essie walked briskly around the dingy upstair rooms, running her finger over chairs and window-sills, tweaking aside lace curtains, and searching for pots and pans in the small, dark kitchenette, before tossing him her reply. 'Afternoon, Harry. Is this the best you could find? Not exactly clean, is it? And how am I supposed to cook a Sunday dinner without a meat tin?'

Not waiting for his answer, she swept into the one bedroom. 'This is going to be mine, Luke. You'll have to sleep on the sofa again if you're too mean to pay for another room.'

The silence greeting her words was explosive. Turning, she met two pairs of outraged eyes. Saucily she smiled, enjoying herself. 'Yes. Well. I've learned a few things, see? I won't be put on any more. And I'm hungry—must be all the travelling. Let's go and find somewhere to eat, shall we?'

Luke sighed, bowed with something approaching reluctant admiration, and she narrowed her eyes to impress her new determination on him. 'And tomorrow I'm going shopping. . .'

'No, you're not. You're coming to the theatre with me to meet the people who matter.' Suddenly he was looking down at her, dominant and tight-lipped as never before.

'Not in these old clothes, I'm not.'

The moment of mutual challenge seemed to last for ever. Then Luke's cold eyes thawed a little. His brow quirked and he looked her up and down. 'They seem all right to me.' Despite his obvious annoyance, she watched his mouth twitch slightly. His voice was low, and for a second her composure was threatened—until she reminded herself of what he'd said in the taxi-cab.

Defiantly, she tilted her head. 'Well, they're not! If you want to impress all your grand friends, I'll have to look better than this.'

'You look lovely to me. You always do. . .' They might have been quite alone, the way he was regarding her now. His gentle words pierced her heart, and had it not been for the untimely sound of Harry's throaty laughter she might have thrown herself into his arms.

'I'll look even lovelier tomorrow!' Provocatively she smiled, and was disappointed to see his eyes grow hard and distant again.

Rapidly he turned away, as if, she thought, horrified, he could no longer bear to be near her. 'Very well. Shop in the morning if you must, and I'll arrange our meeting to take place over luncheon.' Impersonally he glanced back over his shoulder, as if to a stranger. 'I suppose I can rely on you to turn up then?'

Essie's cheeks coloured, but she kept her head. The rebuke, after all, was justified. 'Of course,' she said stiffly. 'I won't run off no more—any more. I know what I'm doing now.'

'Good. Then perhaps we can get on with what matters most—the plans for our career.' He was wandering around the room, and his icy tone seared her.

'All right. Go ahead with your plans. I'm as interested in them as you are, you know.'

And then he was beside her again, fighting the only half-concealed smile that curled his lips upwards, his presence a suddenly draining source of pleasure. She fluttered her hands, distraught, and instantly he took them in his.

'I do know, Estrellita,' he said, very quietly. 'And I'm glad. So glad, in fact, that I'm going to give you an extra large supper as a reward. . .' The skin at the corner of his eyes crinkled in a delightful way that made her feel light-headed. 'Come along; let's go and feed that insatiable appetite of yours—you'll sleep all the better once you're full of meat stew and dumplings, I expect.' He put an arm around her in a quick hug that made her gasp.

As usual, the last words were his. Like a child, she trailed down the stairs behind him and climbed into another taxi-cab, hardly hearing the facetious comments Harry Whitman offered as he walked too closely behind her.

They had been talking, it seemed to Essie, for hours. She had made two pots of tea since their return, and still Luke and Harry were sitting by the empty fireplace, making endless plans about tomorrow, discussing the needs of the tricks and illusions chosen for the new show. Now the teacups were empty once more, and she couldn't face the thought of putting on the kettle yet again.

It had been an amazing day. The first time she had ever left Devon, and, oh, the thrilling excitement of arriving at Paddington's busy terminus, of driving through the London streets to these lodgings. And being so cocky with Luke—even as she yawned, she smiled to herself. Now she knew just how to treat him.

Almost as if he read her thoughts, Luke turned. 'Go to bed, Estrellita,' he told her quietly, his lean face soft and gentle, and with a warmth in his eyes that caught at her heart-strings. 'You must be tired. And tomorrow's going to be an important day.'

Yearningly, she wondered if his gentleness was real, or just another trick. After all, he was a magician. . . The thought made her cut into his words brazenly, rising from the stool by his chair.

'I know it is—shopping!'

He looked up at her tolerantly, eyes openly amused, and she could have bitten her tongue. 'And other things, too. You won't forget our luncheon at Romano's in the Strand, will you?'

'Course I won't. But you'll have to tell me how to get there. I don't know my way about yet.'

'That's all right. You'll have Harry as a guide.'

She stiffened, eyes wide. 'Harry? What do you mean?'

'Exactly what I said. Harry will be with you. . .' Seeing the sheer disbelief on her face, he added, more sharply, 'Good God, Estrellita, you didn't think I was going to let you loose on the town, did you? You and your flighty ways? You're far too valuable to me for that—why, you might get picked up, even fall under an omnibus——'

'Oh!' Her cry of rage was mixed with shame. 'But I've been so looking forward to being on my own— exploring, going round the shops, and—and. . .' Tears pricked behind her eyelids, enraging her even more. She turned to Harry, abruptly shrieking out her disappointment, as if he, and not Luke, were responsible for causing it. 'I don't want you to come with me! I'm not a child—I can find my own way. Got a tongue in my head, haven't I?'

But Harry only put back his head, braying with laughter. 'You're a cracker, Essie! What a gal, eh, Luke?'

Luke rose in one swift movement, his hands on her shoulders, turning her, none too gently, towards him. She saw his beautiful eyes glitter with annoyance, and realised she'd gone too far this time.

'Stop shrieking like a fishwife,' he said, very low, voice taut as wire. 'Remember you're my so-called wife. And remember we're about to star in a show that thousands of people are going to see. Always remember that, Estrellita. . .'

Mortified at his displeasure, her own dismay and hurt remained. Sulkily she pulled away. 'Can't ever forget it, can I? It's the only thing you think and talk about.'

'Of course I do. It's *our* act. Yours and mine.' Now he was half smiling at her, but she wouldn't be charmed out of her rebellion.

'And Harry's.' Sullenly she threw the name at him, watching how his expression immediately changed. Amusement went. Now he looked at her very intently.

'Well, of course—in a way; Harry does the managing, raises the finances, that sort of thing.'

'That's just what I meant.'

'I see. . .'

Was it relief that slid momentarily across his face? Abruptly, she was too weary to care. 'I'm going to bed.'

She went in silence, listlessly going into the next room and closing the door loudly behind her in a last flash of passion. Then she fell on to the bed, closing her heavy eyes at once, too tired to undress, too upset to care. She slept restlessly, and with frustrating dreams, until urban dawn noises awoke her.

For a moment she lay wide-eyed, wondering where she was. There was the sound of a milk cart clattering over cobbles, feet tip-tapping down the pavement, a horse neighing, a distant motor-car hooting and revving its engine. She recalled last night's clash of wills, and then, her volatile spirits restored to their usual energetic level, grinned to herself, making plans for the day ahead.

Shopping! And without that monster, Harry Whitman. . .

She washed in cold water, poured from the jug standing on the marble-topped wash-stand, smoothed her rumpled clothes, tidied her hair, then picked up the cheap straw boater, trimmed with garish ribbon, which was all she had been able to afford on her shopping expedition in Teignmouth, and carefully eased open the bedroom door.

Inevitably, Luke's bare white feet met her searching gaze, and for a second her heart fell. How could she play such a trick on him? He'd be worried, he'd blame Harry, he would have to spend valuable time looking for her. . .

Ruthlessly then, her mind snapped back into the excitement of her plan. No, he wouldn't. He would be far too busy with his own arrangements to even bother with her disappearance. And she'd promised she would be back for luncheon, hadn't she?

She slipped out of the door and out of the house, as silently as a mouse, walking briskly down the street on her way to explore London and buy some entrancing new clothes.

The morning was misty, but not the gentle, clean mistiness that Devon so often spread over its quiet, widely distanced villages. Here there was a sulphuric smell in the grey cloud that made Essie shiver as she walked rapidly towards the square where only last night she and Luke and Harry had eaten that marvellous supper.

She went past the closed restaurant holding her breath, noting the shuttered windows and locked doors, closed to all intruders, and the sight gave her an uneasy foretaste of what might be to come. London was known to be a grim place—was she foolish to be out on her own? Luke's warning words rang in her ears, but she tossed her head and walked all the faster.

Of course she wouldn't fall under an omnibus! And as for someone picking her up—she sniffed. She wasn't that sort of girl, and Luke should have known it.

But when, out of sheer weariness and a growing concern that kept suggesting she was lost, an hour later she stopped at a covered stall tucked away in a shadowy corner of a busy thoroughfare, she was almost too scared to ask for the cup of tea she so badly longed for.

There were evil-looking men hanging around the stall, turning as she approached and exchanging glances with each other. One—a small, rat-faced little man with a black tooth sticking out of his thin lips, said, in a kind of jargon she couldn't quite understand, 'Hang on to yer bees, boys. Here comes a lovely gel. . .'

The coarse guffaws that arose at the quip offended Essie. She forgot she was afraid, and stared coldly at the grinning little man. 'I dunno what you're talking about, but just keep quiet. I've as much right as you to be here.'

Roars of rough laughter greeted her words, and the man behind the counter tipped his curly-brimmed bowler further down over his slitted eyes. 'Now, now, boys—she's right, you know. Just show us yer bees, gel, and then I'll serve you whatever you wants.'

'Bees?' She was baffled. 'What are you talking about? I don't keep bees——'

'Yer money, love. Bees an' honey—talk the King's English, don't yer?' Slit-eyes leaned across the counter, enjoying the mirth he evoked from his regular customers.

'Oh! Money! Well, why didn't you say so? Course I

got money—here. . .' Out of her pocket she drew the five pound note, brandishing it triumphantly.

There was moment's silence, then a hiss of drawn breath. The rat-faced man twitched his ragged moustache and muttered admiringly, 'Musta done well last night, gel.'

Slowly, painfully, his meaning dawned. Essie went bright red, stepped backwards, pocketed her money, and wished the earth could swallow her. She gasped, 'Oh, no! You're wrong! I'm not like that—I mean, I didn't. . .oh, lawks!'

A hand fell on her shoulder, and she nearly jumped out of her skin. Silence again, and the customers began shuffling away from the stall, each of them apparently having thought of something vastly important to do elsewhere.

'What's going on, then?' asked a heavy voice, and Essie turned to look, terrified, into the stern eyes of the law.

The policeman, informed of her predicament, twitched his mouth, looked at her dubiously, before re-adjusting his helmet and becoming more human. 'Not the place to be on your own, miss—not round here. Where exactly do you want to get to?'

Essie gulped. 'The shops. I have to do some shopping.'

'Regent Street? Oxford Street?'

'I—suppose so. I don't know. . .'

'Well, miss, I suggest you go and wait at the omnibus-stop round the corner. A tuppenny ride'll take you into the West End. I'll accompany you there, miss. This way. . .'

Trotting meekly along beside the policeman, Essie felt like a child sent home in disgrace. What on earth would Luke say, if he know how foolish and inexperienced she'd been? She realised now that his warning had been justified. And as for that Harry. . . She scowled, imagining what unkind and prurient comments Harry would make, should he ever hear of her being taken for a tart.

And, even now, after the ride on the omnibus, how would she know where to go? She began to wish she hadn't decided on this childish prank. The image of Luke's white feet, hanging over the edge of the sofa, made her want to weep and run. She should be there with him, not alone, in this cold, dirty, wicked place. . .

At first she didn't hear the footsteps tripping down the road behind them. The policeman walked with squeaking, heavy boots, and the morning traffic was already noisy. But a bright, familiar voice was calling her name. 'Essie. Essie Grimwade!' And she whirled around, nerves jangling. What now? she thought, startled and not a little dismayed.

The girl following them came running up, out of breath, smiling and holding out her hands. 'Eee, thought I'd never catch you up! Essie—what on earth are you doing here? Oh, but I'm pleased to see you again, love. . .'

'Alice! Oh, Alice!'

'A friend of yours, miss?'

The policeman eyed Alice warily, and Essie bubbled with relief. 'Yes, she is! Fancy you being here, Alice——'

'What d'you mean, fancy? Me an' Albie's playing at the Empire—can you believe it? Along with the nobs! I heard as you and Luke were around—thought I'd come and find you in Garrett Street, but he said you'd gone out, so I come looking. . .'

'Well, miss, seeing as how you're in good hands now. . .' The policeman's deep voice reminded Essie of his presence, and she turned, smiling gratefully.

'You've been very kind. Thank you. But I'm all right now.'

'Very well, miss. Good-day.' Touching his helmet, the man strode back down the street.

Alice giggled. 'Trust you to do something daft! Soho's full of tarts! How did you get here?'

'I don't know. How could I? I was trying to find the shops.'

'Well, love, you must've walked in a circle. Shopping, are you?' Alice's eyes shone.

'Yes. Look, I've got money. . .'

'Well, let's get on with it, love. Regent Street, here we come.'

CHAPTER NINE

It had taken a long time, much thought and tireless traipsing from one huge store to another, before finally tracking down the dress Essie had in mind.

At first she had been attracted to a startling red creation, all flounces and swirling skirts, trimmed with bright braid and ribbon, but common sense had prevailed in the end. Luke expected her to be well-dressed, not common and cheap. Recalling the garishness of the street girl's clothes, Essie blushed and put the red dress out of her mind. Something plain, something suitable and becoming. . .

At last, there it was, stylish, expensive-looking and just within her range of spending, draped on a dressmaker's dummy upstairs in Harrod's gown department, the third floor having been reached by a new-fangled escalator, which had both Essie and Alice giggling as they hopped off it at the top.

'Eee, you look a proper elegant lady in that green, love,' Alice said, awestruck, when Essie came out of the fitting-room clad in the plain linen fitted dress that highlighted the richness of her hair and emphasised her tiny waist. The saleswoman smiled encouragement, and Essie looked at her reflection in the big pier mirror by the window, high above London's traffic.

Elegant. Yes, that was undoubtedly the word for it. Enraptured by what she saw—surely a sophisticated woman, no longer the raw young skivvy—Essie preened and turned around until she was quite sure that this dress and no other would do.

'What about a hat? Not going to wear that awful old straw, are you?' Alice was so forthright, and the saleswoman so persuasive, that, before Essie had realised it, she had bought a beautiful new hat which matched the green of the plain dress, but in some magical way seemed lighter and brighter because of the pale cream silk flowers that nestled beneath its wide brim, shadowing her face and giving an extra dimension to her wide, glowing eyes.

'Shoes? Gloves? And you'll need a parasol—go on, love, got enough brass left? After all, he gave it you to spend. . .'

There was—just—enough to pay the bill with a few pence for the ride home in the omnibus. Essie wore all her new finery, carrying the old clothes in a brown paper parcel, soon dumped beneath her bed.

Alice was proving more than just a friend. She made a badly needed pot of reviving tea while Essie practised using her parasol, and then began worrying how she was to get to the restaurant in the Strand for luncheon with Luke. In the middle of her fuming, the door flew open and there was Harry, staring at her as if she had two heads.

'What on earth——?' His face grew an unattractive red shade, and he started shouting. 'Where the hell have you been? I've been chasing round for hours looking for you, you silly bitch.'

Essie froze, giving him a glare. 'Hard luck,' she said sharply. 'Well, now you've found me, and I'm ready for that lunch. Do you want a cup of tea before we go?'

'Damn the tea! We'll have to get a move on if we're to get to Romano's in time. Come on, then—Luke'll be furious if we're late. . .'

Deliberately taking her time, Essie adjusted her new hat. She sent Alice a confidential little grin, then said airily, marching to the door, 'Finish the pot, Alice. And there's biscuits in the tin. I'll come and see you at the Empire when I can. And——' at the door, about to precede the impatient Harry downstairs, she looked back and changed her tone '—and thanks, Alice; you're a real friend. . .'

'Get on with you!' Alice waved a hand as if in blessing. 'Enjoy yer smart lunch! Eee, you look really lovely, Essie.'

'Lovely? More like a tart—mutton dressed as lamb, aping your betters, I'd say.' Harry thumped down the stairs behind Essie, and she spat back at him.

'No one's asking you, Harry Whitman! You wouldn't know an elegant dress if you saw one—but Luke will. He'll like me in this outfit, see if he doesn't.' She sounded confident, but spent the next ten minutes wondering if he would.

Suppose Luke, like Harry, thought she had overdone it? Suppose he told her to go home and change back into her old clothes. . .? Oh, lawks, Essie muttered silently, as she and Harry climbed into a horse-drawn omnibus going in the direction of the Strand, if he does, then it's the finish. I'll run off again. . .

But several male heads turned appreciatively in her direction as she sat down, and gradually her uneasiness disappeared. She *felt* good; surely that was all that mattered?

After a brisk walk from the stop where the omnibus put them down, Essie paused as Harry bundled her towards a broad, open doorway. A bell rang in her head, and suddenly she recalled Luke, back in Exeter, talking about London restaurants. The Ritz. The Savoy. Romano's in the Strand. . .

She particularly remembered Romano's, because it sounded Italian, like her Pa, Vittorio. And there it was. The name stood out, high above her in huge stone letters. 'ROMANO'S'. To the left of the name were moulded the figures 398, and, to the right, 399. Essie was, as yet, unaware of the fame connected with this address, but her entranced gaze slid a little lower, taking in the canopy above the broad doorway, a heavy canopy, providing a dance-floor for nude copper cupids which cavorted delightfully among swags and ropes of entwined metal foliage. Behind this canopy, heavy wrought-iron balcony railings shone in the spring sunlight, and beyond them large windows blinked invitingly.

She gaped, her heart overflowing with excitement. She had never imagined that one day she, an insignificant skivvy from the West Country, would stand here, actually about to enter such a paradise, where carriages and motor-cars were stopping to deliver ladies and gentlemen, all dressed in the height of fashion, all of them smiling graciously, and talking among themselves.

For a second she felt disastrously out of place. Then, 'Get a move on, Essie'—Harry was impatient, nudging her onward, and so she took a deep breath, eyed the regal-looking doorman with slight unease, and made her entrance.

Inside, at first, she saw nothing, for the lights were subdued. The hum of discreetly chattering voices surprised her. But then, as her eyes grew accustomed to the level of artificial lighting, her curiosity became intense.

A dark-haired, neatly moustached waiter appeared, raising an obsequious eyebrow. 'Table for two, sir?'

'Mr Grimwade's party,' Harry answered pompously, and at once the man bowed, and smiled. 'This way, if you please.'

Essie's feet hardly touched the thickly carpeted floor. She felt she was in another world, on a higher plane, perhaps, along with the dancing cupids at the entrance, and these well-dressed, beautiful people who sat at their tables drinking, eating, laughing—and all so clearly enjoying themselves.

The crowded room was long and narrow, with many tables, and red plush seats lining the walls. Mirrors reflected the lighting, and the faces of the diners. Essie's gaze took in a myriad wonderful details as she floated after the waiter, following him down the length of the restaurant.

Men, dressed in expensive dark suits, high stiff collars accentuating their features. The women's hats, large and fantastically trimmed with blowsy roses and gleaming feathers. She noticed plain women, so elegantly dressed that they seemed beautiful, and beautiful women who, in some strange way, had made themselves coarse and unattractive, because of their over-painted faces and petulant expressions.

The restaurant was warm and friendly, redolent of rich food and fragrant wines. Over the reflection of the tables she caught a sudden glimpse of a young girl in a plain dress, wearing a noble hat—a fresh-faced, unpainted girl, who carried her head high, and whose eyes shone like twin morning stars—herself! It was a shock, but a welcome one, to realise how well she compared with the other diners, here at Romano's.

The knowledge excited her. Her emotions surged, and before she knew it she was acting again, throwing foolish, frivolous words over her shoulder to Harry, wanting only to become part of this glamorous new world, finding it almost too easy to ape the manner of the society women she had watched so enviously, outside.

'What a wonderful place. I feel as if I really belong here!'

From behind her, Harry's voice answered coarsely, 'You silly tart. You'll never do that.'

Essie's reply projected theatrically, disturbing the hum of quiet conversation in the big room. 'What a nasty thing to say, Harry, darling—and you're quite wrong; I do belong here, you know. Just remember that you're not the only man in my life, if you please. . .'

And then she saw, at the table ahead of her, Luke's face turning to stare, as if dumbfounded. She watched his anger grow, realised with a plummeting heart that he was offended by her self-indulgent play-acting. She almost ran the last few yards to where he sat. By the time she reached his side, he had risen, and was looking at her stonily, as if she were a stranger.

Ignoring the curious gazes of the men seated around the table, he muttered, 'What the hell are you playing at, Estrellita?' and she nodded, smiling eagerly, trying to reassure him, almost as if her life depended on pleasing him.

She was very conscious of her new clothes, and the words gushed out without restraint. 'Do you like it? My dress? It's a pretty colour, isn't it? Suits my hair. . .' And then, thinking to charm him into a more pleasant mood, she posed prettily with the new parasol, before swirling neatly around, displaying the full skirt and her new, shining, high-heeled shoes.

Dismayed at his still frowning lack of response, she began blustering. 'Well, I like it, anyway, and so did Alice——'

'Alice?'

'You know—on the bill with us in Exeter—my friend. . .' Her voice petered out, for clearly Luke wasn't listening. Instead, he looked past her to Harry, who was fidgeting irritably behind her.

Intrigued, but at the same time instinctively scared by the hostility she sensed rising between the two men, she heard Luke ask grittily, 'So you found her? But you said you had no idea where to look.'

Harry seemed discomfited and sounded angry, as he grunted back, 'Of course I didn't! I searched the streets for hours.'

Unable to understand what the fuss was about, Essie touched Luke's arm. Suspicion shone in his brilliant eyes, and she immediately remembered all that he had said at Plymouth, when she had been out with Harry. Was he still jealous? Oh, but what a fool she had been, play-acting as she did, just now. . . Of course, he thought she had been with Harry all the morning, running off with him, flirting...

Desperately trying to make amends, to convince him of her innocence, she stammered, 'He—he didn't find me. How could he? He didn't know where I'd gone...'

'I suppose not.' Luke's voice was unnaturally hard. He gave Harry a last, terse stare, and then, with a conscious effort, turned back to his watchful guests circling the big table.

'I do apologise, gentlemen.' His smile, flashing around at the three men, was a performer's smile, charismatic and compelling. So great was his charm and magnetism that, in a second, the awkward atmosphere cleared and Essie, looking around, met three pairs of frankly appreciative and curious eyes as their owners waited to be presented to her.

Now Luke had quite recovered his poise. Again the genial host, he took Essie's hand, settling her carefully on the chair beside his, before nodding at Harry to find a seat for himself.

'Gentlemen, my assistant Estrellita Grimwade.' He turned, smiling directly into her eyes, and she blinked at him. Had he forgiven her? She thought so, but, of course, he might just be acting—as she had been.

'My dear, allow me to present Mr Solomon Kurtz, the famous impresario, just over from the States, and interested enough in our act to want to talk about a possible contract on Broadway.'

By now agog with excitement, and at last fully realising the importance of the occasion, Essie had herself under firm control. She nodded, wide-eyed, at the little fat-jowled man with a near-bald head and wispy side-whiskers, who stared at her from serpentine eyes, mumbling, 'Your servant, Mrs Grimwade,' in a thick mid-European accent. Half rising, he made a vague effort to bow, but his immaculately waistcoated stomach made such movement almost impossible.

A CERTAIN MAGIC

Grunting, he re-seated himself, and Essie's gaze moved to the next man, who was already grinning shrewdly at her across the table.

'Our producer, Mr Leonard Rollinson. We'll be seeing a lot of him.'

'Glad to meet you, Mrs Grimwade. Estrellita, isn't it? Splendid. Christian names are more friendly...hope you'll call me Len.' A sallow face, under a thatch of peppery grey hair, regarded her with calculating green eyes, and Essie understood that Mr Rollinson was very much the big boss when it came to putting the show together.

'And this is Sir Jack Martineau, one of our angels——' Luke's vivid smile flashed briefly, intimating his liking for the last guest, who was seated next to Essie. 'An angel is a backer, Estrellita,' he told her quietly. 'Sir Jack is a merchant banker, very important in the city, and a highly respected patron of the arts, too—particularly, I'm glad to say, of the variety theatre.'

The tall, middle-aged man, with the unmistakable military bearing, was already on his feet, a memorable figure, silver-haired, with a monocle on a dark ribbon, and dressed in a grey frock-coat. He bowed deeply, as he said, 'A great pleasure, Mrs Grimwade.' The voice was a lazy drawl, deep and quite charming. Essie looked up into pale blue, astute eyes shining beneath long, sandy lashes, and was instantly captivated.

A proper gentleman! A sir...and how well-dressed, so handsome, and with such lovely manners... Foolishly, she blushed, lowering her eyes and then instinctively restraining her emotion, remembering her position as Luke's wife. She murmured something polite, and Sir Jack's hand reached out to take hers. Firm lips brushed a kiss across her fingertips and, complimented beyond her wildest fantasies, she smiled up into his watchful eyes.

'You're a newcomer to our city, Mrs Grimwade, I believe—and what do you think of it?'

Succumbing instantly to his friendliness, Essie dropped her shyness. 'It's wonderful,' she said openly, 'but, of course, I haven't seen much of it—not yet.' She glanced at Luke for reassurance, and he nodded imperceptibly, a smile of only half-concealed amusement touching his mouth, and she breathed more easily. She vowed to herself not to say or do anything to displease him again.

Raising an indulgent dark brow, he looked across the table, smiling more warmly at Martineau. 'Estrellita is a country girl, Sir Jack, easily impressed by the excitement of dirty old London. As she says, there's been no time to explore the more beautiful parts of it yet. Paddington Station, our lodgings in Soho, and—I think I'm right in concluding. . .' his smile broadened, and a small chuckle of appreciation rippled around the table '. . .Regent Street and its bevy of shops, are the extent of her travels so far.'

Essie flushed, uncertain if he was being complimentary or not, but Luke was still looking at her, his eyes so appreciative and warm that her heart fluttered. Then Harry's surly voice broke into the general mirth. 'Turned down the offer of a knowledgeable guide, too. Females are getting above themselves these days. Before we know it, Essie'll be off with the suffragettes, I'd say.'

'If you think that, Harry, you must be out of your mind,' Luke retorted cuttingly. 'Estrellita would be the last woman in the world to let us down. . .'

There was a moment's awkward pause as he and Harry glowered at each other. Then, masterfully, Luke turned away to signal the waiter before asking his guests if they were ready to order luncheon.

Unused to such social occasions, Essie sat still and silent, waiting for Luke to let her know what he expected from her. Now the euphoria of her entrance had died away, she felt uncomfortably out of place—had Harry been right, saying she was above her station among these sophisticated and knowledgeable men of the world? Even Luke seemed a stranger, sitting beside her but very far away, as he engaged his guests in talk of theatrical matters of which she knew nothing.

The hum of words buzzed around her head like a swarm of menacing bees, and she looked down angrily at her hands, still clutching the elegant new gloves, tightly clasped on her lap. What was she doing here? Luke had said he needed her, but for all the notice he was taking she might as well be sitting at home in their lodgings. Disappointment swelled and grew into self-pity.

Suddenly, the tiniest sound of near-inaudible protest broke from her, and for a second she was seized with a wild urge to fly—to find Alice again, who was someone of her own kind, someone she could talk to, a friend who would listen and sympathise and laugh. Oh, lawks! How badly she needed to laugh. . .

Beside her, Sir Jack shifted in his chair, and the slight movement made her jump. Startled, she glanced at him, and then caught her breath. Relaxed in his chair, he was smiling as he watched her, long fingers idly playing with the ribbon of his monocle, and she thought he was the most attractive man she'd ever seen—even Luke couldn't compete with such well-born features and bright, shining hair. . .

'I fear we're boring you, Mrs Grimwade, which is a great sin. Pretty ladies should be entertained, not ignored.'

In vain she started to protest, but he shook his head, and then bent towards her, as if playfully acting the secret informer. She listened to his lowered voice, amused and instantly restored to a better humour.

'Perhaps you will allow me to make amends, one afternoon? A visit to the National Gallery? Or a trip down the river to Greenwich? I would deem it a very great honour to show you some of the beauty spots of our fine city.' A pause, and then, casually, he added, 'With your husband's permission, of course, dear lady.'

Essie was unsure how to reply. Those last words had broken a lull in the general conversation, and she realised that Luke had overheard. 'Your husband. . .' Her eyes sought his, to find he was smiling, but warily, as if amused at the title.

'That's kind of you, Sir Jack. I know Estrellita would be glad to accept your invitation—but, of course, we'll be rehearsing very hard from now on.'

He sounded unruffled, and, pink-cheeked, Essie looked back at the older man, who nodded amiably.

'I understand. But the invitation still holds. No doubt there will be a few hours when she's not too busy—all work and no play, you know, Grimwade. . .' He shook his silver head in mock warning. 'Shall we say I'll call at the theatre at three o'clock on Thursday next, in the hope that you can spare your wife for an hour or two? I dare say she'd be vastly entertained to take tea at the Ritz. . .'

Essie's exuberance couldn't be contained. 'Please, Luke! Do say yes—tea at the Ritz. . .oh!'

Her expression was so beatific that it raised a wave of kindly laughter around the table, and grudgingly Luke nodded. 'Of course,' he said shortly. 'She'll be delighted to accept. Thank you, Sir Jack.'

And then the meal was served, and Essie was too busy tasting the various courses put before her to wonder at Luke's casual acceptance of Sir Jack's calling her 'your wife'. She ate her way through oysters, rump steak and syllabub, washed down with champagne, and only when the last plates had been deftly cleared away, and she sat replete and rather sleepy, staring into the wonderful green *crème de menthe* Luke had ordered for her, did she begin to try to take in all that was being said.

Harry, on Luke's further side, had been drinking

freely. Even Essie, in her bemused state, had noticed how often his wine glass had been refilled. Now he was loudly and aggressively condemning the fact that 'No Smoking' signs in theatre auditoriums had become an accepted rule.

'Don't think it's right,' he complained, words slurred and heavy voice thicker than usual. 'Who the hell do they think they are, these chappies with their grand ideas? Audiences've always smoked in theatres—why shouldn't they go on, eh? I know I will, anyway!'

In the pause that greeted his outburst, eyes exchanged glances around the table. Luke said smoothly, but with an edge to his voice that warned Essie of his growing hostility towards Harry, 'Because West End theatres are a cut above music halls, that's why.'

'Load of nonsense! What's different about them, I'd like to know?'

'Allow me to tell you, my young friend. . .' Solomon Kurtz puffed at his Havana and turned clumsily in his chair to stare at Harry '. . . West End theatres don't like the free and easy manners of the music hall audiences. And they don't intend to put up with them any longer. So the notices are there.'

Harry mumbled defiantly, but Kurtz's deeply accented voice swiftly silenced him. 'And because I am in control of such theatres, I see to it that the rules are obeyed. Do you follow me, Mr Whitman?'

Harry flushed. Clearly, his addled wits at last realised that he had spoken out of turn. But he had the last word, throwing it spitefully across the table, eyeing Essie as if she, and not Kurtz, were responsible for the unwanted notices. 'You'll do as you want, I suppose—money talks, doesn't it? And we all have to jump to attention. . .like Luke there. . .won't find him arguing with his backers, will you, eh? But it's all really due to female influence. . .do as they like, women do, nowadays. Tell us men how to behave, order us about. . .'

The words tailed off, and Harry looked dolefully into his empty wine glass.

Luke was quick to fill the difficult silence, saying lightly but with a cold smile that put Harry in his place, 'You're talking nonsense. Let's have no more of it.' And then, even as a flood of tempestuous anger rose in Harry's flushed face, Luke turned away, ignoring his reaction. 'Well, come along, Estrellita. You've been looking at that *crème de menthe* for a good ten minutes, instead of drinking it! I promise it won't bite you—hurry up, there's a good girl. We all want to get back to work now that the meal's over. . .'

There was general movement around the table and much shaking of hands as the party broke up. Sir Jack Martineau repeated his invitation, smiling at Essie. 'Until Thursday, then, dear lady,' while Solomon Kurtz and Leonard Rollinson bowed politely but said nothing, forcing her to wonder what sort of effect her presence had had on them.

She was glad to be alone with Luke again, away from the lingering sense of ever-present conflict when Harry was around. Outside the restaurant, blinking in the sunlight and thankfully filling her lungs with fresh air, she stopped Luke calling a cab.

'Let's walk—can we? It was so hot in there, and I've eaten too much.'

'A good idea. We'll go across the park and you can see the ducks.' He kept up a running commentary as they made their way down the busy thoroughfares, finally pausing as they reached a wide space where many roads joined.

'And this is Piccadilly Circus, Estrellita—London's most famous meeting-place.' Luke looked down, laughing at her unconcealed wonder, then took her across the road, dodging cabs, buses and carriages, until they stood below a small statue, poised on a pinnacle above a fountain, beneath which flower-sellers sat with their baskets of bright blossoms.

'That's Eros, the god of love. See, he's aiming his darts at random. Many's the poor fellow who's been pierced with one. Step aside, little star, lest you become a victim, too!' His tone was light, his back half turned as she gazed upwards, not seeing that he bent over one of the flower-girl's baskets.

Still looking at the tiny statue, her delight began to fade as she recalled what he'd just said, and she was ready to argue when he turned around, a bunch of violets in his outstretched hand.

'Some flowers for you. Only violets, I'm afraid—when we're famous I'll buy you roses, dozens and dozens of scarlet roses, enough to twine in your hair and make a garland of, to decorate your pretty new dress!' His voice was as sweet as a song, crystalline eyes soft and kind, and she watched with desperate longing as his lips curved up into a generous smile.

It was wonderful to see him so restored to friendliness, so vital and magnetic. 'Oh, Luke. . .' All her previous thoughts dispersed like snow beneath a rising sun, and she smiled at him with such delight that his own smile deepened in response. 'They're beautiful. Such a lovely smell. And these go with my dress much better than red roses.' She held them to her breast, staring down for a moment to appreciate the melting union of blue mauve blossoms against the calm green of the linen.

'Simple violets in a green Devon hedge. . .' Beneath the hum of the traffic, Luke's voice was low, and she looked up again, abruptly sure that she could read in his brilliant eyes far more than he had allowed his voice to express.

Her heart hammered noisily, and she wondered whether he could hear it. 'What did you call it? That statue?'

'Eros.' He didn't take his eyes away from hers, and the spell of their sea-green depths overcame her. It was a magic moment. She knew she must tell him.

'Eros? Well, I think he *has* hit me. . .' Taking a huge breath, she blundered on. 'I love you, Luke. I can't help it. Just wish I could——'

'Why?'

They stood together, enclosed in a tiny personal world that was suddenly too precious, too rare to even notice the traffic or the people milling about them.

'Because you don't love me back. I know you don't.'

'Oh, you silly child!' Passionately, his arms went around her, pulling her close, squashing the frail violets so that their fragrance erupted, a love-potion so strong that Essie's senses reeled. She lifted her face towards his bent head, surrendering herself willingly for the kiss she knew was to come.

There was a sense of wholeness in their embrace that had not made itself known before. It was, thought Essie ecstatically, as she surfaced for breath, as if love had claimed them for its own.

'So you *do* love me? Oh, Luke, and I thought you didn't. . .'

He removed her smart new hat and buried his face in her hair. 'I've always loved you. Right from the moment I saw you hanging out the washing by the river.' The words were teasing, muffled and at first she thought she must have misheard. She pushed him away, in order to stare deep into his eyes, her expression torn between disbelief and soaring hope.

'It's not true!'

'Yes, it is.' He was laughing, like the mischievous bear-boy he'd once been.

'But you've never told me before, and you haven't loved me—I mean. . .' Modesty dammed the flood of words, and she bent her head to prevent him seeing her embarrassment.

'I've been afraid to. Dear God, do you think I haven't wanted to? When you're so warm and beautiful—so trusting, so full of love yourself? It's been a terrible time for me, little love.' There was an urgency in his voice now that gave her confidence to look up.

He was smiling, his face more open and revealing than she had ever thought to see. His eyes were like sea pearls, deep and rich, the hollows between high cheekbones immaculately angled.

Very carefully, hardly daring to say another word in case it was the wrong word, she whispered, 'But not any longer, Luke? We love each other. You've just said so. And—and I *am* Mrs Grimwade, aren't I? So. . .' Her lips were dry, her throat tight, and desperately she sought for a way to tell him what she so passionately longed for.

Would he understand? The only Luke she knew had so often shown himself to be remote from her that now she wondered, tense and suddenly afraid. True, he had always looked after her, and once or twice they had actually kissed. But, as Essie knew by now, kissing and touching was the common language of theatrical folk. She stared up into his face with a sort of desperation, wondering if it was her cruel fate to be in love with a man who would be content with only the most casual words and gestures of love.

The fearful thought sent a spurt of rage through her. With a burst of strength, she pushed him away, staring beyond him up at the fat little statue that took aim high above London's throbbing traffic.

'Eros!' she shouted. 'Here! Stick one of your darts into my Luke—go on, please. . . I'll do anything, if you will.'

But no arrow thudded down. The nearby flower-seller's face grew animated with curiosity, and then Luke's arms wrapped around her in a rough embrace, and the sound of his unrestrained laughter made all fear flee from her mind.

'You're crazy, Estrellita!' he told her, laughing still, hugging her to him. 'I really believe you'd stand on your head, right here, if you thought it would do any good! Well, it might be a bit of free publicity for the show, but as for making Eros take any notice. . .' He shook her fondly. 'What on earth am I going to do with you, you baggage?'

'Kiss me again, that's what!'

And he did, ignoring the smiles on the faces of the hurrying passers-by, not even hearing the throaty comments of a brewer's drayman, whipping his mighty horses around the Circus. 'An' give 'er one from me, too, guv.'

When at last Essie pulled herself away, she was utterly happy. Luke loved her. Nothing else mattered in the world. 'Let's go home?' Clinging to his arm, she smiled radiantly, and together they turned, ready to cross the busy road.

'Not yet.' He led her briskly down Shaftesbury Avenue. 'We must go down Greasepaint Avenue—to the theatre.'

'Oh, no, Luke—I want to go home!'

'Work comes first, Estrellita.' But he slanted a brilliant smile down at her, allaying her disappointment, and, once she saw the entrance of the Irving Theatre, and listened to him describing how their names would very soon be twinkling up there above the doors in electric lights, love had taken a step back, with ambition overshadowing its gentle influence.

'Luke, show me the stage! I want to see the stage. Want to go on, look at the house, imagine it full of people—all watching us! Oh, isn't it wonderful? Just as you said, we'll be two stars, you and me, up there. . .' Then her eyes caught a glimpse of a man wearing twin sandwich-boards, on which were painted magical words: 'THE RETURN OF THE GREAT GRIMWADE'.

'Look!' she squealed. 'Luke—just see. . .'

But abruptly he seemed to have distanced himself. He stood apart from her, a little taller, more mysterious, standing very still, staring at the board above the theatre entrance as if it held some secret he was reluctant to share with her.

Deflated, she asked, 'Have you been here before?' and he nodded briefly. 'Done a show here?'

'Last year.'

She thought fast. 'Before you came down to Exeter?'

'Yes.'

Some intuitive process suggested to her that he now saw other names up there, on the unlit façade. His and—she swallowed a lump that had just come into her throat—the other girl's name. The assistant who had let him down, who had gone off with Harry Whitman. The girl he had loved.

'Luke?'

Either he had not heard, or he ignored her. He was moving away, walking rapidly towards the stage door, around the corner of the building, walking with clearly only one thought in his mind—to get back into the theatre, to start working on the act that had so nearly brought him the fame he sought. The fame that had eluded him because the other girl had destroyed it.

'Luke!' Again Essie shouted his name, as her pain and dismay turned into a sense of burning rage. Damn the other girl! *She* was here now, Estrellita—the Little Star—who would provide all that Luke needed to take that last, longed-for and well-deserved stride into fame.

'Wait for me, Luke. . .' She ran after him, hardly seeing the people she bumped into in her haste, but the stage door, as she reached it, shut in her face, and by the time she had opened it again he was no longer to be seen.

Essie stared into a long, dim passage, and heard his receding footsteps echo faintly through the empty theatre. Alone, she stood in the shabby corridor, abruptly brought face to face with the truth of the matter. Luke was haunted by a ghost—the ghost of that girl he had loved and trusted. And now it was up to her, his almost-wife, Estrellita Grimwade, to either live with the haunting, or to get rid of it once and for all.

Slowly she walked down the passage, led on by an instinctive knowledge that here, within this theatre, lay the means of resolving the problem of hers and Luke's future happiness.

CHAPTER TEN

ESSIE felt she could sleep for a week. No annual spring cleaning back in Exeter could ever have exhausted her as much as these interminable hours of rehearsal.

'We'll do that again, Estrellita.'

It seemed to her benumbed mind that these were the only words Luke had time to address to her, nowadays. They were sleeping in separate rooms—by her own wish, she reminded herself, mortified at the thought—and breakfast became a rushed snack, eaten by Luke as he dressed, and often finished on his way to the theatre.

'You haven't had your toast, Luke—and I was so careful not to burn it on that old oil stove.' Daily, she watched one powerful hand snatch up the remaining piece as he headed for the door, muttering something unintelligible about meeting Len, or having to see the SM about yesterday's failed trapdoor, and then he was gone, utterly immersed in 'The Act'.

It was the same during the day. If she was lucky, she slipped out of the theatre for a snack after the morning rehearsals, but Luke was never with her. These days he appeared to live solely on nervous energy, fuelled by 'The Act'. In Essie's mind, the words marched about like threatening monsters. At times she wished she had never had a ma who'd been on the stage and passed down that all-consuming dream. That she'd never gone to Monsey's gaff, never met Luke. . .

But at that point her rebellion died. Never met Luke? Never known what love was like? Never experienced such warmth, such security, such contentment? Not to mention the other side of the matter—the frustration and the loneliness, and ever-present ache of yearning for something she longed for, but saw no hope of getting. Shaking her head, uncertain whether to laugh, cry or shout with pent-up rage, Essie always ended by knowing that, however difficult life was, she had no wish to change it.

And once she was in the theatre, the knowledge became engrained certainty, and her disappointment faded as she listened to Luke's words, using all her wit and talent to do as he asked. Yes, this was where she was born to be...

'Let's try that one again, Estrellita.'

His smile dazzled her into weary agreement yet again, and so the trick was repeated. And repeated. She was too proud to complain, and tried hard not to nod off from sheer exhaustion when resting between rehearsals.

She found a cosy little box, all gilt and purple velvet, buttressed by plump, laughing cherubs, hanging high over the auditorium, on the prompt side of the stage, and crept there for solitude and comfort, sitting relaxed on a smart plush chair, arms resting on the velvet of the padded rail, staring around her, eyes sweeping the darkness of the pit immediately below, then the spread of the lordly stalls before climbing high to the tiered rows of the dress circle, topped by the gallery—or the gods, as it was commonly known.

No one ever saw her there, but she could see everything. The stage, with its heavy dark red curtains looped elegantly on each side of the proscenium arch, and even the wings, where carpenters worked and scene-shifters moved endless canvas flats. She saw the other artists in the cast waiting their own few minutes of rehearsal on stage. She even saw Harry watching Luke, suggesting something, then mysteriously disappearing as Luke rehearsed the wonderful illusions that were to be the most spectacular features of the show. She got to know each signature tune, played on a tinny piano, tucked out of sight in the pit, and began to assess the quality of each act she watched with newly critical eyes and ears.

The show, opening all too soon now, was the brainchild of Solomon Kurtz, a new style of variety show which he was certain would quickly replace the riff-raff vulgarity of the old, low-class music hall.

Essie, in her secret eyrie, heard his thickly accented voice rising from the seat in the centre of the stalls where he always sat, telling the lesser mortals, who ran his numerous errands, that this was going to happen. 'Music hall? Pieuw!' It was an indescribable sound, but, accompanied by Kurtz's familiar arm-flapping, expressed exactly and succinctly what he thought.

The first time she heard him speaking so forcefully, Essie remembered her own venture into the even lower layer of theatrical strata—the penny gaff—and hugged herself nervously, hoping he would never find out her shameful secret.

But on the occasions he watched her rehearse—and he was there in the same seat, from ten-thirty until noon, and then again from three to five, every day—slowly she realised she could draw strength and invaluable knowledge from his presence and his immaculate stagecraft.

'So you should bring your girl forward, Luke—two inches, maybe, not three—see, she's in the shadow there, and the audience will watch *you* instead of her.' A wheezy chuckle made Luke pause, rub his chin, reflect and then soberly agree.

'You're right, of course, Solly. And it's at this particular moment they *must* watch her, not me. . .'

Illusions. Secrets. Mysteries. Essie watched, listened, wondered, and learned. She had never before guessed how a magician worked—surely it was all just—well, magic. Now, at last she knew. Everything was trickery, worked by hidden machinery, by expert timing, and effortless concealment.

'Again, Estrellita.'

For the eleventh time that day she played her part in the 'Disappearing Lady' illusion. She concentrated hard, trying to remember the detailed instructions. Everything depended on timing and position.

'All ready, SM?' Luke glanced behind him, received a thumbs-up signal, and then took Essie out on to the stage, introducing her to the non-existent audience. Smiling and taking a bow, Essie knew he had gone to the side to pick up the newspaper carefully left there by Properties. Behind her a crackle told her he had removed one complete page. Then he was centre stage again, holding the paper open for all to see. She watched his face, good-humoured, full of charm, yet tight with intent, as he bent to spread the paper on stage, smoothing it flat with a couple of elegant sweeps of his hands.

Then he brought forward a chair, setting it in the middle of the paper, facing out to the audience. Essie moved carefully, smiling still, throwing a graceful kiss over the footlights, before sitting on the chair. Luke's voice rang out as he waved a large veil between her and the audience, saying, 'She's beautiful, isn't she? Ah, but she's more than that—why, this young lady, my friends, holds the secret of magical knowledge in the palm of her small hand...secrets...mystery ...magic...' The words grew lower, quieter, yet projected so that they could be heard at the back of the gods.

Essie's body quivered. It wasn't magic, of course— no one knew that as well as she did—but, when Luke spoke in that thrilling way, prickles ran down her spine.

Alas, this reaction had proved to be the hitch in the smooth running of the illusion, necessitating more rehearsal and causing Luke to snap at her.

'Why do you wait? I told you to move on *palm*...'

He had grown increasingly impatient as time after

time she failed to move at the right moment. Now, at last, she had finally learned the hard lesson—never think of him as anything but her master when on stage.

The veil covered her now. Luke's deft hands shaped the thin cloth closely around her. She held her breath, pulled on an invisible wire which came up to produce a covering framework, retaining the shape of her head under the concealing veil, then slid the chair seat down and began to force herself through the sliced-out newspaper and on down through the open trapdoor hidden beneath it.

'One, two, three!' Luke removed the veil, and Essie, uncomfortably recovering in the cramped area below the trap, knew that this time the lady had vanished most successfully.

But she received no plaudits. Harry, operating the trap, cursed at her for not moving out of his way fast enough, and Len, whom she bumped into, as she waited for Luke's further instructions back in the wings, had a face like thunder, ignoring her as he marched past, towards a little group of gossiping scene-painters.

Clearly, backstage theatre held none of the lure and glamour that performance did. Essie caught Luke's eyes briefly before he began preparations for the next trick. He nodded, looked as if he had something to say to her, but was quickly distracted by the SM at his elbow.

Suddenly inexpressibly tired and dispirited—surely he could at least have said, 'Well done'?—Essie crept back up the grand, empty staircase leading from the foyer, so richly decorated with photographs of famous men and women of the theatre, into the solace of the little box, there to watch for the rest of the morning, until the tedium of hearing Ray Kelly and his dancing dogs performing the same routine six times in a row addled her brain, and, head resting on outstretched arms, she fell asleep in the middle of the final barks and yaps of the cavorting, fluffy troupe.

Alice found her later in the afternoon, breezing noisily into the silent box. 'Eee, so there you are! I've just come up from our place—we've been rehearsing all morning—and no one knew where you were. I've looked all over.'

Bleary-eyed, Essie stretched and sat up. 'Where's Luke?'

'Gone out with old Solly.'

She leapt to her feet. 'Without me?'

'Seems like it, love.' Alice's pert face softened. 'Come on, then; we'll get a cuppa and a pie ourselves—you don't have to rely on men at times like these.'

'But he's supposed to be my husband——'

'Aye, and Albie's the same, but I'll lay a quid he's down at the boozer, not giving me a minute's thought.' Alice bullied her out of the box, down the stairs, and out into the suddenly brilliant glare of the afternoon sun.

'What's that funny smell? Must be fresh air,' she jested, then took a quick look at Essie's set face, and added, 'Look, love, doesn't mean anything, him going off without you—it's the way they work, all these big names. Oh, yes, they need the little woman on stage—*and* in bed...' she winked, and Essie looked aside quickly '...but otherwise it's them that are the nobs, see? And you'd best learn your place, love. Here, do you want coffee or tea? My treat this time.'

Two cups of strong tea and a meat pie later, Essie at last grudgingly accepted the wisdom of Alice's advice. 'But I tell you what, Alice, if he can behave like that, then so can I.'

'What—going off on your own? You'd never!' Alice's eyes shone with admiration.

'Wouldn't I just.' And then, her smile suddenly

beaming, Essie remembered. 'Oh! Thursday, he said—that's today, isn't it?'

Alice nodded, mystified. 'Aye. And who's he, when he's at home?'

Essie brushed crumbs from her lap and sat up straighter, smoothing her hair before pinning on her beautiful new hat. She smiled excitedly into Alice's curious eyes. 'Sir Jack Martineau, that's who. Said as he'd take me to the Ritz.'

'Get on! He never did! You're telling fibs, Essie Grimwade——'

'No! Yes! Well, I'm going, anyway—what's the time?'

Leaving the little café, they peered down the road at the clock hanging over the nearest office block. 'Ten to three, and he said three o'clock. I've just got time to go to the Ladies', wash my face and shine my shoes...'

Essie was halfway down the street when Alice's voice behind her asked, 'And what about Luke? Suppose he wants you on stage again?'

'Too bad! Anyway, he said it was all right—told Sir Jack I could go with him.' Essie stopped, taking hold of Alice's arm. 'You can tell him I've gone.'

'Not me! Not tell Luke Grimwade something he won't want to know...' For once Alice's pretty face had lost its smile.

Essie said reassuringly, 'Don't be so silly. He's a lovely man. He won't hurt you.'

'But he'll be cross—sure to be...'

'Course he won't.' Essie considered. 'Well, if he is, just tell him as *he* said I could go with Sir Jack.'

'Must I? Eee, Essie, I don't think you should do this——'

'Please, Alice—oh, please! After all, Luke did agree, and you're my friend, and—and I *do* want to have tea at the Ritz...'

Alive wavered. Seeing her friend's resolution collapsing, Essie added craftily, 'I'll bring you back a bit of cake! There, can't do fairer, can I? So say you'll tell him, Alice.'

'Oh—well—all right.'

They parted outside the Ladies', Alice looking doubtful and Essie giggling as she went inside to prepare for the great occasion. When she emerged again, five or six minutes later, Alice had disappeared, but a stagehand was walking down the passage, calling, 'Mrs Grimwade, Mrs Grimwade. . .' Seeing her, the lad grinned. 'A gent outside, askin' for you—in a motor-car too. Goin' places are you, then?' He winked a knowing, amused grey eye. 'Take care, gel—them there stage-johnnies are a wicked lot, you know. . .'

But Essie hardly heard him. She was running towards the stage door, out of the oppressive gloom of the theatre and into the tantalising freedom of the spring afternoon, where a gleaming Rolls-Royce motor was parked at the side of the kerb, a dark-green-uniformed chauffeur standing by the passenger door, and Sir Jack's burnished silver hair and charming smile making her forget all the pain and humiliation of Luke's thoughtlessness.

'My dear Mrs Grimwade—what a pleasure to see you again.' Sir Jack was out of his seat the moment he saw her, sun reflecting on the dangling monocle, hat removed, one hand extended to help her into the car. 'Quite comfortable? Good.' He climbed in beside her, and she felt enjoyably complimented that such a high-born, handsome man should go to all this trouble just for her.

But Sir Jack continued to show his appreciation of her company, as though, she thought, preening herself, she were a friend of his own class. 'Thought we'd have a run down beside the river—take a turn along the Embankment, look at Cleopatra's Needle, perhaps, then drive back beside the Park—would that please you, my dear?' His personable face smiled in such a pleasant manner that she succumbed immediately to whatever he proposed.

To be driving through the heart of London on a glorious spring day like this, with a man as wonderful as Sir Jack Martineau beside her! Essie, speechless, sighed raptly, listening to her escort's mellifluous voice telling her the names of the streets through which they drove, and the buildings they passed. When, finally, the car joined the traffic progressing slowly along the Victoria Embankment, she sat forward, staring at the wide, stately river flowing on through many bridges, comparing it in her mind with the smaller, more rural river Exe, beside which she had, not so long ago, lived. Where she had first met Luke. . .

It was all so beautiful, the sun on the rippling, forceful river, the toots and horns of craft moving up and down the enormous waterway, seagulls reminding her yet again of Exeter. And then, suddenly, unexpectedly, a startling sight made her exclaim aloud. 'Oh, those poor people—look at them! Are they ill? There, on those two benches. . .'

Sir Jack's eyes followed her pointing hand, and for a moment the charming smile switched off. 'Don't worry your pretty head about them, my dear.' His voice was dismissive. 'Every city has its share of down-and-outs, and I'm afraid in London they're actually allowed to sleep on the public benches.'

'But—you mean they have no homes?' Essie's pleasure dissolved instantly. Memories of Tan Court came rushing—the sleazy waterfront where, most evenings, the reeling figures of drunkards and outcasts huddled against sheltering walls. She had not thought to see such shameful things here in London, in this bright, rich city, full of humming prosperity and well-dressed people.

'How—terrible. . .' It was all she could find to say, staring at the figures bundled in grotesque sleeping attitudes on the two seats, as the car passed by.

Sir Jack tapped the glass panel in front of him, nodding curtly as the driver looked back. He said, with a distasteful edge to the words, 'I understand they are given food every evening. A soup-kitchen near by—or some such thing. . .'

The car put on speed, and within seconds the honeyed note was back in his voice and Essie was invited to look at the Houses of Parliament.

And then they were in Birdcage Walk, and she forgot the dark side of the city in her unbounded delight at beautiful St James's Park with its walks, trees and duck-filled lake.

Sir Jack smiled at her obvious enjoyment, and glanced at his gold watch. 'Next time,' he said charmingly, 'we'll have to make it a longer outing—an hour in the afternoon is no time at all in which to show you the many delights of London. Now, we're just approaching Hyde Park Corner, and in a moment you'll see the Parisian arcade outside the Ritz—and then, my dear Mrs Grimwade, you may have the tea I'm certain you must be quite ready for. . .'

The Ritz! Essie stepped out of the car when the chauffeur opened the door, drawing herself up proudly. She might be only a variety performer, but—oh, lawks!—she felt like a queen.

The ornate, light-stone building was decorated in a florid style that impressed her deeply, and when she preceded Sir Jack through the entrance she gasped to see the silver and gilt decorations continuing inside. Everything was light and bright, and the shining foliage of aspidistras and palms seemed to bring the sunlit afternoon right into the restaurant.

'I'll bring you for luncheon one day. The view of Green Park from the windows is superb.' Sir Jack was very clearly at home here. Essie noticed how the uniformed doorman in his top hat saluted instantly, and how the obsequious recognition continued, the waiter showing them to a table in the corner of the pleasant room with a ready smile.

'One of London's favourites places for meeting friends,' said Sir Jack casually, nodding over her head as several faces lifted to smile and bow at him. 'Now, my dear, if you're comfortable. . .'

She eased back in her gilt chair and looked at him admiringly. How good he was to her!

With the waiter hovering at his elbow, he told her quietly, bending forward and smiling playfully, 'You must try one of the famous French pastries, my dear—very good and creamy. Very sinful!'

Nodding happily, she chose the biggest cake of the selection, then poured out very grandly from a silver teapot, and was rewarded by Sir Jack's complimentary comments. 'You have such lovely little hands, my dear.'

'Have I? That's funny. They used to be all raw and red. . .' She bit her lip, trying to cover up the awful mistake by asking swiftly if he didn't think sugar was bad for the figure. Such unsophisticated talk appeared to amuse rather than surprise him, and she couldn't help but recall that Luke hated her to chatter. At the end of the luxurious meal he drew his chair a little nearer, and asked if she would permit him to indulge in a cigarette.

'I don't mind——' She stopped, and then, suddenly filled with excitement and grand ideas, asked in a whisper, 'Can I have one too, please?'

The silvery eyebrows rose.

'Oh, dear, I shouldn't have asked, should I?' She looked around the room defensively. 'But there are some other ladies smoking. . .'

Sir Jack's eyes gleamed. 'It's considered a trifle fast—but your word is my command. Of course you may smoke.' He offered a gold cigarette-case engraved with a wonderful flourish of initials, and she took a cigarette with more assurance than she felt. Whatever would Luke say if he saw her smoking? In public? And with a man. . .?

The first puff was a revelation, and not a pleasant one. Gasping, but acting hard, and trying to appear as if she had smoked for years, Essie smiled across the table defiantly at her amused companion. 'Very—er—nice,' she choked.

Sir Jack's smile broadened. 'Mrs Grimwade. . .' He paused, and then his hand found hers, placed lightly on the table beside her cream-splodged plate. 'My dear, may I call you Estrellita? I feel we're going to be such good friends. Will you indulge an old man by granting him the pleasure of your delightful company again? And soon?'

Unused to such flowery language, she considered his words for a moment or two, before smiling back and allowing his fingers to continue stroking her hand. 'Of course! And you're not old, are you? Not really—more middle-aged, I'd say. . .'

Sir Jack's spontaneous laughter drew the attention of several people seated at nearby tables. Essie, red-cheeked, and not sure what was so funny about her honest reply, stared as the heads turned. Sir Jack's pale eyes followed hers, and suddenly he smiled more directly, bowing at the curious faces turned towards them.

'Ah—good day to you, Marie. . .'

Essie's mouth dropped open, and she stared at Sir Jack in utter disbelief. 'Is that Marie Lloyd? She looks just like the picture I saw in a paper the other day—and who's that with her? That man. Is he—her husband?'

Sir Jack's gaze narrowed, and he looked down at his empty teacup. 'A friend, I believe,' he said smoothly. 'Marie's constant companion these days. Not her husband, of course. No lady comes here with her own husband—someone else's perhaps. . .! No, he's her protector, one might say. . .'

'I see.' But Essie wasn't sure that she did. Why should anyone as marvellous and famous as the great Marie need someone to protect her? And what from? Then, as she watched, she saw the elderly man with balding hair lean forward, putting his hand over Marie's, saw the famous face soften, watched painted lips pout and whisper something in reply, and knew, with a rush of mixed abhorrence and surprise, that the two were lovers. Protector, indeed!

She turned back to face Sir Jack, ready to argue, but his eyes were no longer friendly and easygoing. He looked, she thought quickly, like a hawk watching his next meal, the moment before he pounced... Pulling herself together, she regained her poise and commented, a little archly, 'Fancy them being here, having tea, just like us... Oh, I am enjoying myself, Sir Jack!'

When her companion nodded, the smile returning to his elegant face, clearly amused at such ingenuousness, she looked back warily at Marie's profile. A larger woman than Essie had imagined from the pictures—not that she'd ever seen her perform, but her own skinniness had dictated the idea that all the famous stars of music hall were slender—apart from their hourglass curves, of course. She looked dubiously at Marie's comely but well-upholstered figure, and said bleakly, 'I've got a long way to go, haven't I, before I'm as fat as she is?' which made Sir Jack's laugh ring out again.

He leaned across the table, one hand still playing with hers, and told her, 'Stay as you are, my dear Estrellita; don't ever change.' And for a second she was reminded of Luke saying the same thing—'Don't ever change'.

'Believe me,' went on the honeyed voice, close to her ear, 'your slenderness is eye-catching in a world of—shall we say?—better-developed ladies.' He lowered his tone even more. 'Think of the impact you make on an audience used to seeing large women. . .'

She eyed him suspiciously. Was he making fun of her? 'You mean, they'll like me skinny and small?'

Sir Jack's fingers masterfully turned over her hand, and began caressing the pulse beating at her wrist. 'They'll love you, sweet Estrellita. But not for your youth, or your slim figure alone. You see. . .' His gaze, burning now with an ardour which made her feel awkward, flickered rapidly over her face from brow to chin, and from her throat up again to her wide, startled eyes. 'You see, dear child, there is a certain magic about you.'

That word again. Essie caught her breath, and he went on, 'Something in the way you move, a rare, gamine vitality in your smile, a certain charming sauciness that goes straight to a man's heart.' His fingers paused their feathery stroking, now pressed hard on her racing pulse. 'I should have said, an audience's heart. But you see, my dear, you have such an effect upon me that I find it increasingly hard to keep myself under control. . .'

For a second Essie stared, while she worked out what all the pretty compliments meant, and where they might be leading. Her mind raced, going back over the weeks since this great adventure had begun.

Monsey, with his dirty hands touching her body. The men, backstage at the gaff, and their offensive stares. Harry Whitman and his crude courting. And Luke—yes, even Luke—with that aching look in his darkened eyes, and his honey-sweet kisses that always left her yearning for something more. . .

She dragged her thoughts away from the memories and looked more thoughtfully at the middle-aged man eyeing her so greedily. Now, another admirer. And a sir, no less! Despite the uneasiness the situation was causing her, she giggled to herself. It was a sort of power to have men falling over themselves, and all because of her, little Essie, the skivvy...

The realisation went to her head, banishing finer thoughts. She took a last puff at the ash-tipped cigarette and made sure she didn't choke this time. Thinner and more desirable than the great Marie Lloyd? A certain magic about her? Well, if that was what nice Sir Jack thought—and surely he should know, for a middle-aged man must have had lots of experience, amassed immense worldly knowledge—all right, then. She had nothing to worry about. She was surely destined to become the star Luke had said she would be.

Wriggling on her chair, she gave her watchful companion the most delicious smile, even as she carefully withdrew her hand from his caress. 'Another cup of tea, Sir Jack?' she asked grandly, and refilled his cup with the little finger of her right hand poised at a new, elegant angle. 'And do you know, I think I'll have another pastry—oh, yes, that lovely horn-shaped one...'

How Alice would stare when she heard about this! Then, suddenly, she recalled her parting words. 'And do you think I could take one home for my friend? I promised I would—you see, she was going to do me a favour...'

If Sir Jack was shocked, or even amused, he showed no sign. Instead he raised a casual hand, and gave an order to the immediately attentive waiter. By the time she had waded through the luscious cream concoction placed before her on a clean plate, and drunk her second cup of tea, Essie was presented with a cardboard box, beautifully tied with gold ribbon.

'For your friend,' said Sir Jack, with a twinkle, as he polished his monocle. 'Allow me to carry it to the car for you, my dear...'

They made an impressive exit, with Essie bowing to Marie Lloyd and her consort as they passed their table, and Sir Jack saying graciously, 'I look forward to seeing you after the show tonight, Marie,' as if he were King Edward himself.

Driving back to the theatre, Essie's excited thoughts grew into vast dreams of a wonderful future eclipsing even Marie. . .'a certain magic', he'd said.

She bade Sir Jack goodbye, thanked him prettily for the outing, and readily agreeing to his suggestion of taking her to luncheon the following week. Perhaps Monday would suit her? he asked, screwing the monocle into his left eye and studying a leather diary extracted from his waistcoat pocket. She pretended to consider, then said she thought she could manage it. Sir Jack kissed her hand lingeringly, and watched her disappear into the stage door, before returning to the waiting Rolls.

Essie tripped down the dingy passage, too happy to notice the peeling paint and the sleazy, familiar smell of backstage, her mind entirely filled with thoughts of power, of fame and of personal enjoyment, with Luke by her side and all the nobs in London admiring her at parties and luncheons, both at Romano's and the Ritz. . . The future strung out before her, starry, golden and silver, and blessed in all its wonder and beauty.

And then Harry Whitman turned the corner, strolling towards her with an unpleasant, gloating smile fixed on his weak face.

'So the runaway's returned, has she? Getting to be quite a habit—what's the excuse this time? Not getting enough of Luke's attention? Tired of all the hard work?' He stopped beside her, outside their dressing-room door, and lowered his voice, adding contemptuously, 'You'll never make it to the top, Essie, girl. I know the sort you are, see. Soft, easily get your head turned, a jumped-up scullery maid who thinks all she's got to do is flutter her eyelashes and stick out her chest. . .'

Essie, thrown down to earth with a vengeance, could stand no more. Impulsively she kicked out, catching him what she considered to be a fourpenny one on the calf, her eyes blazing with anger, her mouth set in a hard, straight line.

'Stop your filth!' she exploded. 'You don't know what you're talking about, Harry Whitman—I just wish you'd go away and never come back! We don't need you, Luke and me. . .'

He glared, bending to rub his injured leg, and she took a quick step back, closer to the door, for he scowled menacingly as if he might well hit out in return. Instead, he narrowed his eyes, coming so close that she smelt the whisky fumes on his breath.

'But you *can't* do without me, Essie—that's the joke of it! You and poor old Luke would be finished if I weren't here. Back to conjuring tricks and pulling rabbits out of his sleeve in dreary, provincial theatres. No more magical illusions here, in the West End. . .'

An insidious dismay started to chill her, turning her rage into apprehension. She stared, aghast. What did he mean? How could he possibly be so important to their act, when all he did was manage them, arrange their finances, help with the trapdoor? Her mind ran on—indeed, all he really did was take up too much of Luke's time and thoroughly get under her skin. . .

Before she could pick the right words to upbraid him, the door behind her quietly opened, and there stood Luke, eyes deep and angry, a no-nonsense look on his lean face. He glared at Harry. 'For heaven's sake, stop brawling! What's the row about?'

Harry grinned offensively. 'No row, old man. Just asking your lady wife where she's been——' the smile died '—and who she's been with. . .'

Staring anxiously at Luke, Essie went cold all over. His face was set, and she watched a new expression of near-hatred mask his good looks. 'You *bastard*,' he said, very quietly, before suddenly reaching out and yanking Harry towards him by the lapels of his jacket.

'Hey, wait a minute; I only said——'

'I heard. And I didn't like it.'

Luke's dominance had never been so plain before, and Essie trembled. She heard herself whispering timidly, 'Please, Luke—don't.' But he wasn't listening, and his clipped, intense words made her own peter out.

'Let's get things clear for the last time, Harry. I don't like your dirty remarks about Estrellita. Or your pathetic attempts to make trouble. We're putting on a show—we've got to work together, God help us, because we're both ambitious. . .but it stops there. Understand?'

Uncompromisingly shaken by Luke's powerful hands, Harry struggled in vain to get free, and then resorted to coarse language. 'Damn you, Luke! Let me go! You'll pay for this, I swear.'

Contemptuously, Luke released him, dusting off his hands as if they were contaminated. Not bothering to respond to Harry's continued blusters as he swiftly retreated down the passage, Luke encircled Estrellita with his arm and swept her through the open door into the dressing-room, slamming the door behind him with a force that startled her. Then he stood looking down at her with eyes dark with controlled passion.

Essie was uncertain what to say. His show of strength had alarmed her. The Luke she thought she knew had never shown signs of such primeval anger. Slowly her mind cleared as she realised he was, indeed, a man of many parts, and, if not all of them were admirable, he was at least forthright in his dealings with devious, sly Harry Whitman. A hesitant smile touched her lips as a great surge of love and gratitude rose within her, remembering how he had protected and stood up for her.

Her smile and shining eyes made Luke gently pull

her closer to him. He stroked her cheek, then touched her shoulders, running his hands lightly down her arms, as if he couldn't trust himself too far. 'You're—all right?' His voice was husky, his expression anxious. 'Quite sure?' And then the fire returned to his eyes. 'That damned Harry! If he touched you—or hurt you—I'd——'

'Of course he didn't. He was only being—just—Harry.'

For a long moment they looked at each other, then Luke nodded and dropped his hands. Essie watched his expression become more casual, and knew an intense disappointment. *Did* he love her? Or had he been merely worried that his valuable assistant was at risk?

Her mind clamoured, but then Luke's matter-of-fact voice intruded into her churning thoughts. 'Well? Aren't you going to tell me all about it? It's not like you to be quiet for so long—I thought you'd be chattering non-stop with excitement!' He stopped, and his smile was easier, more expansive as her surprise showed on her face. 'What's in the box, then?' He fingered the cake box curiously. 'Have you brought me back a present? Well, that is kind of you, little star.'

At last she found her tongue, felt, too, a rush of further dismay at having to disappoint him. The box dangled shamingly from one finger. 'No. It's for Alice. I promised, you see. . .' Then her courage began to return, for still he smiled. 'I had to bribe her—poor Alice!—to tell you I'd gone out to tea. It's a French pastry, from the Ritz. They're—very nice. . .'

Luke took the box from her hand, and gently enclosed her in the circle of his arms. He looked very deeply into her anxious eyes, and his voice softened, so that slowly her uneasiness departed. 'Did you have a good time with Sir Jack?'

'Oh, yes—he was so friendly.'

'I'm glad. You deserved an outing. You've worked

so hard and uncomplainingly, and I've been too full of my own worries to wonder how you felt. Forgive me, little star?'

Her throat constricted. She could hardly speak. 'Of—of course, Luke.'

'And are you seeing him again?'

The question was matter-of-fact enough to enable her to reply quite naturally, without second thoughts. 'He's asked me to have lunch one day next week.'

'Very well. If you want to go.'

'I'm—not sure. . .' She was no longer sure of anything. Luke's understanding touched her deep down inside, and because of it all her cravings for excitement had gone.

'You must make up your mind and let him know if you don't wish to keep the appointment,' he told her gravely. 'And—Estrellita. . .' Another pause, his eyes never leaving hers.

'Yes, Luke?'

'Next time you want to go somewhere in particular, why not ask *me* to take you? I'm supposed to be your husband, you know.'

'Yes. But—well, I didn't think you. . .'

She floundered into embarrassed silence, and he said quickly, 'That I would be bothered?'

'You're so busy.'

'Not too busy to be with you.'

Her heart leapt, and at last she was able to smile freely, released from the apprehension that had claimed her since Harry's crude words had broken into her delightful daydreams. 'Oh, Luke! How lovely! Will you really take me out?'

He rocked her gently in his arms, laughing fondly at her sudden childlike excitement. 'Of course. Where would you like to go? Let's see—you've been to Romano's and the Ritz—well, what about the Savoy next? You've heard of it, have you? A famous place, right on the river. . .'

The words touched an echoing chord. Instantly Essie knew where she so badly wanted to go. 'No, not there, but somewhere else, by the river—on the Embankment. Luke. . .' She fidgeted in his embrace, wondering if she dared show her love for him, and then timidly raising her hand to brush aside the dark hair falling over his vivid, black-rimmed eyes. 'There are poor people sleeping on benches there,' she told him, very seriously, 'with no homes, no jobs, and no money. And he said——'

'Sir Jack?'

She nodded. 'That there's a soup-kitchen at night where they get free food. Well——'

'You want to satisfy yourself that that's so?' His arms tightened, and she saw his eyes grow dark with feeling. 'You're too soft-hearted for your own good, little love—but we'll go and see.'

'Thank you! When?' She was ready to show her gratitude by kissing him, but abruptly he let her go, turning away to collect his hat from where it hung, behind the door.

'What's a better time than this evening? I could do with some fresh air after being cooped up in this place all day. We'll take a walk down to the Thames, make sure your poor down-and-outs are being fed, and then have a meal ourselves on the way back.' Looking at her, he sketched a deep bow. 'Would that suit your ladyship?' The note of jaunty mockery in his voice completed her happiness.

Rushing to the mirror, she adjusted her hat, then picked up the cake-box from the shelf, saying brightly, 'That'll be lovely. And I'll just pop into the Empire and leave this for Alice on the way. She'll be so pleased.'

Opening the door, he followed her out into the passage, saying as he shut it behind him, in a quiet, proud voice, so completely unlike his mocking words of a moment ago that she turned to stare, 'I was so busy fighting with Harry that I didn't show you this, did I?'

Essie looked blank, not knowing what he could mean.

'Our names. Starred...' His hand reached up to touch the newly painted sign on the dark door, and suddenly she was filled with a sensation that made her want to laugh and cry, both together.

In bold black lettering were their names.

'THE GREAT GRIMWADE AND ESTRELLITA'

And, yes, a golden star crowned them both.

CHAPTER ELEVEN

'STARS! Both of us, Luke?'

'But of course. Told you, didn't I?'

'And we haven't even opened yet!'

'Only two more days. And enough important people have been in and out of the theatre watching us work to know. Now, stop staring—it won't disappear the moment we leave. Come along. Let's find that soup-kitchen you're so bothered about.'

Essie's joy was unrestrained, walking along with Luke in this easy, affectionate mood. She thought back to the bear-boy and his friendliness, then through the past weeks of Luke's difficult and recurring moods, and knew that this fondness was what she longed for, if only it would continue. She wished the evening could last for ever, there was so much to see and enjoy, and Luke to share it all with. . .

After the cake-box had been left at the Empire stage door—'Don't burst in on her in the middle of the show,' Luke said sagely. 'She wouldn't thank you for the interruption.'—they walked on, hand in hand, through the crowds of Londoners so busily intent on going home after work.

They took an underground tube train part of the way, much to Essie's wide-eyed delight, and, although she found the experience of the rattling, bumping train quite exciting, she was glad to emerge once again into the mischievously slapping wind coming off the wide, rolling river.

'Is this the Embankment?'

'Part of it. Tell me where you saw your starving people.'

She did. But the benches she'd seen earlier were

empty in the fading evening light, and she looked anxiously for the soup-kitchen Sir Jack had told her about. Luke solved the problem by asking a policeman.

'London bobbies are wonderful,' he said, smiling infectiously at Essie, as they followed the constable's directions. 'When you're famous, little star, if anyone asks you what you like about London, remember to mention the Police force. It's the thing to say these days. . .' His eyes twinkled, and she was suddenly overflowing with pleasure. Then she recalled the kindly assistance of the constable who had saved her from untimely embarrassment in the distant square the previous week, but, instead of bursting out with it and telling Luke, she made no reply. She had grown up a lot since that shame-making episode. . .

'This must be it.'

They stared into a dimly lit, cavernous warehouse, crowded with seedy figures. Around trestle-tables sat dejected-looking men and women, in filthy clothes. There was a smell of poverty in the air, a sense of hopelessness that ate away Essie's happiness. The seated figures did not speak but applied themselves to the bowls of steaming soup set in front of them. Long queues wound down the length of the building, and Essie clutched Luke's hand tightly.

'Poor things. How dreadful they look—so tired, so weak. . .'

He bent to catch her low words. 'So drunk, some of them, I'm afraid.' Gesturing, he drew her attention to one or two figures spread-eagled across the table, snoring loudly. 'It's a good thing the Salvation Army runs places like this. An absolute Godsend to these poor souls.'

Essie looked at him, startled. 'I didn't know the Sally Army ran it. . .' And then, almost without thinking, her eyes left the eating, sleeping, yawning figures clustered around the tables to look further into the shadows, down to where the long, waiting queue finally straggled to an end, and then back again, to the huge urn of soup being dished out by several women dressed in the familiar navy blue uniform of the Army.

Instinct made her rapidly search the women's faces. Hadn't Belle said something about maybe coming to London? And wouldn't it be strange if she was here?

Almost unbelievably, she was. Small and unremarkable, yet instantly recognisable to Essie's eyes, full of that indefinable quality that made her stand out from the crowd. Belle held a thick china bowl under the spout of the urn and handed it to the next in line, with a brief smile and a word or two that Essie was unable to hear, but guessed, with tears pricking behind her eyelids, were probably Belle's usual question—'Are you saved?'

She was unaware of her extra grip on Luke's hand, but at once he bent his head to hers, asking quietly, 'What is it? What's the matter?'

Essie, the child, wanted to rush across, shouting Belle's name, attracting her attention. Estrellita stood, watching. She knew from the tone of Luke's voice that he felt her sudden tension, and so she took the time to deliberate before looking up at him with a brilliant, glowing smile. Her voice was low and under control.

'It's my ma! The one holding the bowl—it's Belle. I must go and talk to her.'

Luke's hand tightened. 'How amazing—did you know she was here?'

'No! Oh, she said vaguely we might meet again in London, but I never dreamed—I mean, I had no idea—it's like magic. . .'

'I've always thought you had a spark of it inside you, Estrellita!'

Was he laughing at her? Before she could decide, he added, 'Let's give extra thanks to Sir Jack, then, for mentioning this place.'

She heard the wryness in his voice and turned

swiftly. 'No! It's thanks to *you*, dear Luke, for bringing me.'

The hissing of the gas urn and the regular shuffle of weary feet moving in the long queue was forgotten for one timeless moment as they looked at each other with a sudden, joyous realisation that they had come one step closer—and all through coming to this wretched, sordid place. Then, abruptly, Luke's tender eyes left hers, and he glanced sideways. 'Your mother——' But the words were bitten off, and Essie missed the sharply curious expression filling his face, for her own gaze was directed at Belle, about to leave her position by the urn, giving way to another woman in uniform.

'I must catch her, before she goes—oh, Luke, quickly, I do so want you to meet her. . .' Essie flew down the room, eyes never leaving her mother's figure, now turning away, removing her apron and retying the bows of her dark bonnet.

'Ma! Belle!' Essie put a hand on the thin, stooping shoulders and met her mother's startled eyes with mixed gladness and apprehension. But she needn't have worried. After the initial gasp of surprise, Belle's lined face broke into a hearty smile.

Without thinking further, Essie kissed her mother's cheek. 'Isn't it funny?' she gabbled. 'Fancy you being here and us coming to see what a soup-kitchen was, and. . .' The spontaneous words tailed off as she watched Belle's gaze go past her, settling on Luke.

She turned, immediately awkward. 'This is Luke. Luke, this is my ma—Belle, I mean. . .' And then she caught her breath, seeing how they stared so frostily at each other.

Smiles were absent. Both faces frowned, eyes narrowing unexpectedly in obvious recognition. The silence grew hostile, and Essie's spine prickled with dismay. 'You know each other?' Her voice shook.

Luke was the first to regain self-control. He bowed

distantly towards Belle. 'We do. Not by name, but—yes—we've met before.'

Helpless, Essie turned to her mother. Surely Belle would explain what this mutual dislike was all about? But Belle seemed in no hurry to enlighten her. Her mouth turned down at the edges. 'Yes, we've met. A couple o'years ago.'

Essie heard the urn hissing near by, a clatter of spoons scraping china bowls, and a man's rough voice suddenly shouting something across the room. Someone snoring, further down the table—but all she was aware of was the dragging silence that surrounded the three of them. Then she could stand it no longer, abruptly erupting into rapid, uneven words. 'Well, tell me what's happened! Why are you behaving like this? Like two dogs sniffing at each other. . .what *is* it, for Gawd's sake?'

Disdainfully, Luke said, as if from a great distance, 'It's past history, Estrellita. Nothing to do with you.'

She turned on him, full of desperation. 'Nothing to do with me?' she echoed wildly. 'You and my mother, not talking? Hating each other? Of course it's to do with me! How can you be so stupid—so cruel—both of you? *Please* tell me what's wrong——'

'He can tell you, not me.' Belle fingered the bow below her sharp chin, giving it a final, dismissive tug. 'He's the one who was to blame. Gilda said as how he was impossible—so jealous, so untrusting. . .'

Something only half suspected before suddenly spread out in clear, unmistakable truth in Essie's agitated mind. Gilda and Luke. 'Gilda?' She sobbed the name, not yet able to accept what she instinctively knew. 'You mean my half-sister? The one in America?'

Belle nodded, taking dark cotton gloves from her pocket and carefully easing them down over her work-worn fingers. 'She's home again now. That's why I'm in London. Came up to see her, and then offered to help out here when one of the other women fell ill.

Yes, Gilda...' She darted a look full of malevolence at Luke. 'Ask him about Gilda, maid! He'll tell you all about her—about *them*. As for me, well, I'm off now—can't stand around here all night.' She started to move away, but Essie grabbed her by the arm.

'Ma! You can't just go! Not like this——'

'I can. I will, too. I've got no more to say. Not while *he's* here...' Turning her back on them, she limped down the long building, heading for the open doorway where the evening twilight lingered, taking no notice of either the dejected diners at the table, or of Luke and Essie, who both stood in silence, staring, as she went.

Once Belle had disappeared from sight, Essie rubbed angrily at her swimming eyes. She wanted to shout, even to scream—anything to get rid of the emotions so painfully churning inside her. But life had already proved that problems were resolved more easily by quiet consideration and not by wild outbursts, so, swallowing the threatening tears, she turned to look at Luke, examining his stern face with questioning eyes, willing him to explain.

He seemed as poised as usual, yet she sensed that the whiplash of remembered feeling had touched him as deeply as it affected her. She opened her mouth to ask an agonised why, but he forestalled her, putting a masterful arm around her shoulder.

'Let's get out of here.'

The Embankment was full of shadows. An unfriendly wind ruffled the convector-belt of grey, racing water, and Essie shivered, as much in awe of her unfamiliar surroundings as with unhappiness. Only a short while ago she had been so crammed full with joy that now she could hardly believe she was the same person.

Rapidly Luke walked along in the direction of their lodgings, and she had to move fast to keep pace with him. Stealing an uneasy glance at his brooding profile, she had enough sense not to ask any more questions. When we get home, she thought numbly, I'll make some tea and we'll sit comfortably together, and then he'll tell me his secrets. Tell me about the girl. About Gilda. . .

And then, despite her efforts at self-control, she could not prevent the images and fearful fancies that her unknown half-sister's name evoked from racking her with pain, so that when Luke suddenly crossed the road, with her scurrying along behind him like a forgotten pet dog, she was even closer to tears than before.

At the entrance to a small Italian restaurant, he stopped unexpectedly, his hand on the door-latch. Turning back, as if he'd abruptly remembered he was not alone, he stared down at her, moody eyes turned grey and dull in the half-light. 'Dear God—what've I done to you?'

There was amazement and a hitherto never heard tone of self-reproach in the muttered words, and this proved Essie's complete undoing.

Now her tears fell fast, scalding her cheeks, and she tried desperately to get away before Luke saw the state she was in. But his arms reached out, holding her fast, and one hand slowly and tenderly lifted her contorted face, so that she could no longer avoid meeting his eyes. 'My little love, what pain I've brought you—what unhappiness. Here, little star, dry your face.'

She hiccuped, took the offered handkerchief, and mopped her streaming eyes. There was so much humility in his voice that, once again, she found herself forgiving him everything—whatever it was that she had to forgive.

He sighed very deeply, still staring at her, then drew her closer until her sobs died and at last she lay, relaxed, against his breast.

How many more times, she asked herself wryly but thankfully, sniffing and slowly recovering her self-control, was she to end up in these same powerful, safe arms, hearing the thud of Luke's heart, knowing she could do nothing but love him, no matter what he'd said or done? The thought helped her to smile again.

The door they stood so close to opened as a customer left the restaurant, and the tantalising smell of cooking food brought all her senses into play. Raising her head, she grinned, ashamed, into Luke's anxious face. 'I'm ever so hungry,' she whispered. 'Can we go in now?'

For a second his expression was disbelieving. Then the brilliant, wonderful smile flashed out, delighting and reassuring her. 'You baggage! Sobbing your heart out one minute and demanding a meal the next! What am I to do with you, Estrellita?'

In reply, she took his hand in hers and led him through the restaurant entrance, saying, as they paused to look for an empty table, 'Give me some supper and tell me all about Gilda. It's not too much to ask, Luke, is it?'

Not until the ravioli in tomato sauce was eaten, the coffee-cups filled, and a tiny glass of some strange-sounding liqueur put in front of Luke, did she get the information she sought.

She had watched him slowly mellowing as the simple meal progressed. Now he sat relaxed in his chair, having ordered a cigar, looking at her intently, through the haze of fragrant smoke as he lit up. He drank some coffee, sipped the liqueur, and finally smiled. He was the old Luke, the bear-boy, the friend she longed for almost as much as the lover who had not yet come out of the shadows to claim her as his own.

'All right, little star.' He regarded her thoughtfully, then put back his head and closed his eyes for a moment. 'I said—it seems so long ago,' he mused—'that one day I would tell you about my past.'

'And your secrets.' Essie said the words almost to herself, but he heard, and raised an enquiring eyebrow.

'You think I have secrets?'

'Lots of them. Your past, Gilda, the illusions—all the bits you never talk about.' She leaned one arm on the red and white checkered tablecloth and outlined a series of squares with the forefinger of her free hand. It was easier to talk about his secrets if she didn't meet those probing eyes. 'I'm supposed to be your wife, Luke. I need to know about Gilda. . .'

'Gilda!'

She looked up quickly, caught by the distress and contempt in his tone. 'Yes, Gilda. Ma hinted about you and Gilda when first I found her. Harry told me about the other girl, the one you loved, the girl he ran off with. And once you told me you'd had an assistant, someone you loved. "That's a long story," you said. . . Well, it's time to tell me. *Now*.' Her voice rose urgently, wide eyes full of need, compelling him to answer.

Slowly, stirring his coffee and, in his turn, choosing not to look at her, Luke said, 'Very well. You're right, of course. You deserve to know everything. I've been wrong in shutting you out. But——' He bit off the word sharply, putting down the spoon so that it clattered in the saucer. He met her eyes as if forced to do so. 'But the truth is that in telling you I have to re-open the old wound. I must go through it all again. I have to pull out my problems, look at them, and try to discover if I really can solve them.'

Essie stared. His face was poignant in its unrestrained expression of painful reluctance. She gasped, uncertain how to deal with the desperation in his beseeching eyes. Then common sense came to her aid, and she replied, almost indignantly, 'Well, I hope *you* understand what you're talking about, because I don't! Not a single word. Who wounded you? What problems do you mean?' Swallowing the lump in her throat, she added forcefully, 'I used to think you were a great sort of god, Luke Grimwade—but now it seems you're just a poor little, lost boy!'

They looked at each other for a full minute, Essie's face crimson with tension and her inability to understand, Luke's expression a picture of shock, until finally his tight mouth curved upwards, the grey eyes began to dance, changing rapidly into their usual sunnier blue-green. Then, eventually, their combined laughter rang through the quiet restaurant, causing heads to turn and stare.

Luke put his hands over Essie's, and whispered, 'When I found you on the wasteland by the river—remember, all those years ago?—you made a big impression on me. Then, when I saw you at the gaff, jigging about in that hideous red dress, I had a feeling that we were meant to be together. I knew you could lift the act into a very special performance. I told myself it was a wonderful thing, finding you again. . .'

Essie, listening very carefully, understood now what he was talking about. One thought hit her particularly hard, and she interrupted his quiet flow of words. 'You mean, when you took me home with you that night, it was because you thought I'd make a good assistant? Not because you'd fallen in love with me?'

'That's right.'

She might have been hurt, but his eyes were honest and open as never before and, no, it wasn't pain she felt, not even annoyance, but just a warm understanding of his reason. She nodded. 'And when you said I could be Mrs Grimwade, that was just because of the act, too?'

For a second Luke shut his eyes, as if hiding from himself the unpalatable truth.

'Well, was it?' Essie urged, and he opened them again, looking deep into hers without further excuses.

'I was half in love with you by then. . .but I wouldn't admit it. I'd sworn never to love a woman again. So I told myself I needed you for the act. I was already jealous of your ability to make people laugh—to give them happiness—and I wanted to protect you, keep you from harm—free from the Monseys and the Harrys of the theatrical world. . .'

'Jealous. . .' Essie thought about it. Jealous was a word which had never before touched her life. A word which several people had recently mentioned in connection with Luke. Harry, Gilda, Ma—and now Luke himself.

'Tell me.' The two innocent words seemed to unlock Luke's mind still further.

Slowly he nodded, stroking her hands as he held them. 'I will. But not here. At home. Shall we go?'

She drank up her coffee, smiling at him over the rim of the cup and saying, as she replaced it in the saucer, 'Well, hurry up and finish that smelly old cigar before we go. Can't waste it—not after spending all that money.'

Luke puffed vigorously, then pushed the half-drunk glass of liqueur towards her. He smiled, and there was a new, freer look in his vivid eyes as he told her, 'And you must drink this. One more step in your neglected social education, little star.'

The unexpected potency of the fiery drink made her gasp, but Luke patted her back, teasing her about the ignorance of her country bumpkin ways.

'I know I'm ignorant. But I'm trying to learn.' She sat close beside him in a creaky old hansom cab, leaning her head against his shoulder, delighting in the way his arm tightened around her.

'Your ignorance is more like innocence. Don't ever change, my love.'

The horse's hoofbeats seemed to repeat the last two words. My love. Clip-clop. My love. She drowsed happily until they turned into Soho Square and then down Garrett Street.

By now the night had turned cold, and she was glad when Luke shut the door behind them at the top of the stairs and said quietly, 'Why don't you get into bed? You'll be warm there, and we can talk.'

Something somersaulted inside her, and she stared at his pale, tender face, wondering if there was a hidden motive behind the suggestion. Flashes of memory recalled Harry's eyes, lecherous and eager. And Sir Jack, too—all wanting something which she had instinctively drawn away from. But Luke's smile was guileless, his eyes a clear sea colour, and it was with unbounded pleasure that she did as he'd asked.

The narrow bed was hard and spine-chillingly cold. She slid down, pulling the blankets close around her neck, listening to Luke as he made a pot of tea in the corner of the bleak sitting-room.

'Here you are. It'll warm you up.' He insisted that she sip it at once, sitting on the side of the bed beside her and drinking his own as she obeyed.

Essie stopped shivering, and lay there contentedly, the glow from the small bedside light illuminating her still face. Luke put down his cup and looked into her expectant eyes. 'Gilda was my assistant—about eighteen months ago,' he began, in a quiet, low voice which told her nothing of his emotions.

Her heart began to beat faster. At last the secrets were being disclosed—how would it affect hers and Luke's feelings for each other? Watching his tell-tale eyes, she noticed every change of expression that flitted across his high-cheekboned face, saw his hands lying in repose on the counterpane begin to fidget, and knew that, however casually he was speaking, inside him the wellspring of emotion was coiled tight. It seemed she could do nothing to help but just lie there, listening.

'We worked well together. Gilda had the same sort of vivaciousness as you—well——' a brief smile lifted his lips '—after all, you are half-sisters. Yes, she was quite good. The act began to come alive. And Harry and I perfected an illusion that we knew must succeed in completely mystifying the public. It certainly did. . .' His eyes grew misty, and she knew he was reliving the past. 'We were the talk of the town, for a few weeks.

Stars!' Pausing, his face relaxed into a far-away expression. 'Fame, I thought! Here it is, I'm made, I'm at the top, the greatest magician of the new century—my name in lights, newspaper critics eulogising me, all the theatrical world at my feet. Yes, I got there, all right.'

Essie watched him smiling proudly, full of satisfaction and happiness. His lean face glowed, and his charisma made her want to throw her arms around him. But she lay still. He had only just started to tell her about the past. The bit that concerned Gilda was still to come. . .

And then, as if he read her thoughts, Luke's brilliant smile faded, and his eyes became dark and moody. 'And then the trouble started. Gilda and I——' Abruptly, he rose, turning his back, his voice growing dark and harsh. 'Well, I thought at the time it was love that I felt for her. Certainly I wanted her—she was pretty, we worked closely together, and she was the sort of girl who made herself available.' He was silent for a long moment. Then, turning back, he stared down at Essie's strained face, and threw himself on his knees beside the bed, his fingers cold as they stroked her cheeks. 'I make no excuses, little star. I'm a man, and she gave herself willingly. I thought we loved each other. But. . .'

Very carefully Essie withdrew her arms from the comfort of the bed and clasped them around his neck. They looked deep into each other's eyes in silence, as if neither had really looked before, until at last Luke's choked voice whispered, 'It didn't last. She was only using me as a prop for her own ambition. She wanted fame. And money. And men. . . I discovered there were other lovers. Harry was one of them. We had an almighty row when I found them together that afternoon. . .'

Essie watched the heavy lids hide his troubled eyes,

and raised her head, putting warm lips to his cold, hard face. 'Poor Luke.'

A great sigh erupted from deep inside him, and he opened his eyes again. 'It was my fault as much as theirs, I suppose. I'd grown jealous of her, suspicious of every man she spoke to. Harry and I became enemies. The act suffered, of course, as a result. Our contract was cancelled. And then, finally, they left. Together.'

Secrets, thought Essie, incensed. Such terrible things. If only he hadn't wanted to hide it all. 'Why didn't you tell me before?' she asked accusingly, her face taut with emotion.

Luke smiled faintly. 'Because I wanted to forget it had ever happened. The shame, and the disappointment...'

'But when we met, everything was different.' She held him close. 'I wasn't like Gilda, you must have known I wouldn't play tricks on you—or want other men...' Then she blushed a fiery red, remembering how only this afternoon Sir Jack's smooth compliments had made her feel so wonderfully uplifted and confident.

'I couldn't be sure,' said Luke regretfully. 'You're such a child——'

'I'm not!'

He chuckled, and outlined her pouting mouth with a gentle forefinger. 'Not now, perhaps. You've grown up a lot lately. But you did seem to like Harry—and I couldn't let myself love you, just in case... The thought of losing you has been a constant torture, little star. I can't begin to describe it.'

'And now?' Reminded of her new maturity, Essie used it wisely. Even if the past was unveiled, it didn't necessarily mean that everything was resolved. She needed to know that Luke's transformation from mystery man to a common human being was complete.

'And now...' he echoed her thoughtfully, and she

felt the blood start to sing through her body, for there was an expression on his beloved face that told her all her denied longings were about to be fulfilled. 'We have a lot to make up for, Estrellita—my little love, my wife who is not yet my wife—have I told you all you want to know? And do you forgive me? Oh, my darling—say you do. . .'

Her heart was too full to answer. She knew instinctively that words alone would never convince him. Taking his face in her cupped hands, she raised her head from the pillow and put her lips on his, a kiss that continued until, breathless, she was forced, reluctantly, to let him go.

His eyes smiled at her, deep pools of sea-blue serenity. The look of desire on his face made her tremble. Essie threw aside the bedcovers that separated them, whispering, 'Oh, Luke, I love you so much. . .' and felt his arms enfold her, crush her, moving her gently as he lay down beside her.

She felt the buttons of her nightdress being undone, his lips caressing hers in a long, lingering, erotic kiss that left her dazed and eager for more. From her mouth, his lips moved to her throat and then down to her small, perfect, rosy and erect nipples.

And then there was a noise of feet stumbling up the stairs outside their rooms. A rapping of clumsy knuckles on the closed door. Harry's thick, triumphant voice, slurred with drink, shouting Luke's name. 'Luke! Open up, old man! It's Harry—gotta talk to you. Come on, hurry up—*Luke*. . .'

The banging continued. Essie's eyes were on Luke's face, so close to her on the shared pillow. Suddenly his eyes were rock-hard with anger. 'Dear God! What a time to come calling!'

Sitting up, he shouted out, 'Go away, Harry. It's too late. I need my sleep. We'll meet tomorrow.'

'No!' Now Harry was bellowing like a hungry beast,

and Essie's dismay grew. Surely he would wake the whole house?

'You'd better see him,' she whispered. 'He won't go till you do. He's very drunk——'

'Damn his blasted hide!' Luke leapt out of bed, smoothing his hair and reaching for his discarded waistcoat as he strode across the room.

Some instinct told Essie that she, too, must get up. Rapidly she slipped into Luke's Paisley dressing-robe that had become hers, and followed him to the door. Dismay filled her, although she had no idea what Harry's untimely call could be about. But whatever it might be, she was here, a step behind Luke, supporting him. His wife, at his side.

Luke threw open the door and scowled into Harry's loose-lipped grin. 'For God's sake, stop shouting,' he said in an ice-cold voice. 'Come in, if you must—but surely it could have waited until tomorrow, couldn't it?'

Harry didn't answer. He was still grinning, staggering a little, and reaching out to grasp the door-jamb for support. Essie saw how his brazen eyes glowed, and knew then, with a terrible certainty, that Luke's secrets were still making ripples.

When Harry said thickly, with all his words slurring together, that he'd brought a visitor to see them, she knew at once who it was, and watched a pretty, familiar-looking girl step out of the concealing shadows behind them to smile dazzlingly into Luke's bewildered face.

For, of course, this was the other girl. Her half-sister. This was Gilda.

CHAPTER TWELVE

'HELLO, Luke, love—it's been a long time. Missed me, did you?' Gilda's voice held a hint of a half-Americanised drawl, and seemed to Essie to be all the more attractive because of it.

She stared at her half-sister with hyper-critical eyes, longing to find something she could immediately hate. But Gilda was a decidedly pretty girl, whose bearing and face were strangely familiar. *Because we're alike. . .* The knowledge flooded Essie with cold despair. And Luke had thought he loved Gilda. Maybe that was the only reason why, now, he appeared to love *her*.

Gilda swayed nonchalantly, one hand on hip, the other poised on her parasol. Her husky voice broke through Essie's thoughts. 'Lost your tongue, love? Well, you might at least ask me in. Harry and me have come miles to find you.'

Essie was balancing on a tightrope of indecision. She feared Gilda for coming here, yet she knew that this confrontation was a means of uncovering the most important secret of all—was Luke still in love with her?

He was wondering how he could ever have imagined he loved this flamboyantly dressed, archly smiling girl, who now stared at him with a sickening coyness. Tightly he nodded a greeting. 'Hello, Gilda,' and then spoke his thoughts. 'What is it you want?'

'Why, just to come and talk!' Gilda's bright eyes were smiling, and suddenly danced away to meet Harry's in a sly wink. 'I want to meet your new assistant, Luke. I guess that's her, isn't it, hiding behind you? In the old purple dressing-gown? The one

I used to wear...' Stepping aside nimbly, and, before Essie could retreat, suddenly they were face to face, staring at each other with unbridled curiosity.

'Well! So you're Estrellita!' Gilda's glance raked Essie from the tip of her dishevelled head to her small bare toes, peeping from the hem of the robe.

Essie's courage flared. She said quickly, 'Yes, I am, and you're Gilda. We're half-sisters, so Belle said.'

'Yeah. And I guess it's true. I can see bits of me in you. Well, Belle's told me all about you. Gee, but you're a skinny little scrap!' Gilda's amused smile touched Essie on the raw and she glared back. 'Hey, don't eat me!' Gilda turned to look again at Luke. 'Not really your type, is she, love? Thought you liked a nice armful to cuddle. You did when *I* was your girl...'

Luke's silence during this conversation had made Essie increasingly nervous. Now Gilda's provocative words brought her eyes back to his stern face, dreading what she might see there. But his eyes were thoughtful and chilly, his expression tinged with a wry surprise, and she could almost read his mind as he asked himself, Did I really think I loved her?

With a casualness that mocked Gilda's archness, he said, 'You're wasting your time—and your talent— coming back. We both made mistakes, so let's leave it at that, shall we, Gilda? Let's call it a closed book.'

The vibrancy in his calm voice thrilled Essie. She dared to take a step nearer, slipping her fingers between his arm and his waistcoat, and was rewarded by the brief, fond smile he threw her.

'Gee, how cosy!' Gilda was laughing now. 'Looks as if she adores you—can't really know what you're like, then, can she?' Her voice grew slightly shriller. 'So jealous. Masterful. Bossy. "Do this, Gilda, do that." But maybe you've learned a lesson, Luke, love. Maybe you're not as hard on her as you were on me at times.'

Sharply, Luke said, 'I don't need to be hard, Gilda.

Estrellita has talent and, more than that, she actually listens to what I say. She's not always looking around her for compliments and other men's attention. She works hard. Yes, she's got everything I need in an assistant——'

'Plus a willing little body I guess she's only too happy to share!' Gilda's laugh was no longer good-humoured. Her eyes glinted beneath the glare of the dim electric light bulb above, and her neatly gloved hand tensed on the handle of her parasol.

Abruptly Luke's anger flared, and he stepped forward so fast that Gilda retreated. Laughing quietly, he tilted her chin with one powerful hand and stared down into her uncertain eyes. 'You always had a repertoire of unpleasant thoughts, didn't you? Well, you haven't changed, my girl, not one little bit. But I have. And that's the difference between us.' He stepped away, and Essie saw with relief that his face was serene, his eyes untroubled.

Her gratitude made her want to crow with pride. 'Look!' she cried triumphantly, holding out her hand to show the brass curtain-ring on her finger, 'I may be skinny, and you can say what you like about me, but at least I'm Mrs Luke Grimwade, and that's more than you ever were, isn't it?'

Gilda's arched eyebrows shot up. 'A curtain-ring!' she scoffed contemptuously. 'Is that the best he could do? Oh, well, I guess a ring's a ring. . .' And then, unbelievably, she began to laugh, almost masking Harry's mutterings that it was time to go. 'Well done, sis!' she spluttered, shoulders shaking. 'So you managed to pin him down! Well, I only hope you won't regret it.'

Luke answered for Essie, his voice quiet and controlled, his face wryly amused. 'The only thing I'll ever regret is believing you had a warm, loving heart, Gilda. I know better now.'

They looked at each other steadily for a stretching

moment, and it was Gilda's eyes that fell first. Sulkily, she flung her answer at him.

'Marriage wasn't what I was after. A good time's much more exciting than being tied to one man...' With her eyes flickering back to Essie, she smiled knowingly. 'Well, dearie, maybe you'll find that out for yourself, once you've stopped being so green and innocent.'

Then she pulled roughly at Harry's arm. 'Come on, then, you old drunkard; no more fun to be had here.'

Harry staggered, and Gilda braced herself to take his sagging weight. 'For heaven's sake, man, stay on your feet for a bit longer! Now, where's that automobile of yours? Remember where you left it? Gee, come on, Harry.'

Standing together in the open doorway, Luke and Essie watched the inelegant, stumbling departure along the passage and down the stairs. When, finally, the footsteps faded and the voices dwindled away, Luke drew Essie back into the room and shut the door.

Inside the shabby sitting-room, he pulled her close within the circle of his arms and looked steadily into her eyes. She held her breath, ready to console him, for surely Gilda's unpleasant words must have brought back old memories, and wounded him. To her surprise, he smiled, a warm, carefree smile that brought a twinkle into his deep eyes as he drew her towards him. 'Just like magic, isn't it, little star? One moment it's there, and the next it isn't...yes, love's a very strange thing.'

With her head against his chest, instinctively Essie understood, and felt a great burden of anguish fly away from her. 'You mean it really *is* finished? The way you told her?' Lifting her face, she met the full force of his loving, wondrous gaze, and for a moment felt stunned by the impact.

Very slowly, Luke nodded. 'All gone. Slipped away into the past with everything else that doesn't matter.'

A CERTAIN MAGIC

His eyes suddenly became dark with emotion, and he hugged her to him in an embrace that nearly squeezed out all her breath. 'And now only this one thing matters, my little love—to ask you—no, no. . .' Correcting himself, he unfolded his arms and held her a few inches away, smiling down at her with such laughing vitality that she could only laugh as well. 'I mean, rather, to humbly implore my lady to make an honest man of me.' Then he let her go, dropping on to one knee, clasping his hands and raising them in a dramatic supplication that was quite spoiled by the dancing delight in his vivid eyes.

Essie sighed, a long, pleasurable letting go of all her hurt, her fears and her loneliness. Gently she took his hands in hers, pulling him up beside her, close to her, yet not close enough. . . Her heart was in her mouth when she whispered shakily, 'I will! Oh, yes, please, I will. . .' and pulled his head down so that she could kiss his warm lips.

She kissed him with all the passion she was capable of, holding him so close that once again the beating of his heart was part of her own throbbing body. Breathless, she met his adoring gaze and added unsteadily, 'Oh, isn't it wonderful? Love's like magic, yes, it is! It *can* work miracles, just like Belle said. . .oh, Luke, Luke, let me show you how much I love you—please?'

His answering kiss was the sensual thrill that she longed for, and made her body clamour anew for his loving. Suddenly he swept her up, and, still kissing her, carried her into the bedroom. But there he left her, tucking the covers around her in the narrow, hard bed, and saying teasingly, yet with a tremor in his low voice that told her of his own longing, 'I love you too much to dishonour you, my darling. When that brass ring is changed for a gold one, when you've had the real wedding that I know your romantic spirit longs for, then——' He hesitated, devouring her with his eyes, before quickly turning away, his voice only just audible as he moved. 'Then we'll make love, and—oh, dear God—how good it'll be...'

In the darkness of the little room, Essie lay entranced, her thoughts flying towards the one miraculous fact that she had never dreamed could come true. Luke loved her. He wanted to marry her, to make her a real wife...

She heard him settling down on his own lonely, makeshift bed, and called lovingly across the room, 'Goodnight, darling Luke.'

His voice floated back, quiet, deep and happy. 'Goodnight, my little love—and sweet dreams.'

They were more than sweet. They were filled with love and joy and more happiness than Essie had ever thought herself capable of imagining.

Len Rollinson was shouting. Solly Kurtz, smoking his cigar and shrewdly watching everything, sat in his usual seat, centre stalls. Backstage everyone was rushing and swearing. The dust arose, and with it the familiar smells of size and greasepaint, cigarette smoke and stale food. It was a typical dress-rehearsal day.

Essie had long since lost all contact with Luke. They had walked to the theatre together, deep in joyous conversation.

'We'll be married as soon as I can get a licence,' Luke told her masterfully. 'As soon as the show's opened, we'll arrange our wedding.'

'In a church? Oh, please, in a church—with choirboys and Alice as my bridesmaid, and——'

'And your mother to weep over you!' Luke's hand gripped hers, his voice teasing and happy.

'Of course! But I hope she won't come in her old Sally Army blue...' Essie did a little skip. 'Who'll I have to give me away?'

Luke slid a wry sideways glance at her. 'There's always Harry——'

'No, *thanks*! I know—I'll ask Alice's Albie. Maybe he'll come in his lionskin!'

Such plans. Such shared, wonderful moments of togetherness, making up for the wretched misunderstandings and pains of the past. But, once they had reached the theatre, Luke had kissed her briefly and then, instantly, gone into close consultation with the stage manager. Essie's euphoria was soon melted by an urgent summons to Wardrobe.

'There, fits you nicely,' decided Mrs Kingman, smoothing the bright satin costume. 'Colour's good, too. Move in it, can you, dear?'

Gingerly, Essie crossed the cluttered little room, grimacing as she did so. 'Do I really have to wear this beastly corset? Makes my top stick out one side and my bottom the other.'

'Of course you must. That's the hourglass look—the fashion all the young Gaiety Ladies are wearing now.' Mrs Kingman's plump face was scandalised, and she nipped in an extra quarter of an inch around Essie's minuscule waist.

'Lawks! I can hardly breathe!'

'You don't need to breathe in the finale, just stand there and smile. Do that, can't you?'

Recognising the voice of experience, Essie's grumbles faded away. She did look nice, she had to admit it—even nicer than Gilda last night, decked out in that smart creation of rosy pink silk with lacy sleeves, and an outrageous hat, all floppy flowers and showers of tulle.

Dispatched from Wardrobe, she wandered along the drab, uncarpeted passage behind the cyclorama, at the back of the stage, mind full of dreams and images, forgetting that anyone else was about. Only when the unfamiliar quietness jolted her back to reality did she start to wonder.

Where was everybody? No hurrying scene-shifters, stage hands, carpenters. . .no giggling chorus-girls or anxious-looking comics. No muscle-bound acrobats in lionskins, swearing at each other over mistimed movements.

How strange. No noise. No one here, thought Essie—but surely this is always the part of the show when Luke and Harry are working on the final illusion? So why weren't the backstage staff busy with traps and slides, mirrors and trick-lighting?

She'd seen bits of the illusion, of course. Luke's masterpiece of magic was called 'The Dying Monk', and he and Harry had been working on it ceaselessly. Essie, from her box, had watched, fascinated, as Luke, robed in black with a monk's cowl over his head, came out of a small monastic cell in a forest glade, and was set upon by so-called spirits of the night—hideous faces and claw-like limbs that came streaming in, all around the darkened stage.

Her small knowledge of trickery told her this was done by invisible wires and mirrors, but the end of the illusion had always left her guessing.

Suddenly, footsteps approached around the corner, close to where she stood, and the SM appeared in a hurry, top-hatted head well down, almost knocking her over before she could move away.

Then, 'What the hell are you doing here? Get out of it, Estrellita—go on, hurry up—you know everyone's banned from backstage for The Monk. . .' Scowling, he manhandled her roughly along the passage, taking no notice of her protests.

'Stop it! You've no right to push me around like this!'

'Women! Always get where you don't want 'em. . .now, go in there and stay there for the next three minutes—understand?' He threw open the nearest dressing-room door, thrusting her inside before slamming it shut and then continuing his audible progress.

Essie stared at the surprised faces confronting her.

'Well,' she said crossly, 'don't know what that was all about. . .'

'Course you do.' One of the girls gave her a derisory grin. 'It's "The Dying Monk", isn't it? The one that ends the show. You know—it's the bit where Mr Grimwade lies dying centre stage and then something looking like a ghost floats up from him towards the angel's face that's grinning in the background.' The girl paused to readjust the feathers in her tall head-dress. 'I like the next part, when the angel and the ghost both disappear, the bells ring, and the heavenly choir sings. And then there he is again. . .'

'Who?' asked Essie curiously.

'Why, Mr Grimwade, of course! He's become a saint, or something, standing up there like a statue at the top of the stage, with lovely coloured lights all around him! And yet at the same time you can still see his dead body below. . .fair gives me the creeps, it does, I can tell you!'

'It's only an illusion. . .' But Essie had prickles down her back, too. Secrets, she thought, still more secrets. She'd never actually been backstage when Harry and Luke were working alone on this last illusion. Now it dawned on her that if trapdoors and sliding panels weren't secrets enough, then Luke and Harry must have some really amazing trickery to work, especially if even the rest of the cast were forbidden to watch.

A few minutes later there was the sound of hurrying feet outside, voices raised, a noisy rap on the door, someone shouting down the passage, 'All right, girls. It's over. Back to normal again. Dancers for the Viennese café number on stage, please. And get a bloomin' move on. . .'

It was over. Essie let the girls leave the room before her, and then slowly made her way into the darkened auditorium, searching the shadows longingly for a glimpse of Luke. Solly Kurtz sprawled in his usual place, with Len Rollinson haranguing him from the pit, but neither Luke nor Harry was to be seen.

Essie asked herself curiously, What sort of an illusion was it, that neither Harry nor Luke would allow anyone to be present backstage, even in rehearsal? A little knot of apprehension tied itself very tightly at the depths of her stomach, and lay there, quiet, but menacing, underlying her new-found happiness.

Alice found Essie, as usual, in her private eyrie, after her bouts of rehearsal, just as the clock in the street outside chimed one. She came running in, breathless from the stairs, the empty cake-box in her hand. 'Eee, it were lovely! All that cream! What a job I had, keeping greedy-guts Albie away from it—here, I've brought back the box.'

Essie smiled dreamily. 'Bother that! Oh, Alice, I've got such news!'

'Well, spit it out, love—ee, you look like the cat that ate the canary. . .'

'We're going to be married!' Essie's explosive delight seemed to fill the whole space of the tiny box they sat in.

Alice gasped. 'You never! Oh, but you mean it—I can see it all over your face! Essie, love, that's just grand. . .if it's really what you want.'

Essie came down to earth with a bump. She opened her eyes very wide. 'Of course it is,' she said forcefully. 'Why shouldn't it be?'

'Well——' Alice fidgeted and looked away for a moment '—I thought, maybe—I mean, like, well, that Sir Jack—him with the cream-cakes and the big car——'

'Pooh!' derided Essie, smiling again. 'That's a laugh! He's just a nice kind chap who took me out.'

'Don't you believe it, love. The likes o' him have on'y got one thing in mind—aye, and you know what that is as well as I do.' Alice's knowing wink made

Essie blush. Her mind raced, and sudden dismay hit her. 'Oh, dear! How awful. And do you think *Luke* thought that I was—was——?'

'Nay,' said Alice kindly, seeing the distress on her face. 'Luke trusts you. He loves you—well, you said so, didn't you?'

'Yes, I did.' Essie sighed gratefully. 'Just think—he actually loves me! Oh, Alice, I can hardly believe it...'

'Get on, you silly 'app'orth. You'll soon learn that love's not the only thing in life. Which reminds me— I'm hungry. How about you?'

Essie jumped to her feet, pulling Alice up beside her. 'Yes—I could eat a horse!'

'Nay, love, I'd stick to jellied eels if I was you.'

Still giggling, they stepped out of the doorway of the box into the wide passage that ran beyond the gallery seats to be confronted by a girl just reaching the top of the staircase leading from the foyer below.

Essie halted, pulling at Alice's arm. 'It's Gilda.'

'Looks a bit like you, love—except that she's got a bigger chest than your two little bumps.'

Gilda smiled a little hesitantly as she reached Essie and Alice standing at the top of the stairs. 'Thought you'd be up here. Heard you laughing when I came into the theatre. I—I want to talk to you, sis—if you've got a moment.'

Alice nudged Essie. 'All right, I can take a hint. I'll go and have me dinner, and tell them to keep you something hot. Don't be too long, will you? Dress rehearsal always starts earlier than you think.' She swept past Gilda with a disdainful stare, and ran down the stairs.

Essie was curious, and slightly wary. 'Well?' she asked bluntly. 'What is it, then?'

'I saw Belle this morning.' Gilda's face held an unfathomable expression.

'Yes?'

'Well, she's upset that we don't seem to get on.'

'You mean you told her about last night?' Essie's curiosity grew. Had Belle's unpredictable heart softened towards Luke, after all?

'She got it out of me. Guess you know what Belle's like...' Gilda smiled faintly.

'Not really,' Essie answered. 'I only found her a few weeks ago, and she wasn't exactly pleased to see me.'

Gilda shrugged. 'I should think not! A daughter, out of the blue, suddenly arriving on her doorstep?'

'She shouldn't have given me away—then I wouldn't have had to surprise her like that, would I?' Essie's caution had gone, and she found she could talk openly to this half-sister of hers. 'I want her to love me, but——'

'She does. Only she'd rather die than tell you so.' Gilda's gaze had softened. 'Belle's like that, you see. She's been hurt, and so I guess she's scared it could happen again.'

Just like Luke. Essie kept the fact to herself. Aloud, she said, 'I didn't know.'

'Well, you do now, sis.'

'Ye-es...' She looked at Gilda with increased interest and an emerging sense of affection. If Belle's seeming coldness of heart was only self-defence, then perhaps Gilda herself was more sympathetic than she seemed? Abruptly, Essie asked, 'Can we be friends?' and watched as Gilda's artificially pinkened cheeks became a deeper red.

'Gee, I don't see why not.' She sounded slightly unsure, but there was a glow in her eyes that softened their rather frosty blueness. 'What about His Highness, though? What about Luke?'

Essie nodded, remembering. 'You were horrid to him last night,' she accused, her voice hard.

'He'll get over it. Men are like children—tantrums one minute and then pleased with the world again the next. Luke's an exceptionally talented artist, too—

guess he can't help being so moody.' Gilda stopped abruptly, then asked, 'You haven't had much experience of men, have you, sis? Only with Luke?'

Essie considered, and then longed to show off. 'Harry. And Ned. And then, of course, Sir Jack. . .'

Gilda's stare became amused. 'Who's he?'

'One of our backers.' Essie grinned, suddenly eager to share confidences. 'An angel, Luke called him.'

'Is he your lover?'

The question shocked her, and recalled Alice's unpleasant home-truth. 'No, of course he's not!' she said indignantly. 'He's just a friend. He took me out to tea, and he's taking me to luncheon on Monday, and——'

'And the next thing you know,' cut in Gilda, with a knowing wink, 'he'll be setting you up in a cosy little house in Chelsea and visiting you every night!'

'Stop it!' Essie covered her ears, distressed beyond all reasoning. 'It's nothing like that——'

'Of course it is, sis! All those stage-door johnnies keep girls in love-nests. Why should your Sir Jack be any different?'

'Because I love Luke——'

'Then you're a fool.' Gilda fidgeted with her parasol, before walking to a nearby mirror, where she patted her hair and preened, still talking over her shoulder. 'I'd give anything to be set up like that. You could be a really lucky girl if you played your cards right.' Glancing back, she smiled saucily. 'Tell you what, if you don't want good old Sir Jack Somebody-or-Other, why not pass him on to me? It'd be a good swap; I'm more experienced than you. And he sounds just my type—a title, money——'

'He's got a Rolls-Royce motor-car. And a chauffeur.' Essie's tone was grim. 'And he holds your hand at teatime, and encourages you to be fast and make a fool of yourself. . .' Her voice made Gilda suddenly flush again. 'Yes, sounds *just* your type; take him, with my blessing, Gilda.'

'No need to be like that. A girl's got to look to the future, hasn't she?' Gilda was aggrieved.

Essie savoured her reply, hugging it to herself before the words came out. 'I know where my future is. With Luke.'

Their eyes met with a clash of momentary hostility, and silence grew between them. Then, tossing her head, Gilda stepped away from the mirror and began descending the wide staircase. 'Where were you meeting him, this Sir Jack of yours?'

Essie let the taunt pass. 'Outside the theatre, noon on Monday.'

'Guess I'll be there. He won't mind switching. His sort never do. Well, sis—good luck for tomorrow. . .' Her voice drifted back up the stairs.

'Thanks.' Essie smiled reluctantly.

'Don't mention it. Toodle-oo for now. . .' Gilda went gracefully into the foyer, humming to herself. The words drifted back to Essie's ears and made her smile broaden.

'A little of what you fancy does you good. . .'

Alone, Essie stared blindly at the shadowy corridor in which she stood, thinking about Sir Jack Martineau. Gilda had called her green and innocent last night, and how right she'd been. I never thought—never imagined—that he. . .a house in Chelsea? A love-nest? The images were offensive. Suddenly, Essie knew she must find Luke, and never again leave him. Then another thought struck her, a thought so dreadful that she cried aloud, 'What if Luke thought we were lovers? Oh, lawks, I've got to tell him we weren't—tell him I've never loved anyone but him and I never will! I've got to tell him now. . .'

She raced down the stairs in a state of acute distress, calling Luke's name and searching the auditorium for him, but to no avail. When a figure loomed up beside her, she whirled around hopefully. 'Luke?'

But it was Harry. 'Hello, Essie, darlin'...here, have a drink with good old Harry. I've got a thirst like a dried-up river-bed after last night...' He held out an opened beer-bottle, and she stepped away distastefully.

'You've been drinking. *Again*.'

'And why not? "The Monk" went well, just now. It's going to take us to the top, you know...we open tomorrow, and we'll be the most stu—stupendous show in town. Luke and me'll bring the roof down.' His voice was slurred, his eyes pin-pointed with alcohol. 'But Luke can't do it without me. Poor old Luke, always needs Harry to help him out——' His voice cracked into a drunken laugh and, disgusted, Essie slipped away.

At last she found Luke, sitting quietly at the back of the stalls, asleep. His head lolled to one side, and his hands were clasped loosely over his stomach. He looked peaceful, but exhausted, and all traces of Essie's anxiety were diminished by her concern for him, as she recalled how hard he'd been driving himself these last weeks. And the opening tomorrow meant so much to him—this was his great chance to make good. His second chance—and a second chance never came again, did it? She slid into the seat beside him, sitting as still as a mouse, eyes on his sleeping face, heart overflowing with love.

Nothing mattered any more except Luke and her love for him. She could easily forget what Gilda had said, even forget her fears that Luke might suspect her fidelity to him. That was all behind her now. Just as Harry's drunken ravings could be ignored, along with Belle's unexpected change of heart.

In the thirty-five minutes that Luke continued to sleep, it seemed to Essie that she experienced a lifetime's growth of wisdom and knowledge. She felt remade, and resolved to use the new strength in any and every way that Luke needed.

When, eventually, he lifted his head and opened his eyes, she did no more than smile and watch him, until Luke discovered she was beside him. He yawned, stretched, suddenly leaped up.

'What's the time? God, I must have nodded off——' Then he stopped, smiling fondly. 'How long have you been here?'

'Half an hour? I don't know.'

'Why didn't you wake me?' He was smoothing the creases out of his coat, gazing down at her, looking refreshed and eager to get back to work.

'Because I knew you needed to rest.'

'Estrellita—my dear love—you never cease to amaze me.' Taking her hand, he drew her up to stand beside him in the aisle, between the tiered seats. 'You, sitting there in silence, for so long?' His smile was jaunty, his voice light, and her heart expanded.

'It wasn't hard, Luke. I was just—looking after you.' She smiled tenderly, knowledgeably, as if she was far wiser than him, and was rewarded by his gentle touch on her face.

His fingers stroked her cheeks, then hovered about her lips. A little hoarsely, he said, 'I don't think I deserve all that you give me, little star——' but she cut in quickly, seizing his hand and pressing it to her mouth.

'Oh, yes, you do—and now I'm going to take you out and make you eat something. You can't live on air, you know.'

'Not even on love?'

His low question brought a rosy flush to her face, and her eyes glowed as she answered quietly, 'No, Luke. Not even on love.' Then she smiled more cockily, restored to her usual good spirits. 'Come on; a good plateful of cod and chips will do you more good at the moment than all the love in the world!'

CHAPTER THIRTEEN

NEVER before had Essie been so nervous, in spite of the fact that last night's dress rehearsal had gone quite well, apart from the few inevitable hitches with scenery changes, and entrances and exits, that she had been warned to expect.

Now the all-important day was here, the actual opening of the show which was to bring success and fame to her and Luke—or failure. The alternative thought had never occurred to her before. Suppose—just suppose—the show flopped? Would it make any difference to their love? Of course not! Nothing could ever do that. But today she felt something in the atmosphere, causing her to become uneasy.

Naturally, Luke noticed. 'I thought you'd be excited today, not quiet, like this.'

'I am excited. Oh, lawks, I am!' But she couldn't explain the other apprehensive tension that was winding her up so tightly.

'You'll be fine once we get to the theatre,' he assured her, snatching up the usual last mouthful of toast as he headed for the door.

And he was right. The comfortable awareness of being with friends and colleagues worked wonders on Essie's nerves. There was a welcome hurry and bustle throughout the whole building. The auditorium was being tidied and polished, and the cleaning-women's chatter added to the happy hum of noise throbbing through the theatre.

Essie was snatched into Wardrobe for a final costume fitting as she left the dressing-room, ready to prepare for one of Luke's inevitable last-minute rehearsals.

'There—look a proper treat, you do.'

In the long mirror, she considered herself, and was impressed more with the serenity in her wide brown eyes than the artificial glitter of the tight-fitting, sequinned and tinselled costume that she would wear for her first entrance with Luke.

She hadn't thought she looked as calm as this, yet deep inside her, hidden and refusing to emerge, the old uneasiness lurked. The show couldn't really bring failure, could it?

When, after an hour of brisk rehearsal, a message reached her that someone waited at the stage door, she ran there to find Belle standing outside in the sunshine, and her joy suddenly took wing.

'You've come! Oh, how lovely to see you—come in, Belle; the dressing-room'll be quiet. And I want you to see our star on the door—and—and I've got something to tell you!'

But Belle silenced her enthusiastic greeting with a hard look, squaring her thin shoulders resolutely. 'You won't get me stepping inside this den of iniquity,' she said acidly. 'Drunkenness, that's what goes on backstage—always did, always will. I can smell it, too. . .ugh! Thank the good Lord I took the Pledge when I did.' Her peaky face grimaced, and cautiously she took a step nearer the door to smell the air.

'It's not as bad as all that, Belle.' Essie's voice fell. Was there always to be a prickly barrier between them?

Belle stared, as if she shared the thought, and then, with a redeeming although brief smile, added, 'Another thing—when I was in the business, we had gas fumes! Whew! What a smell.'

'Worse than the drink?' suggested Essie hopefully.

'Just as dangerous,' Belle replied sternly, but her face had softened, and Essie guessed she was remembering—maybe even wishing she was back among the rough camaraderie and bawdy goings-on of theatre folk. 'Those gas jets were naked flames, you know—

many a girl I saw catch fire. All those feathers and gauze petticoats. . .nasty, it was. Still, it can't happen now you've got electrical lighting.'

'Course not. The only way we'd have a fire nowadays is a cigarette end on a heap of rubbish.' Essie's hopes rose again. 'Belle, please come in. Perhaps you and Luke could——'

Belle shook her head firmly. 'I don't want to see him, but I had to come to wish you luck.' She hesitated. 'You're my girl, after all. I want things to go right for you.'

They looked at each other for a long moment, exchanging understanding smiles, then the older woman added, a little grudgingly, 'and for that Luke of yours, too. I don't know the rights an' wrongs of him and Gilda, but—well, doesn't do to bear grievances. "Turn the other cheek", says the Good Book, an' so I will. You tell him from me, maid, as I said good luck.'

'I will. Oh, Belle—Ma—thank you. . .' Essie's voice shook. She hadn't expected such a generous gift. Touched by her mother's understanding, suddenly words tumbled out in a spate of excitement as she tried to share her happiness. 'We're going to be married! Next week some time—soon as the show's on its way; oh, Ma, you'll come, won't you? Please?' Emotion made her quickly reach forward to touch her mother, but Belle pulled back, her smile gone.

'Now don't get weepy—can't abide tears all over the place. Married, eh?'

'I'm not crying. I—there's something in my eyes.'

'Get on with you.' Belle sounded scornful, but she smiled again. 'So he wants to marry you—just hope he knows what he's taking on—a wayward, flighty maid like you. . .' But her smile was warmer, and her husky voice had lost its edge. 'Course I'll come to the wedding. Make sure you tell me where and when.' She grinned wickedly. 'I might even treat meself to a new hat. No promises, mind.'

They smiled at each other, then Belle said, matter-of-factly, 'Well, must be on me way. Taking part in a procession in the East End at dinnertime. Lovely. Banners, and the band, and lots of testimonies. Oh, we'll save a few, see if we don't.'

Essie blinked hard. 'Are you going to stay in London? Now that Gilda's home?'

Her mother sniffed. 'That young madam doesn't want me around! Got ideas of her own, she has. No, I've got a nice lodging with Captain Mrs Forester and her husband, and we get on all right. I'll bide here a bit longer.' She gave Essie a final nod. 'Bye-bye, then, maid.'

'G-goodbye, Ma. Belle. . .'

Essie stood at the open doorway, watching her mother's slight figure limping hurriedly down the street. A few yards away, Belle turned, stared, and then shouted back hoarsely, 'Don't forget, if you need a bed for yer honeymoon, the cottage is empty.' Then she was on her way again, disappearing among the crowds without any further backward glances.

The day had acquired a sort of power, a greater meaning, Essie mused, as she went back down the passage. Fancy Belle saying that, about the cottage. Almost as if she was inviting her back to Teignmouth, but could only do so in a roundabout way that couldn't possibly be mistaken for mother-love! Essie grinned, then skipped the next few steps, suddenly transported out of her introspection. Today! It was becoming a wonderful day. Why, anything—everything—could happen today!

The afternoon slid past in a procession of further chaotic run-throughs, none of them long enough to warrant the term rehearsal. 'We'll do that bit with the scarves again. Make sure you're dead centre when I go behind the table.' Luke smiled at her with such devotion in his eyes that her heart glowed. Seldom before had he ever allowed their love to show while he was working.

He was in his element, she thought, standing in the wings, forgotten, watching the other acts polishing their performances, bringing everything and everyone up to his personal standard of near-perfection.

Around her the other artistes crowded, full of their own problems and tensions. Scene-shifters, carpenters and electricians, all hurrying down the labyrinthine passages in the dim fustiness of backstage, or crowding each other in the wings, shouting messages, cursing, paying no heed to anyone else's business but their own.

The orchestra arrived during the afternoon, adding to the cacophony of sound, running through music cues and snatches of song. Essie's head began to whirl, and, once Luke had nodded at her across the group of property men and scene-shifters filling the stage, she thankfully escaped to the comparative peace of the dressing-room to rest her unexpectedly tired legs and sit quietly, trying to concentrate on what lay ahead. But her mind refused to do anything except flash from one muddled thought to the next.

A knock at the door broke into her reverie, and she stared in astonished pleasure at the flowers handed in. A bright posy of cottage flowers with a card from Gilda: 'From one showgirl to another. Good luck tonight, sis.'

A note from Alice, rather crumpled and smudged, that said formally, 'Best Wishes From The Francarti Twins.' Then there was a 'please turn over' in Alice's scrawled, scratchy writing, and a brief scribble on the back. 'Lots of love and enjoy yerself.'

Essie's eyes grew moist and her heart threatened to burst. Sniffing, she stared next at the large, expensive-looking bouquet of iris, freesias and pink carnations, wrapped and beribboned, and seeming too stiff and elegant to be real. But the fragrance of the freesias was real enough, and she pulled out a small gilt-rimmed card from their midst with a feeling of disbelief.

'To Estrellita, born to be a star,' the thick, beautiful writing stated proudly. Essie hiccuped, then read on, wide-eyed. 'From one who waits impatiently for our next meeting. Devotedly, Jack Martineau.'

She was busy with her thoughts for the next few minutes. All these people, sending her flowers and their love—did she deserve it? Suddenly she needed Luke to make her joy complete—but of course he wouldn't be here yet; he had too many other things to think about.

But she'd maligned him. For abruptly the door opened and he entered hurriedly, carrying slopping mugs of tea, smiling at her surprised face in such an understanding manner that immediately she reached for a handkerchief to mop her tell-tale eyes. 'Oh, Luke—how lovely!'

He sat very close to her, both chairs facing the mirror above the make-up bench, the naked electric light bulb behind them glaring down harshly so that their reflections seemed colourless and hard.

His brilliant eyes sought hers in the mirror. 'Anything wrong?'

'No!' She wanted to blurt it all out, her need for him, her overflowing happiness, but drank the reviving tea instead.

'Don't tell fibs, little star. I know you so well. There's a far-away look on your face.' His steady gaze was reassuring, his presence a new source of strength.

Unevenly, over the rim of her cup, Essie muttered, 'Nerves. That's all.'

His lips twitched. 'I don't believe you. Tell me the truth.' There was a new, masterful note in his voice that made her turn sideways, forgetting the reflections in the mirror. She stared yearningly as he, too, turned in his seat, and then, without more thought, his arms were around her, pulling her up as he rose, kicking the chair aside in the passion of his movement.

He was strong, thrilling, loving, and suddenly she was laughing and crying, both at the same time. 'I want us to be famous, Luke! And I can't wait to be truly married—to make love—I'm so tired of being just a make-pretend wife...'

And then, even as his arms tightened around her trembling body, she felt the exciting hard strength of him against her. He was laughing, kissing her wet eyes, her cheeks, her mouth, her throat, nuzzling her hair and her ears, and all the time his laughter and desire vibrated through her, setting her senses afire with the knowledge that they truly meant so much to each other.

'My little love! What a torrent of passion to come from such a small, skinny person!' At last he held her away from him, smiling down with such delight that she could only sniff and feebly smile back.

'I'm not—so—skinny as I was,' she murmured defensively. 'I'm trying to eat more, so I'll get fat.'

'Don't you dare! You're perfect as you are.' His face grew abruptly serious, his sensitive mouth very gentle. His voice dropped, the low resonance making her blood race. 'Perfect. Yes, that's exactly the right word. My perfect woman, my Leda of the statue, warm and soft and the very essence of all things feminine.' The rich voice dropped even lower. 'My goddess,' he whispered, and Essie shivered. She was transported to a state where nothing seemed real save Luke's touch, the sound of him, and the subtle, haunting smell of his masculinity.

In silence, she could only shake her head as joy burned through her, igniting all the old fears and unresolved problems until her mind was one brilliant orb of light, conveying pure happiness and unbelievable revelation.

Eventually, she found her voice. 'You mean you really *do* love me?' It was almost too much to accept.

Again, Luke laughed. 'How many times do I have to tell you?' He drew away, a hand in his coat pocket, and then gave her a small square wrapped package. 'For you, little star. The wedding present I couldn't afford to buy until now.'

With shaking fingers, she undid the wrapping, opened the little brown leather case, and then stared in utter astonishment at the creamy starburst of pearls that lay on the dark, rich velvet.

'It's a pendant. And—oh, Luke!—it's a star. . .'

'Of course it is. Better than the china egg, don't you think? And much luckier.' His voice grew softer. 'After all, what else could I possibly give to Estrellita, my own little star?'

'But——' foolish tears threatened again '—but it must have cost so much—where did you get the money?'

'We'll be earning at least four hundred pounds a week from now on—this is just a loan. It'll be paid off in no time at all. . .'

'Oh!' Hardly daring to touch the beautiful thing, gingerly she took it from its box to hold against her pale throat. 'It's——' she swallowed '—it's lovely. . .'

'I'm glad you like it.' His eyes reflected her own pleasure, and she recognised the expression of longing once again touching his vulnerable mouth.

'Luke——' She sought for words, but found none, so reached out, touching him, kissing his dear face, loving the warmth of him, the harshness of his afternoon stubble, the salty taste of his skin.

Time stood still while a world of sensuous delight enveloped them both. Then Luke clumsily disengaged her clinging arms, and stepped back. His breathing was fast, his voice thick as he said unevenly, 'My darling girl—oh, God, how badly I want you; I can't wait any longer—but not here, not now. At home, my little love. Tonight, after the show.'

'Yes! Oh, yes, Luke—tonight. . .'

He left her then, his vivid eyes shining with blazing happiness and a new serenity that had eluded him until this precious moment, his loving glance clinging to hers until the door closed and she was left alone with her joy and sense of impending ecstasy.

Luke truly loved her! All the secrets had been revealed, never more to threaten and separate them. After tonight they would be forever man and wife, with nothing in the wide world to come between them again. . .

Then, slowly, as she replaced the beautiful pendant in the case, Essie's floating mind at last came down to earth, and she recalled that there were other things to live for besides love.

The show. Their act. And—oh, lawks!—the time was flying past. Soon, she knew, with a tremor of anticipation knotting her stomach, and making her look around the room in a flutter of excitement, she must get dressed, put on her make-up, prepare for the performance on which depended so much. Luke's lifetime ambition, and her own small share in his well-deserved success.

And then her eyes were, in some strange way, drawn back to the pearl pendant, shining so blandly in its case beneath the light bulb. Someone, somewhere, had told her once that pearls meant tears. . .

Through her radiant happiness, the old uneasy feeling slid menacingly a step nearer. Essie's smile died. Firmly, she closed the leather case and put everything out of her mind but the show. As if it were a holy amulet, she picked up the china egg which always stood near by, and stroked it, willing good luck to override the apprehension that the pearls had brought with them. And Belle's photograph, too, helped to put away the fears that nudged her so darkly. Why was she worrying like this? Nothing could go wrong now.

But the atmosphere in the little room still tore at her mind. She thought, grasping desperately at reality, I'll go and look through the spyhole in the curtain. I want to see the audience come in, the way I did at Exeter. It was lucky then; perhaps it'll make us lucky again. . .

As she ran down the passage, dodging bodies and bits of moving scenery, she knew, deep down inside her, that she and Luke needed every scrap of luck they could get tonight.

Somehow, she escaped the SM's all-seeing eye, creeping into the darkest, stuffiest corner of the wings, and then inching out, on stage, until she found the spyhole. Putting one eye to it, stifling sneezes as the dust enveloped her, she concentrated on what she saw.

If the Theatre Royal in Exeter had opened an unknown world to her, then the Irving was cosmic in its revelation. The auditorium, usually darkened and almost unnoticeable, was lit now by a blaze of light. Electric light standards shone down like huge opalescent jewels, flashing and hissing as they did so, and reflecting on the shiny gilt of the laughing cherubs and ornamental swags of acanthus buttressing the boxes above the rows of raked seats.

Gasping, Essie looked further back to the dress circle, then upwards again to the cheap seats of the gallery. Already the gods were filling up, the benches half hidden by people. But it was the stalls that captivated her, for the aisles between the rows were crowded with groups of elegantly dressed men and women.

Silk and satin swayed, luscious velvets billowed, and on the palely gleaming bosoms of the women myriad gems twinkled as heads bowed and bare shoulders turned to acknowledge friends. And—Essie caught her breath—there was Sir Jack, escorting a pretty young girl to her seat. His silvery thatch stood out like a beacon among the women's frothy concoctions of head-coverings, and his soldierly bearing was unmistakable.

He was attentive to the girl in the white, gold-tissued gown, and Essie could almost imagine what he was saying—and in what smooth and experienced tone of voice. For a second her mind raced back to their tea at the Ritz, and she felt her face become red as she recalled how green she had been—a love-nest in Chelsea? 'Oh, lawks!' she muttered, and for the first time felt a stab of surprising gratitude to Gilda for having enlightened her. Then she dismissed Sir Jack and his compliments completely. Tonight there were better things to do than regret what was past and done with.

Her wandering eye went on exploring the mass of humanity beyond the curtains, and she paused to stare very hard at one or two wonderfully gowned young women who stalked up and down the aisles, staring very directly at men as they passed. She had no need to wonder who they were, for theatrical gossip had already laid bare the intriguing and shameful world of the courtesan.

Tarts, thought Essie, and curled her lip wryly. Ladies of the night. Well—good luck to them. That brought her back to reality—And good luck to everyone tonight, she thought.

She was still staring through the peep-hole, fascinated by all that she saw, when she was abruptly shouldered aside by a gruff scene-shifter. 'Move yer bum, dearie; this flat's gotta go jest where you're standing.'

Then the dreamworld disappeared and she was back among unmannerly backstage friendliness. Returning to the dressing-room, Essie knew she had learned yet another lesson: Sir Jack and his retinue of moneyed, idle, pleasure-seeking friends were not for her. Now she knew herself to be a true child of the theatre.

Greasepaint was in her blood. This was where she—and Luke—belonged.

Someone collided with her as she went down the passage—Harry. The moment she met his eyes she knew, with sickening dismay, that he'd been drinking. His face was an unhealthy grey, the pupils of his eyes as tiny as pin-points. He swayed, and his vapid grin grew suddenly lecherous and loose-mouthed. 'Come to w-wish you g-g-good luck, darlin'. . .' Staggering forward, he pushed through the doorway of the dressing-room, clasping her roughly as he did so, pulling her towards him.

'Stop it! Leave me alone! You stink of whisky and cigarettes—ugh.' Disgusted, Essie pushed him away, and the door slammed, leaving them together in the room. Spread-eagled against the bench, Harry shook his head and glared back at her.

She watched a degree of sobriety return to his face, and was afraid. Harry drunk she could deal with, but Harry clear-headed and in an evil mood was definitely dangerous. She blustered, acting desperately in the hopes of vanquishing him. 'Get out of here, Harry—you'll be needed with the trap for the "Vanishing Lady" soon.'

'Not going till I get what I came for. . .' His voice had grown hard and ugly, matching the expression on his face, and she instinctively backed away.

'What's that, then, Harry?' Only too well did she know, for a hungry greed filled his inflamed eyes. Every minute mattered. If only she could just keep him talking. . .

But he was upon her, his mouth stifling her cries in a crudely wanton kiss. When she tried to escape he grabbed her hair so that she was unable to move. Lasciviously, he grinned at her.

'Kiss me, darlin' Essie, or I won't play tonight——'

'What do you mean, won't play?' It hurt even to speak, so tightly was her hair being pulled, causing the mask of her face to stretch uncomfortably, but even now she still hoped to keep him at bay.

'Shan't be where Luke expects me to be.'

She gasped at the sudden hatred in the words, and went on questioning him, trying to prevent the onset of more violence. 'Not by the trap when I come off the chair, you mean? But you must be there, or the trick won't work. No one else has rehearsed the timing the way you have, Harry.'

'Eg-zackly. . .' He yanked her even closer, so that his sour breath made her blench. 'No one else can take my place. . .' The triumphant whisper ran around her frantic mind, the threat of his words filling her with despair. 'So you'd better be nice to me, Essie, my darlin'—or else no "Vanishing Lady". . .' He began to laugh, a high, gloating cackle that made her blood turn cold. 'And no Dying bloody Monk, either!' As the laughter faded, he saw the contempt in her staring eyes, and gave her hair another sharp, painful tug. 'Kiss me, damn you.'

There was no escape. It was a moment of living horror to have his mouth close on hers, to feel his tongue sliding over her lips. The smell and taste of him revolted her, and she fought like a caged lioness for her freedom.

For a few seconds they grappled fiercely, and then Harry's drunkenness allowed her to get free. Stepping back from him, she lashed out with her foot, and had the satisfaction of hearing his howl of pain, of seeing him double up, one hand stretching down to his injured calf. 'You bitch! You little tart! I'll get you for that——'

But Essie was at the door in two frantic steps, opening it to find herself face to face with Luke.

'What on earth——?'

Abruptly, her bravery collapsed. She clung to his arm, hiding her head against his breast, thinking only that he mustn't know what Harry had done—what

Harry was threatening to do. Luke needed peace and quiet before the performance. If he thought Harry had been betraying him, what might happen?

Wearily, she raised her head. 'It's all right. It's—nothing. Honestly. Harry—just——'

Luke's eyes were like circles of ice, and she realised with dismay that all her excuses were in vain. Luke knew what Harry had done. He stared through the doorway at Harry, who was still crouching, rubbing his leg. 'What are you doing here?' The low voice was harsh with suspicion and dislike.

'Wishing Essie good luck, of course.' Harry recovered his self-control with an adroitness that Essie couldn't help but admire.

'Then if you've done so, I'd like you to go and check the trap for a last time.' Luke's face was stern, but Harry merely nodded, sullenly limping off down the passage. Staring over his shoulder, Luke shouted forcefully, 'And don't forget to put out your fag-end before you go down there—I've told you about it before. . .'

Alone again, Luke looked at Essie, and she thought he seemed as tense as she herself felt. Pushing aside her own fears, she reached for his hands and smiled, managing to say, quite casually, 'Nice of him to come and wish me luck——'

'Very nice.' The sarcasm was emphatic, and the old feeling of uneasiness that had haunted her all day was strong, hearing his low words.

Searching his unfathomable eyes, she said impulsively, 'Nothing can spoil it for us, Luke, surely? Not Harry? Not now. . .now that we love each other. . .?'

His expression changed swiftly, and he pulled her to him, kissing her with a desperation that made her uneasiness grow. His hands were warm and caressing about her body, and his answer so soft that she hardly heard it.

'Don't say such things, my darling,' he muttered into

her hair. 'Remember we've got to keep the luck going. . .'

Half laughing at his superstition, half crying with the joy of knowing herself so deeply loved, she watched his hand rise to touch the silver earring. 'You're such a silly creature, Luke Grimwade!'

He let her go then, slapping her bottom teasingly as he turned to the make-up shelf to pick up the china egg. 'And this makes two of us, doesn't it? A superstitious pair. . .' The gleam of fond mockery in his eyes disappeared, and then in its place she watched a more sombre, brooding expression arise. 'Don't laugh at luck, little star. Don't ever risk it.' And then, quickly, he was laughing again, leaving her by the mirror, smiling over his shoulder as he left the room. 'I'll be back to dress very soon.'

The door closed, and Essie sat down, still dreaming of the success that must surely come tonight.

She could hear the faint sounds of the orchestra tuning up over the ceaseless chatter from the dressing-rooms along the passage. The chorus-girls seemed noisier than ever, and she guessed they would all be brandishing their rabbit's feet and horse-shoes, flitting from one room to the next as they wished each other good luck. Kisses smearing the make-up, and even the dour stage staff smiling instead of scowling. Dreamily, she reached for her make-up. She put bistre shadow on her eyelids, mascara on her lashes, and a faintly purple rouge on her lips. She saw herself change from the small, ordinary girl of a few minutes ago to a new, fairy-tale princess. There was a living radiance that appeared to come from deep within her, and she realised, gratefully, that she had needed these few precious minutes of stillness to prepare herself mentally for what was to come.

Next, she dressed her hair, and then put on the tight, saucy silver costume for her first appearance. In her mind, she ran through the routine. Scarves from

Luke's pocket, cigarettes appearing out of nowhere. The rabbit from his sleeve, six pigeons fluttering out of the magic cabinet. Chinese rings, and then 'The Vanishing Lady'. All well rehearsed, and nothing to worry about. Then an interval before their next act, in which Luke was allowing her a two-minute song-and-dance spot.

She repeated the words of the sentimental ballad, seeing an image of herself in the centre of the big, empty stage, twirling, swaying, pirouetting, in a gorgeous gown of pale blue tulle, with a shepherdess's straw bonnet decked with bright cornflowers pinned on top of her errant red hair. Estrellita, singing and dancing. . .

She thought, then, of how often, as Essie, at the stone sink in Exeter, she had wistfully wondered if her dream would ever come true, and felt her heart race with excitement and gratitude that the moment was here.

And then Luke returned, her heart abruptly missing a beat as she sought his reflected, loving eyes in the mirror.

He smiled at her, and she continued to sit quietly, sharing the mirror with him as he put on his own pale make-up. She watched him in silence putting on his specially made frock-coat with the deep, hidden pockets that supported so many properties in the act. Then, satisfied that everything hung well, that he looked the epitome of a well-dressed gentleman, he reached for the scarlet-lined cloak and fastened it at his neck, pushing back the full folds over his wide shoulders. He touched the silver star in his ear and then looked down at Essie, smiling, love shining through the veil of tension that had, until that moment, darkened his vivid, absorbed eyes.

She met his gaze calmly and waited, strangely uplifted and serene. A new wisdom shone in her returning smile, and she thought she had never seen him look so handsome and so magnetic.

'I can't kiss you,' he said quietly. 'Mustn't spoil my make-up—or yours.' They looked at each other in silence for a long, stretching moment, then he moved a step nearer. 'We're not on yet, but I must go and see that all's ready—that Harry's not drinking himself to death. Wait here until you're called, Estrellita, my darling.'

'Yes, Luke.' She put out her hand, and he grasped it hungrily, carrying it to his lips, eyes still on hers, as he turned her hand over and gently kissed her warm palm. 'Good luck, my little star. . .'

'Good luck, Luke—darling Luke.'

He left quickly, not looking back, and she heard his rapid footsteps recede down the passage outside. For a while she thought only of Luke, and of what awaited both of them this evening. The moments slid past, unchecked, and she was startled, yet exuberant, when she heard a rap on the door, and the rough voice of the call-boy on his first round.

'Overture and beginners, please.'

Then the skivvy called Essie became an unimportant memory, and Estrellita, the concentrated and committed star-in-the-making, took over. Calmly she left the dressing-room, making her way to the wings, where, soon, Luke found her.

They looked into each other's brilliantly glowing eyes, and smiled, as if they had, by some magic, been fused into one person. Luke reached for her hands and folded them on his chest, against his heart. There was no need for words now, just the beauty of unspoken love and understanding.

They stood there in the hot darkness while the show unfolded itself in a riot of colour and noise only inches away from them. The troupe of Japanese acrobats flung themselves around the stage in dust-raising flim-flams and somersaults. Applause rose. The sweating little men came running off. There was a heart-catching pause while the orchestra sorted out its music, and then started playing a slow and mysterious introduction.

'We're on, little star.'

Essie ran on stage, feeling hot and ice-cold at the same time, terrified, yet more alive than ever before in her life. She smiled brightly at the waiting sea of faces beyond the glowing footlights and then, turning, made a graceful obeisance towards the wings where Luke waited.

All eyes turned, and he strolled on very slowly, timing his entrance impeccably so that the expectant audience broke into a flurry of hand-clapping at his eventual appearance.

Essie allowed herself a second of unprofessional indulgence to look across the stage to where he stood, top hat in hand, acknowledging the audience's greeting. Dark hair glinted beneath the lights, and his lean, angled face was projected into a masculine beauty that set her blood singing anew.

His eyes were brilliant, and the silver earring shone like a star of heaven. Essie's emotions rose inside her, and she had a moment's revelation, knowing suddenly that Luke's own personal magic would bring their performance tonight to the highest realms of contemporary theatrical art.

And then the act began. . .

CHAPTER FOURTEEN

ESSIE was never to forget that wonderful, yet terrible night. The heat and the dust, the ceaseless concentration and feeling of being wound up like a tight spring, somehow carried her through the hours she spent either—briefly—on stage, or merely waiting, huddled backstage, jammed against uncomfortable beams and timbers, in over-heated, dirty passages, endangering the beauty of her various costumes by leaning wearily against the years-old grease stains of other reclining bodies on plastered walls.

Smiles surrounded her, not only from Luke, but planted on unlikely faces. The small, impassive Japanese acrobats. The over-painted, cynical dancing-girls. The middle-aged lady ballad-singer, the wary-eyed, ageing soubrette, neither of whom had even noticed her before, now smiled warmly as they passed.

Solly Kurtz came backstage during the first interval, holding her hand tightly in his massive paw as he said, with a great grin creasing his fat, smiling face, 'Very goot. Yes, yes—very goot inteed. . .'

Even Len Rollinson gave her a pat on the bottom and muttered, 'Not bad for a beginner, dear.' And Luke—Luke smiled tautly, and told her that the evening wasn't over yet.

'Keep concentrating. Don't let your excitement take over——' Then he broke off, turning away, to call back into the shadows in a sharper voice, 'Harry, for God's sake—put that cigarette out.'

A rare new confidence filled Essie, and now she knew that, whatever mistakes of either staging or performance might occur, every member of this wonderful band of professional performers—herself included—was possessed of a sixth sense that would, somehow, cover up, and even create something new of, the error itself.

When the time came for her song and dance solo, she was ready for it. Oh, the magic of being in command of that vast stage. Of communicating joyously, cheekily, lovingly, with the audience, who, by now, she knew intuitively, were willing to eat out of her hand. All too soon the two-minute spot ended.

Scarlet beneath her make-up, sweating and exhilarated, hardly daring to believe the warmth of the applause that followed her, she ran off straight into Luke's arms. He hugged her fiercely, and his whispered voice was an echo of her own happiness. 'My little star!'

Then again, as he released her, he became cool, in control of his feelings. 'Go and rest. You'll need all you've got for the next act. We're doing the Monk now. . .' He stared deep into her eyes and touched her red, parted lips with a caressing finger. 'I'll see you after the finale.' His voice dropped, its resonance throbbing through her sensuously. 'Dear God, how I love you, Estrellita. . .'

Then he was gone, talking to the SM, shouting at Harry, and Essie obediently, as in a dream, returned to the quiet dressing-room to get back her breath and regain some vitality before changing into her finale costume.

But the finale never came that night.

There was a sudden hush creeping over the whole backstage maze of rooms and passages as Luke and Harry took the darkened stage for 'The Dying Monk' act. Essie sensed it, sitting in her hard chair staring at her reflection in the blotchy mirror. An eerie silence that made her abruptly glance down at the pearl pendant, gleaming in its open box beside the china egg and Ma's photograph.

Were pearls really unshed tears? But everything was

going so well—the show was a tremendous success, and surely the Monk illusion would establish Luke's fame as the illusionist of all time? Nothing could go wrong now.

But something tingled through her, cold and frightening, so that her skin crept, in spite of her heat, and she jumped to her feet. Luke had said she must stay here—but, no, she knew she must get back to the wings. The urge to go was so compelling that she ran down the empty, hushed passages like a figure possessed.

I have to find Luke. I must be close to him... No other thoughts pierced her distraught mind but that. She reached the spot where, such a short while ago, Luke and she had stood together, and then halted, as the SM loomed out of the darkness, glaring at her as he whispered throatily, 'What in hell's name are you doing here? Get back to the dressing-room——'

'No.' She shook her head fiercely, fixing him with her burning gaze. 'No, I won't. I have to be here.'

The orchestra was playing a slow, solemn air, and she knew that Harry and Luke were well into the act by now. This music heralded the appearance of the angelic face.

The SM grunted as he pushed past her, and 'Women! Well, just keep still and don't let Luke see you there,' before rapidly disappearing backstage, with a burly scene-shifter following in his footsteps. They were going to engineer the mysterious transformation, she realised, which somehow would reveal two Lukes on stage at the same time.

Mirrors. Trick lighting. Traps. Slides. *Secrets*...

She shivered, despite the unremitting heat of the lights, and wished wretchedly that this haunting fear, deep down inside her, would go. What could it mean?

Within the next two seconds she knew. An acrid smell made her tremble. *Fire*! Swiftly, turning, she caught sight of a veil of sweeping smoke loom up out of the shadows. She heard crackling, and then a wall of brilliant fire suddenly erupted, reaching ever upwards in all directions, tendrils of flames catching at everything within reach.

Essie screamed with all the power she could find, and fled in the opposite direction. Abruptly, all backstage was in chaos. Doors of dressing-rooms opened, and scene-shifters and waiting performers came from nowhere, hurtling past her, one thought only in their fearful minds—to get out before the whole building went up.

She was jammed in a dark corner. Terrified, she watched the SM trying to contain the fire. 'Bring down the drop-curtain!' he bellowed, and above the increasing noise of flames and frightened screams she heard the rollers above the cat-walk releasing the heavy canvas. 'Now the fire-curtain—for God's sake, hurry. . .'

The fire-curtain came down, only to jam thirty inches above the stage, fouled by the drop, blown out of alignment by the draught from an open door backstage.

'They're getting out safely from the auditorium,' shouted a passing electrician, 'but it's getting worse here. Where's the bloody fire brigade?'

'Keep yer hair on, mate—on'y just sent for it, haven't we? Where's those buckets. . .?'

Essie became part of the heaving, swearing, fighting mass of bodies that were pushing past, heading for the open door and the blessed fresh air that would disperse the clouds of black, choking smoke swirling down the passages.

One thought alone hammered in her head—*Luke*. Dear God, where was he? In her frenzy, she caught at the SM's arm as he hurried past. 'Help me find Luke— you've got to help me.'

The man stopped dead, his eyes abruptly even more desperate than before. 'First things first,' he shouted roughly, tearing away her hand. 'Let's get the buckets o' water moving before we look for the bodies. . .' And he disappeared from her side.

A kind of reckless, blistering rage grew inside Essie, and she turned, knowing that she alone must do what no one else had time for. Somehow she fought her way back on to the smoke-filled stage, coughing and spluttering, masking her streaming eyes with a shawl dropped by a fleeing chorus-girl. All around her timbers were splintering and crashing. Debris fell heavily as she paused, staring into the veil of smoke. There—that dark mound; was it? It must be. . .oh, no—no!

She screamed as she knelt by the prostrate form, sweating hands trying to pull back the heavily charred and still burning robe that hid the face she sought so wildly to see. Her scream, piercing in its intensity and despair, at last brought a pair of helpers on stage behind her.

They threw buckets of water over both Essie and the dark heap beside her, then, swearing and puffing, pulled the body off stage.

'Get away, miss—this ain't no place for you,' shouted the young lad who always had a cheeky smile for her, but she stayed immobile, unable to think of anything except that the silent heap of charred clothing they had taken away was Luke, and that their life together was over. Finished, before it had truly started.

She knew then, in that surging, emotional moment, what her uneasiness had foretold. That unnerving, nameless fear in the pit of her stomach. Wildly she started to sob, knowing numbly that pearls were, indeed, tears waiting to be shed, and that their luck had turned. . . It was some ten minutes later, when the fire was at last under control, that the SM came to her as she sat, shivering from shock and dismay, in a small room leading off the box office, at the front of the charred, still smoking building.

He stared down and bent to shake her arm. Startled

out of her nightmare of numb apathy, Essie looked up slowly to meet his beetle-browed eyes. 'You all right, gel?'

'Yes, thank you.' She wasn't aware of speaking. She was made of ice now, and thank goodness for it. Being frozen was a way of not feeling, and she prayed that she would never thaw out.

'About—er—Luke. . .'

A huge iceberg formed in her throat. She shut her eyes and tried to stop thinking.

'It wasn't him, you know—not that—er—body on stage. . .'

Minutes passed before she understood and was able to open her staring eyes. She looked up at the grim face above her.

'N-not Luke?' Then something began to move inside her, a small nudge of warmth, trying to break down the frosted barrier that was denying thought and feeling.

'No. Not Luke. It was Harry Whitman.'

'I—don't understand.' Her head swam, the blood in her frozen veins was thawing, and the pain was excruciating.

'The illusion—"The Dying Monk"—well, that's how they did it—the trick. Only a few knew, of course— just Harry and Luke and me and the master carpenter, and one of the electricians.'

'But—it *was* Luke—at the beginning? I saw his face, his earring. . .' The clamour in her mind threatened to swamp her wits, but somehow she kept a hold on that one hope. Not Luke. *Not Luke*.

'Harry wore a mask.' The SM's heavy face broke into a brief, swiftly wiped away grin. 'An' the earring was a bit o' tinsel.'

An explosion burst through Essie's weakness, and suddenly she was on her feet, confronting the SM with a raw fierceness that made him step away.

A CERTAIN MAGIC

'So where is he? Where's Luke? Tell me—oh, God, tell me—*where is Luke*?'

'Safe,' said the SM, nodding vigorously. 'A bit smoked up and choked, down in that secret room for two minutes or so—we couldn't get there till we'd doused the worst of the flames. But he's quite safe. Hey—you all right, gel?'

Essie swayed, but her pallor and swimminess were only momentary weaknesses. 'Safe!' She sobbed the one word in a great shout of thankfulness, kissed the SM's startled, blackened cheek and rushed out of the room, her thoughts churning and soaring in a maelstrom of gratitude and love.

Instinctively, she knew where to find him, sitting weakly in the back row of the stalls, holding his head in his hands, and not immediately hearing her as she rushed to his side.

'Luke! Are you all right? You're quite safe? Not burned? Not hurt?'

He turned then, his eyes a strange, pale, exhausted shade of dull grey, but his soot-stained face smiled, and his arms reached out for her. 'Estrellita, my darling—yes, I'm safe. With you. Thank God.'

The stumbling, quiet words told her all that she needed to know. Looking deep into his weary eyes, she felt the tears in her own brimming over. Then his hands released her, and he spread them out for her to see. There were angry red blisters on both scorched palms, but nothing that time and loving care couldn't heal.

Essie lifted them to her lips, kissing them repeatedly, willing them to recover. 'I'll make them better! I'll give them back to you! You'll still be the best magician in the world, Luke.'

Slowly he shook his head. His voice was low, but no longer despairing. He sounded content. 'I don't care any more now,' he told her, his lips beginning to curve at the edges. 'Nothing matters, after this, except that you're here with me. That we're safe—and together...'

She watched the colour return to his pale, smudged cheeks, saw his eyes regain their sea-green beauty, and knew, with her heart singing, that out of disaster and terror had come a gift far greater than anything the theatre and stardom could ever convey.

She and Luke had found each other.

Like a blessing, the sun shone on the glittering river Teign as it steadily danced towards the Point and the open sea. Seagulls were following a small fishing-boat into the harbour, their harsh screams all part of the contented hum of the noise of holiday-makers enjoying themselves on the sandy, sloping beach.

Luke did his palming exercises, sitting on the sand, leaning against the boarded front of a friendly fisherman's boat-hut, fine eyes staring up-river to the faraway hazy humps and bumps of distant Dartmoor.

Essie, toes braced against the tide, watched the clear water magnify her bare legs as she paddled along dreamily, a faint smile wreathing her face, hair untidy in the soft wind that followed the river. Many thoughts filled her mind, and chief among them was the memory of Luke's white feet spilling out of his uncomfortable makeshift bed in their recent lodgings. Suddenly she laughed aloud, and raced back up the beach, throwing herself down beside him, causing the golden sand to spurt up in tiny fluffy explosions.

'They won't ever have to be cold and lonely any more, Luke.' She answered the question in his eyes laughingly. 'Your feet! They can always be with me now, in a warm bed, never hanging over the edge of that old couch.'

In reply Luke took her left hand and lifted it to his lips, kissing the gold wedding-ring encircling her third finger. 'I'm afraid it wasn't quite the sort of wedding you dreamed of, my darling, was it? A register office in a busy London street, a bridegroom with bandaged hands and charred hair. . .'

'And Ma—I mean Belle—with her tambourine because she was off to join in a procession!' Essie lay beside him, remembering.

'Alice all dolled up in shrimp-pink, with what looked like a dead flamingo on her hat——'

'And Albie bursting out of his suit! Oh, Luke—I'll never forget; it was so lovely.'

His silence penetrated her memories, and she moved her head to search his suddenly preoccupied face. 'And neither of us will ever forget that dreadful night—or poor Harry. . .' Her voice dwindled away.

Luke sighed, his gaze lost in the distance. 'No, we won't forget him. Poor old Harry. He was a rogue, a fool—but I owed him so much.' Briefly he paused, then looked back at her anxious eyes. 'And he helped to make us stars, Estrellita—never forget that. "The Dying Monk" wasn't possible without him. So the Monk's dead, as well as Harry.'

Essie shivered, then forced her thoughts away from the nightmare images. 'Stars!' she whispered exultantly. 'Twin stars. . . Oh, Luke, the papers said such wonderful things about us! And all those flowers and telegrams and letters. . .'

Luke nodded, a smile of satisfaction wreathing his face. 'Accolades, bigger and better contracts being offered—yes, my love, fame is certainly very pleasant.'

'And all that money! But we need it, don't we?' Suddenly she felt very practical. 'I mean, the loan you got to buy my pearl pendant. If only it hadn't got burned in the fire. . .' But secretly she was glad. Pearls were tears. The china egg and Luke's earring had been far healthier good-luck charms.

'Just a drop in the ocean,' Luke assured her smoothly. 'At the moment we're wealthy, my darling. And yet—I don't know that I really want either money or fame any more. . .'

Turning on his side, his brilliant eyes questioned her very seriously. 'Tell me, little love, would you be disappointed if we didn't return to London, once the theatre's repaired, and the show goes on again?'

Curiously, Essie asked, 'You mean stay here? In Teignmouth? For ever?'

A wry smile lifted Luke's lips. 'Hardly! A nice enough place for a honeymoon, but. . .' He sat up straighter, eyes suddenly afire with excitement. 'We could start again, travelling the world with our act. Not caring so much for stardom, as for the joy of being together and performing.'

'Without Harry.' Essie's voice was thoughtful. Inside her a small germ of certainty had begun to sprout. She and Luke could never live away from the theatre, but they would never again chase elusive, dangerous stardom, for that way lay too great a price to be paid—the price of losing their new, hard-won happiness.

Lazily she began to make plans. 'All the usual things. The scarves, the rabbits, the magic cabinet.'

'Your song-and-dance spot.' Once more, Luke was practising his palming movements, and she watched his slender, powerful fingers, thankful that every day brought greater strength and expertise to them.

Suddenly she gasped, turning to him with shining, excited eyes. 'Leda! Of course! They loved Leda in Plymouth—so why can't we build our new act around Leda?'

Luke considered for a long, silent moment. Then— 'If I wanted magic, I couldn't have anything better,' he said huskily, looking deep into her eyes. 'I'll never forget the way you looked at me; everyone there could see the love in your face—you really were a statue coming to life. Yes, we'll replace the Monk with Leda.' Abruptly his face was revitalised, full of new enthusiasm, and his body tensed. 'Maybe we should start rehearsing soon.'

Essie put her free hand on their entwined fingers,

and her touch relaxed him again. 'Not yet,' she said, smiling into his adoring eyes. 'You still need rest. And it's so lovely here. The sun, the warmth, and the river. . .'

Luke stirred, returning her smile. She saw memory fill his gaze. 'Remember that other river?' he asked fondly. 'The river down which I hollered your name—so long ago?'

'Exeter. The sheets cracking in the wind. Me, full of dreams and hopes. . .' She laughed, a little sadly. 'I can still hear your voice shouting, "Estrellita"—and the wind carrying it off to goodness knows where. Oh, Luke—what a lot has happened since then.' Her smile fading, she turned to him. 'Do you think we were really meant to meet—that time, in Exeter? And afterwards?'

'Just as much as I believe we are meant to be here now, by another river, planning our future together.' He dropped a kiss on her forehead. 'Now stop dreaming, little star, and let's think of what is to come.'

Essie allowed the warmth of the sinking sun to enclose her. It was sheer heaven, being here with Luke, her husband, knowing that nothing in the world could harm them again.

The heat, the yielding softness of sand beneath her, and the singing of the flowing waters, wove a pulsating spell within her body. She moved restlessly, hand tightening on Luke's, her gaze searching his face.

She watched the brilliance of his eyes darken until they seemed like icebergs drowning in a flooding torrent of hot desire. Her own answering need arose swiftly. She stared hungrily at his sensitive mouth.

'Belle said love can work miracles. . .' Her whisper made him bend closer, his hands releasing her fingers, moving to her upturned face, stroking her cheeks with a moth's-wing delicacy, then to her parted lips, outlining them with a tender, almost reverential touch, before sliding down to encircle her pale, throbbing throat. Closer still, he kissed the tip of her sun-freckled nose.

Suddenly she saw bubbles of laughter lightening his crystal-clear eyes, and instinctively read his thoughts. Her blood sang and, squinting against the sun, through half-shut eyes, she murmured, 'Let's go home——' But before the words were out, Luke was on his feet, pulling her up beside him. His eyes glowed with an urgency that excited her even further, his smile sending a shiver through her willing body.

'Time enough to plan our new act in a day or two. . .' His voice deepened, rousing all her senses with its erotic music. 'But let's make a little magic of our own—*now*.'

He swept her up in one strong, lithe movement, and swiftly carried her home, along the beach, towards Belle's cottage.

Lying against the creaky old brass bedstead, where all her dreams had come true, Essie stared adoringly at Luke, and no longer saw the tense being with ambition burning in his deepset eyes, but, instead, a happier man, whose vivid smile now held only the relaxed expression of serenity.

And something was missing—something so familiar and taken for granted that, for a moment, she couldn't think what it was.

Sitting up quickly, she said, 'Luke? Where's your earring? Your lovely silver star?'

He came to the bed and lay down, smiling enigmatically, before turning to her and slowly unbuttoning the front of her print dress. 'Gone,' he told her wryly. 'I don't need it any longer.' His insistent hands gently drew her down beside him. 'You see, I don't need luck, or fame—and certainly not the earring.'

'But——'

He silenced her, one finger on her lips. Bending his head closer, she felt his breath, warm and sweet, slowly growing ragged with passion. 'I've found what I've been searching for all my life. I've got you, Estrellita—my own little star...'

He kissed her, and her body began to arch to meet his in a moment of mounting sensation and love, and then Essie forgot everything in the world, except the truth that Belle had told her.

Oh, yes—love *could* work miracles.

The other exciting

MASQUERADE
Historical

available this month is:

JUST DESERTS
Elizabeth Bailey

Christopher, Baron Chiddingly, would have liked more money to fund his passion for horses, but he had no real urge to marry a fortune. Not until Miss Persephone Winsford, newly returned from India with a fortune from her Nabob father, and reputedly as horse-mad as the Baron, came into his ken.

Bluntly autocratic, the Baron met his match in Miss Winsford – she didn't suffer fools gladly either! And neither seemed prepared to compromise . . .

Look out for the two intriguing

| MASQUERADE *Historical* |

Romances coming next month

TO PLEASE A LADY
Valentina Luellen

Despite all the scandal that inevitably followed from his gambling, Dominy Granville was determined to find her father in America. Tracing him to San Francisco, she found he had not mended his ways, which resulted in Dominy falling into the clutches of Lance Beautrellis, wealthy riverboat gambler.

The only way to pay off Lord Granville's debts was to work for Beau, but Dominy made it *very* clear, both to Beau and his friend Austen LaMotte, that her body was not for sale! How could she foresee that his desire would persuade Austen into actions that seemed destined to keep Dominy and Beau apart?

SHARED DREAMS
Janet Grace

The feud between the Finderbys and the Chenes had begun in Elizabethan times, and in this year of 1798, showed no sign of abating.

Which made things rather difficult for Marcus, the new Earl of Chene, because he wanted to acquire a corner of Finderby land to cut a new canal. Old Lord Finderby cherished the feud, but his granddaughter, Susan, brought into regular contact with Marcus as he tried to pursue his goal, knew she didn't want to be at odds with him . . .

Available in April

FOUR REGENCY ROMANCES

Four short stories featuring four determined women with their dreams of love, independence, wealth and position.

Can their dreams come true?

Published: April 1992   Price: £3.99

Available from Boots, Martins, John Menzies, W.H. Smith, most supermarkets and other paperback stockists. Also available from Mills & Boon Reader Service, PO Box 236, Thornton Road, Croydon, Surrey CR9 3RU.